# Codename Enigma

**Other Books by Colin M. Barron**

# Codename Enigma

Colin M. Barron

Published by New Generation Publishing in 2019

ISBN: 978-1-78955-719-0


www.newgeneration-publishing.com

New Generation Publishing

*To the memory of my father*

**Non Vi Sed Arte**
*(- not by strength by guile)*

The motto of the Long Range Desert Group (LRDG)

# Prologue

## Cardiff, 17 December 1941

*My life is so ordinary*, thought Dr Peter Lee, M. B. Ch. B. as he brushed soap suds onto his face. After popping a new blade into his Gillette safety razor, he shaved his cheeks, jaw and chin, avoiding his neatly-trimmed black moustache. A large crimson spot of blood appeared on the rim of his washbasin. 'Dammit,' he muttered as he staunched his bleeding chin with a white towel and searched in the bathroom cupboard for a styptic pencil. *Why do they call these things safety razors? They seem pretty dangerous!*

The styptic pencil didn't work so Lee stuck a small Elastoplast on his chin, wiped off the remaining suds, put on his vest and shirt, and contemplated his surroundings. A dingy, damp bedroom in a rented flat with a single naked light bulb hanging from the ceiling. Peeling cream paint and blistering yellow and white striped wallpaper. A linoleum-covered floor with an ill-fitting, faded wool carpet on top. Rain pattered on the window as leaden clouds crossed the sky. Beyond it, the landscape was grey and depressing. Rows of tenements and terraced houses with smoke-stained stonework and shining, wet slate roofs. A single, grey merchant ship with rust-streaked paintwork lay at anchor in Cardiff Bay. It carried a single Hawker Hurricane fighter on a catapult. Lee reckoned it was one of the new Catapult Armed Merchantmen he had read about.

It was more than two years since the conflict had started, yet Lee had done little to help the war effort, apart from a stint in the Home Guard in 1940. He had graduated from Glasgow University Medical School in April 1941 and had spent the last few months in Wales as a G.P. Pretty boring stuff. Coughs and colds. Diarrhoea and stomach pains. Sore backs. Headaches. How he wished he could be given a chance to serve his country, to really make a difference.

As he was brushing his teeth with Eucryl tooth powder and reflecting on his humdrum existence, Lee heard the sound of something being popped through the letterbox. He walked downstairs while knotting his tie and noticed a large manila envelope lying on the floor next to the front door. It had a black 'W.D.' stamp on it. He took it into the kitchen and slit it open with a table knife.

It was his call-up papers. On 16 January he was to report to the British Army training camp at Catterick, Yorkshire. At the end of his basic training he would become a Captain the Royal Army Medical Corps. He knew there was a fair chance he would be posted abroad, possibly Egypt or the Far East. At last he was being given a chance to make a difference. Lee didn't know it at the time, but his whole life would never be the same again.

# Chapter 1

## Welcome to Tobruk!

**20 June 1942, 06.30 hrs**
**HMS *Kiwi*, off the Libyan coast.**

A brilliant sun rose in the cloudless Mediterranean sky. Golden rays sparkled on the calm sea. It should have been a welcome sight. But to Captain Peter Lee of the Royal Army Medical Corps, it meant danger. *The ship would have been spotted.* Lee took off his peaked cap and wiped the sweat from his forehead with a handkerchief. Drops of perspiration ran from his short black wavy hair,down the side of his generously proportioned nose into his neatly trimmed moustache. Libya was one of the hottest places on Earth and the following day was the summer solstice. The RAMC Captain looked down at his short, slightly bandy legs. When he got the opportunity, he would change his Eighth Army shorts for long trousers, which gave better protection from the sun and insects. He had been in North Africa for only a few weeks and so far had spent his time treating soldiers for minor ailments. All that was about to change. *He was going to see some action.*

An hour earlier, as the sky reddened in the east, an Italian Caproni Ca.309 *Ghibli* twin- engine reconnaissance plane had overflown the 2,500 ton *Tribal* class destroyer, and narrowly avoided the blizzard of anti-aircraft fire which greeted it. By now, the *Kiwi's* position would have been plotted in Axis control bunkers as it raced east at its maximum speed of thirty – six knots, towards the dubious safety of Tobruk harbour.

Lee imagined enemy pilots strapping themselves into their aircraft. Engines starting. Propellor blades whirling round on numerous desert airstrips. Groundcrew engulfed in clouds of noxious, white exhaust smoke as they pulled away wooden chocks. Aircraft taxiing onto desert runways. And what would the Germans and Italians send against them? Junkers Ju 87 and Ju 88 dive bombers perhaps? Or maybe even deadly Savoia - Marchetti S.M. 79 tri- motor torpedo bombers?

HMS *Kiwi* was well-armed, with four 4.7inch guns for'ard in two twin turrets and another pair in the aft 'D' Turret. There was also a pair of 4 -inch weapons aft in 'C' turret. All these large guns could engage aircraft but were aimed from remote gun directors, which meant they often missed as the old technology wasn't designed to cope with fast - moving targets. In addition, the 4.7 - inch weapons had problems engaging dive bombers as they couldn't elevate to a high angle. Only the two 4 - inch guns could elevate above 40 degrees. The *Kiwi* also had a quadruple 40mm quick – firing, two - pounder pom-pom amidships and a pair of four-barrelled Vickers fifty- calibre water-cooled guns close to the bridge wings. Its armament had recently been augmented with four 20mm Oerlikon cannon with armoured shields, one of which stood near Lee.

But despite the *Kiwi's* impressive anti-aircraft firepower, Lee worried because he knew that in any contest between a plane and a ship, the aircraft usually won. Events at Taranto, Pearl Harbour and Crete in the last two years had proved that beyond doubt. Still, the *Kiwi* was a fast ship with two powerful Parsons steam turbines producing 44,000 horsepower and it was this nimble pace, combined with her manoeuvrability, which might prove crucial in the coming battle.

Lee ground his teeth and furrowed his brow as he ruminated about what had gone wrong. The original plan was for the *Kiwi* to discharge her cargo of soldiers and war *materiel* during the hours of darkness. By now she should have been on her way back to Alexandria, well east of her current location and beyond the range of enemy aircraft, but a leaking steam pipe had delayed her departure. It had been a cock–up, just like all the other Allied military blunders in the past three years. Now the 190 crew of the

*Kiwi* were about to pay the price for this error.

Lee felt sweat trickling down the back of his neck as the sun rose. Two wet patches had formed under the armpits of his beige battledress shirt. And the crews manning the guns had it even worse as they were compelled to wear white anti-flash hoods, gloves and steel helmets when they were at action stations.

Lee grabbed a handrail to stop himself falling as the deck tilted. The ship rolled and Lee felt a wave of nausea sweep over him. Then his stomach contents rose up his gullet and he threw up over the side. Lee felt the burning taste of hydrochloric acid in his mouth and nose. The wind blew some of the vomit back onto the deck and Lee noticed that his spew contained what looked like diced carrot. How is that possible, he thought, as he never ate diced carrot? Lee didn't know that four decades later a Glasgow comedian called Billy Connolly would have audiences rollicking with laughter after making the same observation.

'You haven't got your sea legs, yet mate!' said Able Seaman Newley, the short, dark-haired Scouse Oerlikon gunner, as he looked over his right shoulder at Lee. 'You need to get yourself down to the galley and have some porridge and bacon and eggs with plenty of tea and toast!' The other three members of the gun crew guffawed with laughter.

Lee felt sick at the thought. Apart from anything else, his religion forbade him from eating bacon. Now the crew of the quad pom-pom on a higher deck also roared with laughter at the sight of the short, slightly - built Royal Army Medical Corps officer feeling ill in what they would consider calm conditions.

As the sailors chuckled, four dark shapes swept towards the ship from the east with the sun behind them. A brilliant tactical move by the Italian pilots. They had flown just above the sea and couldn't be seen because of the low, bright sun. The first the crew knew of the attack was the noise of the fighters' 870 horsepower Fiat radial engines and the staccato bang-bang-bang of 12.7mm machine – gun bullets hitting the *Kiwi's* superstructure. The aircraft flew overhead and then banked to make another pass. Lee recognised them as Italian Macchi C. 200 *Saetta* fighters. With their sand and brown mottled camouflage and yellow engine cowlings, they looked rather beautiful in the golden morning sunlight and Lee had to remind himself that their pilots intended to kill him and everyone else on board.

The crew of the *Kiwi* soon recovered from the shock of the sudden assault. Now, as the Macchis banked for a second pass, every gun that could be brought to bear opened fire on the attackers. Lee's ears were assaulted by a cacophony of sounds from the various naval anti-aircraft weapons. The loud thump of the 4.7 -inch and 4 -inch guns, the chatter of the Vickers 0.5s and the slower bang - bang - bang of the pom - poms and Oerlikons as they filled the sky with glowing red tracer rounds and small puffs of black smoke. Brass cartridge cases tinkled on the deck. Choking, white acrid smoke swirled everywhere. Lee smelt burnt gunpowder and cordite. Some of the soldiers on deck joined in, firing their Lee-Enfield short magazine 0.303 rifles and Bren guns at the attackers. A moment later, the battle was over and the four Macchis retreated south at high speed, their ammunition expended. One of them had been hit and was trailing black smoke from its engine. Lee wondered if it would make it back to base.

So far so good. They had survived a strafing attack by fighters but they were no real threat. With their puny armament of just two machine guns, the Macchis could inflict only superficial damage on a 2,500 ton vessel. Lee knew the real danger would come from the slower bombers that followed the fighters.

Ten minutes later they arrived. Six black dots on the horizon. Lee recognised them as German Junker Ju 87 Stuka dive bombers in tight formation. As they got closer, the pilots executed a well-practised move and formed up into a large circle above the ship, taking care to stay outside the range of *Kiwi's* anti-aircraft weaponry.

On the port bridge wing, Captain Harrison spoke into a microphone. His deep voice boomed over the Tannoy system:

'All gun crews, track the Stukas but do not open fire until they come within effective range.'

The Junkers Ju 87 had been a deadly dive bomber during the Polish and French campaigns but was vulnerable to fighter attack, as had been proved during the Battle of Britain when it was shot down in large numbers. In 1940, RAF fighter pilots had talked about 'Stuka parties.' *Just two RAF Curtiss P-40B Tomahawks or Hawker Hurricanes would have taken care of the whole bloody lot*, thought Lee, but,with recent Axis advances on the battlefield, there were no RAF fighters within range of Tobruk.

Lee knew the best way to thwart a Stuka attack on a naval target was to keep the ship's speed as high as possible and make violent evasive manoeuvres once the Junker's bombs had been released. He guessed that would be the Captain's plan. The only snag of this tactic was that these sudden alterations in course would also make the job of the anti-aircraft gunners harder. Hitting a speeding aircraft from the deck of a moving ship was difficult as there were so many variables.

Now the Stukas circled the ship, making that eerie warbling sound that had terrified thousands of civilians across Europe. Ju 87s were fitted with a wind-driven siren on one of their fixed, spatted undercarriage legs,a so - called 'Jericho's Trumpet' – which made a screaming noise that could frighten even hardened troops. One of the bent- winged aircraft peeled off and dived towards the destroyer, flying through puffs of black smoke from exploding anti-aircraft rounds. Lee spotted a 550 kilogram bomb suspended on an extended trapeze below the lower fuselage of the aircraft and noticed the aircraft was a long range 'R' version with underwing fuel tanks. The Stuka reached the lowest point of its dive and released its ordnance just as Captain Harrison ordered a hard turn to port.

Lee nearly lost his footing as the destroyer heeled over violently, and grabbed a railing to stop himself from falling. A bomb fell through the sky, apparently heading directly for him. A moment later it landed in the sea and exploded in the ocean off the starboard bow, drenching the crew with cold salt water and leaving them with ringing ears and temporary deafness.

Now a second Stuka bore down on the ship from the east but, before it could release its payload, it exploded in mid – air with an orange flash. Hot, smoking pieces of airframe, including the spatted undercarriage, clattered down on the aft deck. The aircraft's Junkers Jumo twelve - cylinder engine ended up on top of 'D' turret. Coolant spilled out from the plane's burst radiator and dripped over the side of turret.

It had been a lucky shot from one of the twin 4 -inch guns in 'C' turret. The crew cheered loudly but their celebrations were short - lived as a third Stuka dived down and released its ordnance. Once again Captain Harrison ordered a violent last - minute evasive manoeuvre, this time to starboard and the bomb exploded well clear of the ship, sending up a cloud of white spray.

Now a fourth Stuka attacked. This time it approached from directly ahead. The *Kiwi* would be a harder target from this angle, but the Ju 87 would also be much more difficult to shoot down as it could only be engaged by the 4.7-inch guns, which were usually ineffective against dive – bombers. Lee cursed the lack of light anti-aircraft weapons which could fire straight ahead as the Stuka dived down, making its terrifying banshee wail. The 550 kilogram bomb left its trapeze just as Captain Harrison ordered a turn to port.

Time seemed to slow down for Lee as he followed the bomb down. It just missed the ship but exploded very close to the starboard side of the hull causing a violent concussion which could be felt on deck. Dozens of rivets popped and hull plates buckled as thousands of gallons of seawater poured into the ship. One of the two Parsons steam turbines stopped, the lights in the lower decks went out and the vessel slowed to twenty knots as it began to list to starboard. Lee grabbed a davit to stop himself from falling over.

Up on the bridge, Captain Harrison gave his orders over the Tannoy with calm efficiency. Nobody ever panicked in the Royal Navy.

'Start counter- flooding on the port side. Damage control parties to shore up leaks on the starboard side. Emergency generators on.' There was no need to order all watertight doors and hatches to be closed as this had been done more than an hour earlier when the vessel had gone to action stations after it had been spotted by the Italian reconnaissance aircraft.

Now the fifth Stuka took advantage of the momentary confusion caused by the list to attack from the starboard side, hoping to cause further damage to the weakened hull. This time the pilot opened fire with his twin wing – mounted 7.9mm machine – guns as he dived on the stricken ship. Several rounds pattered off the armoured shield of the Oerlikon mount next to Lee and one passed through the gap between the gun barrel and the shield and penetrated Able Seaman Newley's heart. He fell dead at Lee's feet. The gun's loader also collapsed as he had taken a bullet in his right arm. A spare circular drum magazine containing 20mm rounds clattered on the deck.

Without a moment's hesitation, Lee grabbed the gun, pressed his shoulders against the two semi-circular handles and aimed the Oerlikon at the diving Stuka using the crude mechanical sight. It was a perfect zero-deflection shot and he simply could not miss as he pulled the trigger and unleashed a hail of deadly 20mm shells at the attacker. One round hit the Stuka's chin – mounted radiator causing coolant to spew out, two struck its engine block and a fourth decapitated the pilot. The German dive bomber clipped the ship's forward mast and crashed into the sea, taking some of the rigging with it. It sank in seconds, weighed down by its heavy bomb and twelve – cylinder engine. The rear gunner drowned.

Now the *Kiwi* was only three hundred yards from the entrance to Tobruk harbour which was marked by the rusting wreck of the four – funnelled Italian cruiser, *San Giorgio* which had been scuttled earlier in the war. Once the British ship was inside the harbour, it would be compelled to slow down and be unable to manoeuvre. On the other hand, the port was ringed by a large number of 40mm Bofors and 3.7-inch anti-aircraft guns which were a formidable deterrent to dive – bombers.

The helmsman steered the *Kiwi* around the rusting hulk of the cruiser and into the entrance of the harbour just as the last Stuka made its attack. But now the British defences opened up and the Stuka pilot was distracted by anti-aircraft shells bursting all round him. He aimed badly. The 550 kilogram bomb exploded just ahead of *Kiwi*, ripping off part of its bow. Water flooded into the forward compartments.

The ship began to sink, but at least she was now in shallow water, and Lee knew the Captain could save the crew and cargo by beaching her. Harrison ordered his helmsman to steer for a patch of beach between two jetties. A couple of moments later, the *Kiwi* rode up onto the sand, its hull plates buckling and groaning as its bottom struck rocks. Harrison's actions had wrecked the ship beyond economical repair but its cargo and passengers had been saved. The crew threw nets over the side and Lee scrambled down one, only to lose his footing and fall into the filthy harbour water. A moment later he was pulled from the sea, his uniform soaked in salt water and his hair matted with oil. A squaddie offered him a cup of Army tea made with lots of sugar and tinned Carnation milk.

'Welcome to Tobruk, Captain.'

# Chapter 2

# Enigma

The beige British Army Humber Heavy Utility car steered its way through the potholed, rubble -strewn streets of Tobruk and halted outside the dilapidated sandstone building which served as a temporary HQ. All the cream-painted wooden shutters were open, revealing glassless windows. Two steel - helmeted sentries stood on either side of the sandbagged entrance carrying Lee Enfield Short Magazine 0.303 inch rifles with fitted bayonets. Both soldiers wore shorts and battledress tops with full webbing kit and suede desert boots.

Lee opened the passenger door, thanked his driver, and took in the view. In the far distance Tobruk harbour was filled with half - submerged rusting, wrecked ships, their broken masts lying at drunken angles. A slick of fuel oil lay on the filthy water. Black smoke rose from burning oil tanks and formed a large cloud above the town which threatened to block out the sun. Three Junkers Ju 88 bombers painted in mottled brown and sand camouflage with light blue bellies escaped south as AA shells exploded around them. Lee heard the thump of the big 3.7 - inch anti-aircraft guns, the familiar cadumph – cadumph - cadumph of multiple Bofors guns and the chatter of various small arms as they fired in vain at the receding attackers. The Humber's metal bodywork was already scorching from the mid-morning sun and the bonnet was hot enough to fry an egg. The characteristic smell of the Middle East was in the air, a mixture of sand, sweat, urine, camel dung, exotic spices and the aroma of the hookah pipes smoked by the locals.

Inside the HQ building, the brilliant North African sun streamed through the open windows of the briefing room. Two officers studied maps of the Western Desert that were spread out on an old wooden table. They sipped tin mugs of tea as the ceiling – mounted electric fans struggled to keep the room at a comfortable temperature. One officer looked about forty - five, of medium height with greying dark hair, and sported a black patch over his left eye. The other was about six foot two inches tall , well –built , with dark hair and a thin reddish beard and appeared fit, muscular and tanned. He was wearing an officer's cap with a unit badge which Lee had never seen before. It consisted of a winged dagger with the words *Who Dares Wins* written beneath it. The officer with the eyepatch looked up as Lee entered.

'Ah, Captain Lee. My name is Brigadier Scobie and for the time being I am your commanding officer. Scobie offered Lee a rather limp, sweaty handshake.

'I understand you had a rather …*interesting* journey.'

'Yes sir, we were attacked by Stukas a few miles from Tobruk,' said Lee in a cultured Glasgow accent. 'We shot down two of them but *Kiwi* was badly hit and had to be beached.'

'So I heard. I was also informed you played a part in the action.'

' Yes sir, I manned an Oerlikon and brought down a Stuka.'

Scobie's face reddened and his brow furrowed.

'Captain Lee, may I remind you that you are an officer in the Royal Army Medical Corps. Your primary duty is medical care of our soldiers and any prisoners of war. You are not supposed to go squirting lead at any passing Jerry aircraft, even if it is a tempting target.'

'Sorry sir. It won't happen again. But the Stuka was diving directly towards the ship and about to release its bomb. All I did was grab the gun, centre the target in the sight and pull the trigger. I couldn't miss. A seven - year old could have hit the bugger!'

Scobie's facial muscles relaxed and he grinned, revealing nicotine - stained teeth.

'I know Captain, I know. According to King's

Regulations I am required to give you a bollocking, but just between you and me, all I can say is … bloody good show! We all hate these bloody Stukas. By the way, how did you know how to fire an Oerlikon?'

'Always been interested in guns, sir. Before the war I was a member of a rifle club in Glasgow. In 1940 I joined the Home Guard and became an instructor on the Bren gun. I also learned to fire the American Thompson sub - machine gun and the B.A.R. – the Browning Automatic Rifle. The Yanks shipped lots of them to Britain in 1940 and they were passed to the Home Guard. And before I was transferred to the Middle East, I visited one of my old school chums at HMS *Excellent*, the Royal Navy's gunnery school at Whale Island, near Portsmouth. He let me have a go at shooting an Oerlikon at a sleeve target towed behind a Fleet Air Arm Boulton - Paul Defiant. Quite an experience.'

'I see, so you are a doctor with many talents.'

Scobie opened the drawer of an old, battered oak desk and pulled out a bottle of Bell's whisky.

'Here, accept this little gift in recognition of your shooting skills.'

'Sorry sir, but I don't drink. It makes me drowsy and gives me gastritis. I may even have the beginnings of a duodenal ulcer. And I don't smoke either.'

Scobie looked astonished.

'Surely as a medical man, you must know the health benefits of smoking. A mild antiseptic action on the lungs and all that.'

'Sorry, I must disagree on that point, sir. Cigarette smoke contains a number of substances that are known to cause cancer, such as coal tar. I believe this has already been discovered by Nazi scientists. Hitler is even planning to introduce smoking bans.'

'So the Nazis have actually done something to benefit mankind …………apart from the Volkswagen Beetle and the autobahns?' said Scobie. 'I'll be damned!'

Scobie's face fell. The tall officer who was standing

behind the table grinned and gave Lee a bone-crushing handshake. He spoke in a broad Ulster accent.

'Major Paddy Mayne of the Special Air Service – or SAS for short. Pleased to meet you, Captain!'

Scobie turned to Mayne.

'So Captain Lee is a British Army officer who doesn't smoke and doesn't drink. How unusual. I hope the two of you are going to get along. I know you like your fags and your booze, Paddy.'

Mayne laughed as Scobie continued.

'Now that we have got the introductions out of the way I must explain the reason for this meeting. Captain Lee, you have been ordered to participate in a crucial mission to deliver a certain … item to our intelligence services in Cairo. Do you know what this is?'

Scobie opened a wooden ammunition crate filled with straw to reveal what looked like an American electric typewriter. Yet, it was like no typewriter that Lee had ever seen. There was a keyboard but no rollers or ribbon. Around the keyboard were a few coloured lights and several discs which fitted into slots. There were also numerous wires, single - pin plugs and sockets. Lee had no idea what he was looking at but all the same he had a feeling that he had seen one of these machines before. Then he remembered.

'It's a German Enigma coding machine.'

Scobie and Mayne both looked surprised that a Captain in the RAMC had recognised a top - secret German coding apparatus. But Lee had an explanation.

'I used to build radios before the war and have always been interested in electronics and science. The Enigma machine itself is no secret. The first examples were built in 1923 and have been freely available for purchase by civilians. I saw a photo of one in *Practical Wireless* magazine in 1935. While the machine itself is not secret, the exact details of the code settings and the crucial rotors are. There are tens of millions of possible combinations of rotors and plug-board settings. I imagine that the Germans think Enigma is unbreakable but I 'm sure we must have a team working on it right now.'

Scobie recovered his composure and laughed.

'Well, Captain Lee, your powers of deduction are remarkable. You're quite correct in everything you say. Four days ago a Long Range Desert Group patrol captured a German radio truck intact. The vehicle had broken down, and the crew died of thirst before they could be rescued. It seems they got lost. The German search party looked for them in the wrong part of the desert. The truck contained the machine you see here, plus a codebook and a set of the latest rotors

'We hoped to get the machine back to Britain via Alexandria and Cairo. The original plan was to take it back on HMS *Kiwi* but that is now impossible. There isn't time to send another vessel as we expect Tobruk to fall soon so we will have to get the Enigma out by road.'

'How exactly are you going to do that, with Axis forces closing in?' asked Lee.

'We're going tonight under cover of darkness. We can't go due east because Rommel's forces are moving into blocking positions to prevent an evacuation along the coast road. No, we think the best plan is to head south through a gap in the Axis lines. I think it would be best if Major Mayne explained further.'

Mayne picked up a pencil and indicated a road on the map.

'As Brigadier Scobie indicated, our plan is to go south and head towards the Qattara Depression. This is largely impassable to vehicles, even the latest American Willys MB jeeps and the LRDG's Chevy trucks, so we intend to follow a road that runs east along the northern edge of the Depression. There is a network of tracks across the Great Sand Sea, which we can use to get back to Alexandria without making contact with Axis forces. As you know, most of the fighting in the North African campaign so far has taken place in the narrow coastal strip. The Axis forces tend to avoid the Qattara Depression as it is a death trap with its areas of treacherous salt marshes and quicksands. There are a few tracks that light vehicles can use to cross the Depression but it is highly risky.'

Lee's brow furrowed.

'It sounds like a dangerous plan to me. With the Enigma machine being so important why don't you fly it out?'

'We did consider that option,' answered Scobie. 'But with the Axis now having air superiority over Tobruk, any aircraft we use is likely to be shot down. However, we *do* intend to fly the Enigma back to Cairo but *not* from Tobruk. The first stage of the mission involves getting to this forward landing ground north of the Qattara Depression.'

Scobie indicated a small point on the map with his pencil.

'The Desert Air Force based Hurricanes here during Operation Crusader. Currently, the airstrip is not in use and the runway is just flattened sand, but an RAF Bristol Bombay transport will land there two days from now to pick up the Enigma and take it back to Egypt.'

Scobie continued as Lee and Mayne listened attentively.

'Major Mayne, your orders are to avoid contact with the enemy until the Enigma has been picked up. Once you have completed this part of the mission, you have permission to engage any targets of opportunity on the way back to Alexandria.'

Lee's mouth felt dry. This all sounded dangerous.

'One question, sir. What do we do if we bump into an Axis patrol?'

' I think I will ask Major Mayne to answer,' replied Scobie.

'First of all, I should explain that we will be passing through the Axis lines at night,' said Mayne. Secondly, about three-quarters of the trucks used by Rommel's forces in North Africa are captured British Army vehicles. Furthermore, my men are painting out the British Army markings on our trucks and applying Afrika Korps insignia using captured stencils. We always carry Afrika Korps caps in our vehicles and some of my men speak a little German and Italian so we don't foresee any problem getting through their lines. We have done the same thing many times during our raids on their airfields and ammunition dumps.

'I should also explain that this will be a joint mission between the SAS and the Long Range Desert Group. We'll be using six of the LRDG's latest vehicle, the American Chevrolet 1533, thirty – hundredweight truck. Although it only has two-wheel drive to the rear axle, it has good performance in sandy conditions. If we get stuck we can use the metal sand channels we carry on the sides of all our vehicles. The Chevy also has better fuel consumption than a four- wheel drive truck. The LRDG has been getting twelve miles per gallon. Quite impressive for a big six-cylinder petrol engine. We will be taking as much food, water and petrol as we can carry and will be well-armed.'

Mayne turned to Scobie as he concluded his impromptu presentation.

'I 've also beefed up the armament on the Chevys, sir. I 've ordered all the Lewis guns to be removed and replaced with Vickers Ks which are lighter and have double the rate of fire. I've also obtained a couple of American fifty - calibre M2 Brownings. They have excellent range and hitting power and can pierce almost an inch of armour plate at close range. We also have some Nobel 808 plastic explosive and time pencils in case we feel like getting up to some mischief on the way home.'

'But why do you need me on this mission?' asked Lee. 'As you said yourself, I am a medical officer, a qualified doctor. I can handle firearms as you know, but I am not a commando.'

'The LRDG always takes a medical orderly on their missions. Unfortunately, the only available man has developed acute appendicitis so General Auchinleck has suggested you go in his place. As it happens, with the rapid changes in the war situation, the RAMC now wants you back in Alexandria rather than becoming a POW here in Tobruk. You should be grateful that you are being offered an opportunity to get out as many of us are going to end up in the bag. And you will be taking part in an important mission that has been personally approved by Churchill himself.'

'I'll try to look at it that way, sir!'

Scobie and Mayne smiled but Lee felt a gnawing pain in his stomach. Was it gastritis or just anxiety? It was a good plan but as the saying goes, no plan ever survives contact with the enemy. And if the Germans found out what was going on, they would do everything they could to thwart the mission. Lee didn't know it at the time, but they were all heading for more danger than they could ever have foreseen. And few of them would survive to see Alexandria.

# Chapter 3

## Spies Like Us

Abdul Rashid hated the British. His visceral loathing began when he was a boy in Cairo. Like many Arab families in that hot, stinking, fly – ridden city, he had known only poverty and disease. With two brothers and three sisters, Abdul lived in a small hovel on the outskirts of the city near the Great Pyramids at Giza. All the children shared one bedroom and there was no bath or shower, just a single cold water tap. His father, Hoshi worked as a waiter at a British Army officers' club in the centre of the city while his mother Leyla struggled to bring up six children in their filthy, cramped accommodation.

Egypt had supposedly become an independent country in 1922 but the British Forces refused to leave and had actually increased their garrison, particularly around the Suez Canal, which was vital to the British Empire. Then in 1925 his father had been arrested on a charge of murder. A British major had been found dead in an alleyway, his throat cut and his wallet stolen. Word on the street was that it was the work of a fellow soldier who had got involved in a drunken argument with the major over a woman. But the Cairo police were under pressure to arrest someone quickly, put them on trial and give them the harshest possible sentence. And the British authorities didn't want one of their soldiers to be prosecuted as it would worsen relations with the local population.

Within three days, Hoshi had been arrested. The following week he was put on trial. There was only circumstantial evidence against him but the prosecutor was very skilled and Hoshi was inarticulate. He was hanged five days later.

The incident shocked Abdul and he vowed that he would do everything possible to bring about a British withdrawal from Egypt. A new radical organisation called the Muslim Brotherhood had recently become established in Egypt, and Abdul became a member. But the young Egyptian was sufficiently intelligent to understand that his goal might take twenty years to achieve. For the time being he would have to blend in to Cairo society. To maintain his cover he would have to pretend to like the British.

At the age of sixteen, he went to technical college in Cairo and learned to repair radios. When he wasn't studying or going to college, he worked as a waiter at the posh Shepheard's Hotel which was frequented by British officers and diplomats. Abdul was popular with the customers and became highly adept at hiding his true feelings. He became known as a friendly waiter who always put his customers first, and so got a lot of tips. He seemed to like the British and knew a lot about their culture. Fish and chips, football, Dundee cake and the Piccadilly Line. Arthur Askey and Noel Coward.

In 1936 Abdul visited a cinema and saw a foreign newsreel. It showed a man called Adolf Hitler addressing a huge rally in Nuremberg, Germany. Abdul thought Hitler didn't look physically impressive with his Charlie Chaplin moustache and possibly the worst haircut in history. But he was bowled over by the man's personal magnetism and powerful delivery. Abdul didn't understand German but there were caption cards in Arabic which explained everything.

Hitler explained that all the world's problems were caused by the Jews. International Jewry had caused the Great War and Jewish bankers were behind Wall Street crash and the Great Depression.

Abdul left the cinema a changed man. Hitler spoke the truth. Almost certainly the British Empire was allied to International Jewry. He had to destroy both the British and the Jews. But how?

In 1938 Abdul completed his studies and saved enough money to open a small radio shop in the centre of Cairo. It sold all the latest brands such as Bush, Phillips and Blaupunkt and offered a quick repair service at competitive prices.

Then one afternoon in June 1941, a bespectacled middle-aged European man in a white tropical suit called at Abdul's shop. He was carrying a large, portable Bush radio that required urgent repair. As the visitor polished his glasses with his handkerchief and then mopped his sweaty brow he explained he was a Swiss businessman called Gumbold and handed Abdul his business card.

After Gumbold had left, Abdul studied the card and found a message on the back scribbled in blue ink which told him that the strange visitor wanted to meet him at 7.00 p.m. at a nearby café on a matter of national importance.

Three hours later, Abdul sat at a table in the café sipping a glass of hot cinnamon tea with lots of sugar. The open door let in a blast of warm air with the usual Cairo pong. Outside, market traders had set up stalls which sold flat bread and watermelons. Rather emaciated donkeys and camels laden with goods sauntered down the heavily potholed street, dropping dung everywhere. A maroon Austin Seven with a dented front wing and a missing headlight drove past. It was covered with yellow dust and looked as though it hadn't been washed for years.

Abdul looked at his cheap watch. It was 7.03 p.m. Was Gumbold going to show? A moment later the Swiss man appeared, pink-faced and puffing.

'Sorry I'm late,' explained Gumbold. 'My taxi got stuck behind a slow - moving donkey cart. Let's go to the room at the back where we can talk in private.'

A minute later the two men sat in a small private room, cooled by a single electric ceiling fan which made a faint whump – whump – whump sound. Gumbold enjoyed the welcome blast of cold air, which dried the sweat on his brow. A waiter brought two glasses of hot mint tea in silver holders, some sugar cubes and a plate of sweet baklava and then left, closing the door behind him. Gumbold dropped two sugar cubes into his glass, stirred the tea with a long-handled silver spoon and then spoke to Abdul in perfect Arabic.

'First of all I must explain that I am a representative of the Third Reich. My real name is Major Heinrich Strasser and I am a member of the Abwehr, German Military Intelligence. We are aware that you are a member of the Muslim Brotherhood and consequently have no love of the British. That is the reason I am not afraid to tell you my true identity. I take it that you would be glad to see the British leave Egypt permanently?'

Abdul nodded as he sipped his tea. Strasser continued.

'Good. Our leader, Adolf Hitler has similar aims. Earlier this year, the Führer sent a newly created force, the Deutsche Afrika Korps, under the command of General Rommel, to Libya to assist Mussolini's armies. The Afrika Korps has been successful beyond our wildest dreams and, equipped with our latest Panzer IIIs and Panzer IVs, is expected to push all the way to Cairo and beyond. Eventually we hope to capture Palestine and prevent it from ever becoming a Jewish state. We will then capture the oilfields in Iran and link up with our forces in Russia. At that point we will effectively have won the war and the British will be forced to sue for peace. We will then mass all our forces against the Bolsheviks and defeat them completely.'

Abdul listened with great interest. He knew the Jews were hoping to establish a homeland in Palestine after the war had ended. That had to be stopped at all costs. Strasser ate a piece of baklava as the young man reflected on what he had said. Then he continued.

'The Führer is very sympathetic to Arab aspirations. He would welcome the removal of French and British dominance of North Africa and the establishment of truly independent Arab states. All we ask in return is control of the Suez Canal, the use of ports such as Alexandria and access to the oilfields in Iran. So I hope you can see that for all your organisation's goals to be achieved, it will first be necessary for Germany to win the war.'

Abdul nodded in agreement.

'So what do you want me to do?'

Strasser smiled. Outside the café a taxi driver was hooting noisily at a Ford pick – up truck which had broken down.

'We already have enough spies in Cairo but we are keen to have a pair of eyes in Tobruk. As you may know, this key port in Libya has been a thorn in our flesh for some time. Although we have helped our Italian allies to recapture Libya and threaten Egypt, the port of Tobruk remains in British hands. Currently the garrison includes many Australian troops who are very tough fighters. The port is being resupplied by sea, despite the efforts of the Luftwaffe and the Kriegsmarine.

'So, to answer your question, we want you to move your business to Tobruk. You will be taken there in an Italian submarine and dropped off at night in a deserted cove. We have already found a suitable shop near the British Army HQ. There is a comfortable flat over the shop and you will be well paid for serving the Reich.'

A month later, Abdul had relocated to Tobruk and began his spying activities. Details of troop deployments, anti-aircraft and artillery positions and shipping movements were all logged and sent back to Tripoli by coded radio messages. At the same time, he spent a lot of time establishing his radio repair business and making friends with the locals. He was well-liked by the British and Commonwealth forces garrisoning the port and soon gained a reputation for a quick, friendly service and low prices.

Then on 20 June 1942, Abdul noticed something unusual happening. For some months he had observed the British Army vehicle compound next to their HQ and had become quite adept at identifying the different trucks used by the enemy, such as the Bedford QL three-tonners and the large, six-wheeled AEC Matadors.

But the six odd-looking vehicles which were parked in the compound were of a type he had never seen before.

Abdul consulted a folder of photographs that had been supplied by his Abwehr handler and discovered they were Canadian – manufactured Chevrolet trucks which had been stripped of much of their bodywork to lighten them for desert operations. The entire cab, including the doors and windscreen, had been removed, and a rubber hose lead from the top of the radiator to a cylindrical metal condenser can. Sitting on the top of the dash was what looked like a sundial.

Abdul looked at his folder again and discovered more about the vehicles. They were Chevrolet 1533 30cwt trucks. The newest variant. They were used by only one unit – the legendary Long Range Desert Group, LRDG for short. From reading his notes, Abdul learned that the sundial was actually a gadget called the Bagnold Sun Compass which was more effective than a traditional magnetic compass in the vast reaches of the desert. The can and hose device which he had seen was a clever yet simple way of recycling radiator water.

So what was the LRDG doing in Tobruk? Abdul knew that this unit had two main activities-carrying out raids on airfields and ammo dumps, and also establishing road watches to report on vehicle movements. Usually the LRDG operated from a number of bases deep in the desert which had so far escaped detection. Something big was happening so Abdul decided to close his shop early and keep the compound under observation from his bedroom window using a pair of Zeiss binoculars. He had already hung a net curtain so he could not be seen.

All that day, mechanics and fitters swarmed over the vehicles, inflating tyres, loading stores, checking the oil, changing spark plugs and air filters and fitting additional machine guns. One squaddie was even painting what looked like white Afrika Korps insignia on the sides of the trucks using stencils held on with masking tape.

At 11.00 hrs a tall, well – built man wearing an officers cap appeared and started giving orders. Through his binoculars, Abdul could see that the cap had an unusual badge consisting of a winged dagger. Again he consulted his folder and found that the officer was none other than Major Paddy Mayne of the Special Air Service, better known as the SAS.

So the Special Air Service was teaming up with the Long Range Desert Group for a clandestine mission . What could that be? And what was in that ammunition box that had been loaded into the first truck? The soldiers carrying it were treating it as though it contained bone china. And the trucks were now guarded by an armed sentry. That was something new.

Could they be planning a raid on an airfield or ammunition dump? Or could it be something even more important? Abdul knew that he must inform his handler who would get a coded radio message through to the Abwehr unit in Tripoli. Then the Germans and their Italian allies could take defensive measures. The only problem was that once the convoy of LRDG vehicles headed out of Tobruk they would be impossible to track and would soon get lost in the vastness of the desert. He had to find a way of keeping tabs on them. But how? Then Abdul spotted a dismantled radio on his workbench and had an idea.

# Chapter 4

# Making Waves

Abdul took a few minutes to find it. Inside a dusty cupboard in his hall he kept a tattered cardboard box filled with old American and British radio magazines that he had acquired during his college days. And there it was, just as he remembered it. An article in the December 1936 edition of the US journal, *Radio Engineering* that explained how to convert a domestic radio receiver into a simple transmitter.

The author, Al Finkelstein III (what strange names these Yankees had!), had gone into great detail about how to create a 'home broadcaster' which could transmit speech to other radios in a house. The principle was quite simple. In a modern multi- valve super- heterodyne receiver, the local oscillator could be disconnected and used to generate a radio signal. Then, the moving coil speaker could be employed as a microphone and its output fed into the input of the audio amplifier which, in turn was rewired to modulate the carrier wave. Yet, Abdul realised he didn't even need anything that complex . All he required was a modification to the local oscillator so that it would generate a simple carrier wave with a constant audio tone that could be picked up by the German Army's radio direction finding equipment. He would increase the signal strength by putting the signal through a radio frequency amplifier employing two thermionic valves. Abdul plugged in his Solon soldering iron, selected his other tools, and got to work. It should only take about an hour.

*******

The briefing room at the Army HQ in Tobruk stank of

stale sweat and cigarette smoke, the walls stained with nicotine. Despite a couple of whirling ceiling fans and open shutters, the heat was oppressive, and Lee could feel his beige short – sleeved battledress shirt sticking to his back as he sat on a wooden folding chair at the front of the room. He faced sixteen soldiers with sunburnt faces and noticed that many of them had beards. Some had longish hair. Could this gang of scoundrels - who resembled thieves or pirates - really be some of Britain's best fighting men?

Mayne stood beside a blackboard and waited for the nervous chatter to die down before he began his presentation. On the wall behind him was a large colour map of the Western Desert affixed with ten brass drawing pins.

'Your attention please. You may not know it but this evening you are going to embark on one of the most important missions of the war. Two of you are members of the Special Air Service, the rest of you are from the Long Range Desert Group. We have worked together before. SAS troops have been taken to enemy airfield targets and back in LRDG vehicles on numerous occasions. We also do many of the same things, like attacks on ammunition dumps and airfields and road watches.

'But tonight, for the very first time, a mixed force of SAS and LRDG soldiers will be departing Tobruk on a vital mission which has been sanctioned by Churchill himself. We will be heading south through Axis lines, heading towards the Qattara Depression. Then we will turn east along the northern edge of the Depression until we reach a former Desert Air Force Advanced Landing Ground at Al - Balad.'

Mayne touched the map with his pointer. ' Al-Balad is here though the airfield itself is not shown on any map.'

'We've allowed ourselves two days to get there. At 19.00hrs on 22nd June an RAF Bristol Bombay transport plane will land on the strip and we will hand over a package which will be flown to Cairo via Alexandria,and from there back to the UK in an RAF B-24 Liberator bomber. You are probably all wondering what is in that package that is so important. I can't give you exact details for reasons of national security. All I can say is that it is vital for the Allied war effort. So important that we consider its safe delivery to be more important than the fate of Tobruk. We expect this port to fall into enemy hands within forty-eight hours. It will be a severe blow to Allied morale, but in the long-term the fate of this package is more important to the outcome of this war than the loss of a town. Are there any questions at this stage?'

A young sergeant with blond curly hair and a thin beard put up his hand. He spoke in a Yorkshire accent.

'Sergeant Binns, LRDG. Will we have any opportunity to engage the enemy, sir? We're all fighting soldiers, not delivery boys. Surely we should be staying behind to cause as much damage to the enemy as possible.'

Mayne leaned on his pointer and looked the soldier straight in the eye.

'I take your point, Binns. I like a good scrap myself, but the Prime Minister himself has ordered us to carry out this mission. Once the package is safely aboard the Bombay and on its way back to Cairo then we have permission to engage any targets of opportunity on our way home. We will be packing plenty of firepower and carrying copious quantities of plastic explosives …..our beloved Nobel 808 …. so we will have our fun on the back to Alex.'

Mayne gave a knowing wink. All the men roared with laughter.

'Now, I want to talk about the details of the mission. We will be using our latest patrol vehicle, the Canadian Chevrolet 1533, thirty hundredweight truck. As you know, it has a very reliable six - cylinder engine which gives twelve miles per gallon in desert conditions. That will give us a range of 240 miles on a full tank of petrol so we will carry as many spare fuel cans as we can cram into the vehicles. We also have the option of topping up our supplies of food, water and ammunition from a number of LRDG dumps which have been established across the desert. Some have been established around an oasis such as the base at Siwa, others in abandoned forts.

'We will be taking six trucks on this mission. I will be in the number one truck along with a driver and gunner. All the trucks will carry three personnel. The number five truck will carry a captured 20 mm Breda autocannon and the number six truck will be our radio vehicle containing our standard Number 11 set. If you look at the typed sheets that are on the green felt notice board at the back of the room you will find out which vehicle you have been allocated to. All the Lewis guns have been replaced with twin Vickers Ks with a much higher rate of fire, and we will be taking a couple of the latest American M2 fifty-calibre Brownings, which can even pierce thin armour. Their armour - penetrating capability is similar to the Boys anti-tank rifles we already use.

'One other thing. The number four truck will be the only one with a canvas cover over the truck bed. That is because it is configured as the Medical Officer's vehicle. Normally we carry a medical orderly on our patrols but on this occasion we will have an actual medical doctor, Captain Peter Lee of the Royal Army Medical Corps who is sitting here in front of you.'

Lee blushed at the sudden attention.

'Captain Lee is Scottish by the way. He graduated from Glasgow University Medical School last year so no jibes please about haggis, kilts or why the Scottish football team hasn't been doing so well recently!'

The men laughed. Lee grinned.

Mayne continued. 'By the way we have two other Scots in this patrol, Corporal McAleese and Private McTavish , both members of the SAS. We also have a first- class mechanic in our team, Davy Atkins. I have known Davy for a year. He was a motor mechanic before the war and is great at repairing engines and fixing punctures. He can also drive any kind of motor vehicle, whether wheeled or tracked, and can handle just about any firearm. Now are there any more questions at this stage?'

*******

While Mayne concluded his briefing, Abdul completed his makeshift radio transmitter, which consisted of a mess of wires and electronic components attached to a simple metal chassis. He connected the black, cotton – covered power lead to a six-volt lead - acid battery using chunky crocodile clips and noticed the filaments of the thermionic valves glow cherry red. Then he used a radio receiver to check that the device was emitting a signal which could be picked up as a constant sound of 100 cycles per second audio frequency.

All he had to do now was fit the apparatus inside a suitable wooden box. There was no shortage of them round the back of his shop. Abdul selected one which was ten inches long and six inches wide and deep. His transmitter fitted snugly inside and Abdul secured it to the base of the box with four short woodscrews. Then he drilled a small hole in the side with a hand- drill to allow the power cable to exit and fitted the top of the box, which he secured with four screws.

Abdul prised open a tin of quick - drying, sand - coloured cellulose paint with a screwdriver, applied a coat of the matt finish to the box and left it outside to dry in the hot sun while he selected a few British Army vehicle stencils which he kept in a drawer. Once the paint on the box had dried, he used the stencils to apply some lettering with matt black paint which read 'W.D.' plus the well - known 'arrow' symbol. Underneath it he put the words 'Radio Amp No 17.'

Abdul stood back and admired his work. Even he had to admit that it now looked like a piece of British Army radio equipment. All he had to do now was infiltrate the Army compound next door, fit his device to the patrol's radio truck and connect the power lead to the existing

Number 11 radio set's supply which he knew - from reading the Chevrolet truck's manual - would be six volts with a positive earth. Abdul prepared to leave the shop with his radio transmitter and bag of tools just as Mayne completed his presentation.

*******

'If there are no other questions then I would like you all to retire to your barracks and get your heads down for a few hours because we will be driving all night and we are not going to get much sleep in the next few days. Your trucks are being loaded by Royal Army Ordnance Corps And Royal Army Service Corps fitters and an armed sentry is guarding them. At 22.00 hours the cookhouse will give you all a good feed and at 23.00 hours we will get moving. I hope you manage to get some kip because you are all going to need it.'

The soldiers left the briefing room, puffing at their fags and headed to their beds. Even the hard metal-framed beds and itchy blankets in their barracks were luxury compared to sleeping in the back of a truck or on the desert floor. Lee picked up his bulky kitbag and moved to the door. Mayne stopped him by standing in the doorway.

'So how do you feel, going on a dangerous mission behind enemy lines for the first time?'

'Scared,' replied Lee.

'Me too. The worst part is the few hours before the mission begins. Once you're in action you'll be fine. Now I suggest we both grab some sleep for a few hours. See you at dinner.'

*******

Just thirty yards away, Abdul arrived at the gates of the compound carrying the 'Radio Amp' and a small bag of tools. A military policeman with a holstered pistol let him through the gates but he was immediately challenged by an

LRDG Corporal who carried a Thompson sub-machine gun.

'Halt! Where do you think you're going?'

'My name is Abdul Rashid. I run the radio store next door. Major Mayne authorised me to repair this radio amplifier and fit it into one of these trucks.'

'That doesn't sound right. We have our own RAOC radio technicians who do that kind of thing!'

'Ah , but this is the latest American equipment. Gifted by our good friend President Roosevelt. Your own people do not know how to fix it as it uses a new type of thermionic valve created by RCA in the USA. But Abdul is up-to-date with the latest technology and reads radio magazines. I fix it good.'

'I'm still not sure about this. I'm going to phone Major Mayne right now. He told me that no-one was to be allowed anywhere near the trucks.'

The sentry, Corporal Forbes, picked up the phone in the sentry box and got through to the HQ's switchboard but found that Major Mayne had gone to bed and had given instructions that he was to be woken only if there was an emergency. Forbes put the receiver down and walked towards Abdul.

'Let me see what's inside that box. I want to make sure you don't have a bomb there.'

Abdul put the box on the ground and retrieved a small screwdriver from his tool bag. Then he removed the four screws and prised open the lid to reveal a jumble of electronic components. Forbes was no expert in technical matters but he recognised thermionic valves, wires, capacitors , resistors, a terminal block and a tuning coil. There was no sign of an explosive charge so maybe the Arab was telling the truth.

'OK, I believe you. You can fit your device but be quick about it. The radio truck is the last one on the left.'

Abdul scrambled onto the truck bed and put the box on the wooden floor as close as possible to the Number 11 set. Then he secured the apparatus to the planks using four stout screws and put the lid back on. To make it harder to open, he applied a thick blob of sand - coloured paint to each screw-head. His last job was to connect the transmitter to the power feed for the existing radio using a small , hidden junction box. He stood back and admired his work. The box looked as though it had always been a part of the truck's equipment and he was sure that no - one would ever guess its true purpose.

Abdul jumped down from the truck, flashing white teeth as Corporal Forbes came over.

'Thank you, my British friend. Now you have a more powerful radio you can go and beat my enemies, the Germans and Italians. We work together to win the war, eh! One more thing. My brother Anwar, he runs a club in Cairo called *The Kasbah*. British soldiers always welcome.'

Abdul handed Forbes a card.

' You go there if you get to Cairo on your next leave. You tell Anwar that Abdul sent you. He get you prettiest girls who do anything you ask. Abdul winked and gave Forbes a sly grin.

Forbes smiled and his pupils dilated. One thing lacking in Tobruk was pretty women.

Abdul chuckled. What Forbes didn't know was that the *Abwehr* used the *Kasbah* as a base for a 'honey-trap'. British servicemen would be lured into the club and then photographed during the sexual act by a hidden photographer. A few married British Officers had been blackmailed into revealing military secrets by this method. Still, Forbes would probably be a POW within a day or two so it didn't matter too much. And Abdul's important task had been completed. Now the Germans and Italians could monitor the location of the British raiding force. There would be nowhere for them to hide. They would be found and hunted down. It was only a matter of time.

# Chapter 5

# Escape From Tobruk

Lee tossed and turned in his metal-framed Army bed as anxious thoughts flitted through his mind. Soon he would set out on a dangerous mission. He could be killed, mutilated or captured by the enemy. And if he became a POW, the Germans might discover he was Jewish and things could become very difficult for him.

German forces in North Africa had behaved well, scrupulously observing the provisions of the Geneva Convention. Rommel had even ignored direct orders from Hitler to kill Jews, and a lack of SS units in North Africa meant that old-fashioned chivalry prevailed. But all that might change if he was taken prisoner and shipped to Germany.

A year earlier, he had changed his name from Levy to Lee to make his religion less obvious. A lot of Jewish serviceman had done this. There was even a German Jew who had joined the RAF and had changed his name from Klaus Adam to Ken Adam.

Lee was soaked in sweat and the rough woollen blankets irritated his skin, but the bed was probably as comfortable as any you would find in Tobruk in June 1942. All the other soldiers were fast asleep, including Major Mayne, who snored loudly. But they were all hardened combat veterans who had learned to nod off just about anywhere. On the desert floor. In the back of a truck. In a trench or foxhole. So a metal- framed bed with a hard mattress and coarse blankets in a hot dormitory would seem like luxury to them.

Lee could have taken a barbiturate sleeping pill, which would give him a few hours of rest. He had a bottle of them in his medical kit. But then he would be groggy for the first few hours of the mission, a time when he needed to be fully alert. For the hundredth time, Lee turned over in bed in the hope of finding a more comfortable position and heard the distant crump of British 25-pounder field guns as they engaged in an artillery duel with their German and Italian counterparts. Since Lee had arrived in the North African theatre a few weeks earlier, he had learned to identify different weapons by their unique sounds. The buzzsaw noise of a German MG34 or MG42 which the British always referred to as a 'Spandau.' The more leisurely chatter of a Vickers Maxim gun. And the slow, precise bang – bang – bang of a Bren, which was usually fired in short bursts. Despite the racket, Lee's eyes eventually closed and he enjoyed a few hours of blissful sleep.

While the members of the British patrol rested before their mission, a dozen fitters from the Royal Army Ordnance Corps (RAOC) and Royal Army Service Corps (RASC) completed their work on the six Chevrolet trucks. Petrol tanks were topped up, oil levels measured with dipsticks and the engine cooling system checked for leaks. Spark plugs were cleaned and replaced if required. New air filters were fitted. The heavy duty tyres were inflated with compressed air to the correct pressure and all lights tested. One Chevy had a broken headlamp which was replaced by a unit taken from a shot- up vehicle.

Five of the six vehicles were loaded with ammunition. Metal boxes of 0.303 inch rounds and spare magazines for the Brens. As many 100 round drums for the Vickers K machine guns as could be carried. And boxes of grenades, Nobel 808 plastic explosive, time pencils and detonators. The fitters were particularly impressed by the two big shiny, black Browning M2 fifty-calibre machine guns which had been recently been delivered. Although their rate of fire wasn't that much greater than a Bren or Vickers Maxim, they used a heavy bullet which had tremendous stopping power. A single round could decapitate a man or pierce thin armour. It wouldn't be effective against the thick frontal armour of a tank but could defeat the thinner plating of a half-track or armoured car. It gave the patrol a great increase in firepower. Both Brownings were new and were coated in Cosmoline, a protective grease which had to be removed. Along with the other machine guns, they were cleaned, oiled and tested by the technicians.

Then the soldiers loaded as much food, water and petrol onto the Chevys as they could carry, their leaf-spring suspensions groaning under the weight. Mayne had asked for two-thirds of the petrol to be carried in captured German 'jerrycans', far superior to the British 'flimsies' which were like giant square food cans, and tended to leak at the seams. The flimsies would be used first and could then be employed as 'desert cookers', filled with sand drenched in petrol.

Truck Four was filled with medical supplies, consisting of various drugs including morphine , dressings , bandages and a simple surgical kit. Truck Five was fitted with a captured Italian 20mm Breda cannon while the last truck in the patrol carried a standard Number 11 radio set. The fitter noted a sand – coloured box had been installed on the truck floor.

'What's this for?' he asked his sergeant as he pointed at the new addition. ' I haven't seen one of these before'

'Well judging by the lettering, I would say it's a radio frequency amplifier to increase the range of transmissions. Now get a move on so we can have our tea!' The fitter nodded. That seemed like a reasonable explanation.

At 21.30 hrs. the members of the patrol rose, had a quick wash and made their way to the cookhouse where they had a meal of tinned Irish stew, canned carrots and mashed potatoes washed down with plenty of strong Army tea. At 22 .30 hrs they mounted their vehicles and did final checks on their weapons and equipment. At 22.57 hrs Mayne gave the order to start engines and half -a-dozen six - cylinder petrol motors sprung into life, clouds of white exhaust smoke blowing everywhere. Two MPs opened the gates of the compound and the trucks rolled forward, headlights blazing.

After the heat of the barracks, Lee welcomed the cooler night air which was now blowing through the truck and drying his sweat – soaked body. To save weight, the Chevys had the entire cab removed including both front doors and the windscreen, requiring the driver and front-seat passenger to wear goggles when at speed, but these modifications made the vehicle cooler when it was in motion. Some of the soldiers donned woollen caps but many wore traditional Arab *shemaghs* which gave them good protection from the sun. They could also double as dishcloths.

The streets of Tobruk were now deserted and most of the population remained indoors in their hovels, illuminated only by the weak light of a kerosene lamp. The potholed streets were littered with piles of camel dung. Wooden tables stood at the side of the road. They would become traders' stalls in the morning, selling local produce, such as figs, dates, eggs and flatbread.

A few flashes of gunfire lit up the horizon as artillery duels continued throughout the night. Searchlight beams criss-crossed the sky in an attempt to pick up the few Junkers Ju- 88 and Heinkel He-111 bombers that operated during the hours of darkness. No British night-fighters took to the skies to challenge them. Within 24 hours the port would be in Axis hands and 35,000 British and Commonwealth troops would be taken prisoner. The Allies weren't giving up without a fight though, and, as the convoy of six Chevys headed south, Lee saw a dozen tracked Universal Carriers towing six – pounder anti-tank guns heading west towards the battlefield at Gazala.

After twenty minutes, the column reached the southern outskirts of the port and all the vehicles switched off their lights as previously arranged. Mayne's plan was to get as far south of Tobruk as possible before dawn. Driving in the dark without lights was dangerous but it would cover their escape.

Just fifteen kilometres away, an Afrika Korps radio operator in the back of an Opel Blitz radio truck turned a small varnished, wooden wheel attached to a system of chains and gears which rotated a roof - mounted aerial. After checking his signal strength meter, he had a bearing on the source of the transmission which he heard in his headphones as a single tone. It was north-east of their truck's current position. Although he couldn't get an exact location fix without a second bearing from another radio van in a different location, the information supplied by the *Abwehr* was that this signal would be emanating from a joint SAS and LRDG convoy which was heading south out of Tobruk in six thirty-hundredweight Chevrolet trucks. The Afrika Korps *Landser* turned to his *Unteroffizier* as he listened to the steady tone in his headphones.

'There's no doubt about it. That's the signal we've been asked to look out for.'

The *Unteroffizier* smiled. 'Excellent. We can now set up an ambush. I will arrange for two other trucks to move into position to keep a track on the position of the target.'

'Are we going to ambush them at night?'

'I think that would be too risky. At night, the desert is as dark as a coal mine and some of the British soldiers might escape. Don't forget we only have a tracking device on one of the six trucks. If they split up, we could only locate the radio vehicle. No, I think we should intercept them at dawn as the sun as rising. One detachment will block the road to the north, another to the south and then strong forces backed by light armour will attack from the east and west simultaneously. They will be caught like rats in a trap. If they don't surrender they will all be killed!'

# Chapter 6

## Surrender!

**The Cabinet War Rooms, Whitehall**
**20 June 1942, 09.00 hrs**

Deputy Prime Minister Clement Attlee puffed at a Player's cigarette, stubbed it out in a round, pewter ashtray and studied the faces of the War Cabinet, who were sitting round the large mahogany conference table. On this occasion they had been joined by two of the Government's scientific advisors, Dr R.V. Jones and Professor Frederick Lindemann. Also present were the Government's chief military advisor, Field Marshall Alan Brooke, Sir Stewart Menzies, head of M.I.5, and Lieutenant Commander Ian Fleming, an officer in the Royal Navy Volunteer Reserve who now worked in Naval Intelligence at Admiralty Arch in Whitehall.

'Thank you for joining me today, gentleman,' said Attlee. 'As you know, Winston is in Washington for talks with the American President, so I have been asked to hold the fort while he is away. Unfortunately there has been some bad news from North Africa. The port of Tobruk in Eastern Libya has been held by British and Commonwealth forces for some time. For several months in 1941 it was besieged and cut off. In November 1941 the siege was finally lifted after our advances during Operation Crusader.

'Our forces are currently engaged in a desperate tank and artillery battle at Gazala, west of Tobruk. If the Germans and Italians win, as now seems highly likely, then Tobruk will fall tomorrow.'

There was a collective gasp round the room followed by a silence. Then Sir Stewart Menzies spoke.

'How many troops are likely to be captured?'

'We estimate 35,000,' replied Attlee. 'But even worse will be the considerable war booty that will fall into the hands of our enemies. Tens of thousands of gallons of petrol. Food. Ammunition. Guns. And trucks. Lots of trucks. They will be very useful to Rommel as the Germans are desperately short of motor transport.'

'But how could this happen?' asked Field Marshall Alan Brooke. 'Our forces have just received the latest equipment. The new six-pounder anti-tank gun which can pierce any enemy armoured vehicle. And the American M3 Grant tank which has two cannon, a 37mm plus a big 75mm on a side sponson. We should be winning, not losing.'

'You are quite correct,' said Attlee. 'The Army has indeed received a lot of new equipment but that doesn't make up for poor tactics and bad leadership. Once Winston gets back from the USA he is going to put a new General in charge of the Eighth Army. And rumour has it that President Roosevelt is about to send two hundred and fifty of the latest American M4 Sherman tanks to North Africa to equip our forces. They have a 75mm gun like the Grants but in a fully revolving turret. They also have reliable engines and decent armour protection.

'There is another factor I must tell you about, which has contributed to our recent military disasters. As some of you already know, the Americans have a military attaché in Egypt called Major Bonner Fellers. He has been sending detailed reports on our military operations back to Washington by means of coded radio messages. With our approval, of course. Unfortunately we have just discovered that this code has been compromised since last year as a result of the activities of the Italian Secret Service. Apparently they broke into the US Embassy in Rome last September before the USA entered the war, and stole the codes from a safe. This means that Rommel has known our every move for the last nine months. So it has no wonder that so many of our military operations in North Africa and the Mediterranean have gone wrong.

'However, now that the leak has been identified we are taking measures to stop it. Commander Fleming has even suggested that we start feeding the enemy false information from now on. If I may say so Ian, you seem to have a remarkable talent for dreaming up fantastic schemes. After the war you should write spy novels.'

Fleming smiled as he lit his tenth cigarette of the day. Everyone else laughed.

'However, let us not get things out of proportion. In the short term, the loss of Tobruk will be a great psychological blow to our forces. But in the long - term, I cannot see how Hitler can win because we now have Russia on our side, plus the Americans, who have a huge industrial capability which cannot be bombed.

'In addition, there are signs that we will soon break the Enigma code again. We did it once before but then the Germans added extra rotors and changed the settings. However, there has been a significant development which, rather ironically, involves Tobruk. A few days ago a Long Range Desert Group patrol captured a German radio truck in the desert which contained the latest Army Enigma machine plus spare rotors and code books. The crew died of thirst and the LRDG completely destroyed the truck with plastic explosives so the Germans won't know we've got one of their coding machines. As far as the Germans are concerned the truck was hit by an artillery shell and completely burned out.

'The machine was transported to Army HQ in Tobruk and will be taken out by road tonight in a convoy of trucks manned by men of the SAS and the LRDG. If all goes to plan it will be picked up by an RAF Bombay transport aircraft in two days' time and flown to Cairo via Alexandria and from there back to Britain in a B-24 Liberator bomber.'

'What landing ground will the Bombay be using?' asked Sir Stewart Menzies.

'I understand the Bombay will land at a disused forward landing strip at Al -Balad, north of the Qattara

Depression. The RAF based Hurricanes and Blenheims there during *Operation Crusader*. If all goes to plan, then we should have one of the latest German coding machines in our hands within a week. Our codebreakers at Bletchley Park will be glad to get their hands on it. I think that should please you, Ian.'

Fleming blew a cloud of smoke and stubbed out his cigarette in an ashtray before replying. Attlee noticed that his fingers were heavily stained with nicotine.

'It will indeed,' answered Fleming in his posh, Eton - educated voice. 'I must explain though, that the machine that has been captured in North Africa is an Army Enigma. For our code-breaking efforts to be completely successful, we must also have the latest *Kriegsmarine* Enigma which will enable us to fight the U–boats more effectively. The example that was captured by the crew of HMS *Bulldog* in May 1941 helped our codebreakers enormously. But the Germans recently upgraded their Enigmas by adding new rotors and plug- board settings. It is essential that we grab one of the latest models. For that reason we are planning a raid on the French port of Dieppe this summer. After the event, the official line will be that the raid was to test the feasibility of capturing an enemy port and to give us experience of amphibious landings.

'The real purpose of the mission though, will be the capture of a naval Enigma machine from a building within the town. To distract the Germans, we are going to take a squadron of our new Churchill tanks with us and ensure they get stuck on the shingle beach. This will reinforce the impression that the raid was a failure. But I predict that once we have both an Army and a Naval Enigma machine, then the tide of the war will start to turn in our favour.'

All the men round the table listened intently to every word that Fleming spoke. Even though he was a bit of a maverick, they had to admire his ingenuity and imagination. Earlier in the war, Fleming had proposed a number of madcap schemes to aid the war effort. He even had a plan – *Operation Ruthless* - to seize a naval Enigma machine. A German Heinkel He-111 bomber which had crashed in Britain in 1940, and been returned to airworthy condition for evaluation, would be deliberately ditched in the Channel by an RAF crew wearing Luftwaffe uniforms. When a German Air Sea rescue launch arrived on the scene, the British crew would overpower the sailors using hidden weapons, capture the launch, and sail it to a British port. Thus, the Intelligence Services would obtain an intact Naval Enigma machine. The plan was seriously considered but was eventually vetoed by the RAF who said it was too risky as ditched Heinkels tended to sink immediately because their glasshouse noses always caved in when they hit the sea. Yet, although the idea was never put into practice, Fleming recorded all the details in a moleskin note book which he always carried in a pocket in his uniform jacket. One day, after the war, when he became a thriller writer, these notes might be very useful, he thought.

Fleming lit up another of his favourite custom-made cigarettes using an American Zippo lighter. They were made especially for him by a tobacconist in Morland Street using a blend of Turkish and Balkan tobaccos and delivered to him by his girlfriend Muriel, who worked as a WREN.

'That all sounds very encouraging,' said Attlee. 'But first, our truck convoy must make it to Al-Balad without incident. There are a lot of enemy forces in the area and at present the Axis has air superiority over Libya and Western Egypt. Major Mayne will need to use all his skills to survive and I have a horrible feeling that things might go wrong.'

'I have heard of Al – Balad,' interrupted Dr R.V. Jones. 'It is on the edge of an area of the desert that is noted for its magnetic anomalies. When we had Blenheims based there during *Operation Crusader* their compasses wouldn't work. Over the years a number of aircraft have gone missing in the area. In 1938 a flight of five Vickers Wellesleys from 19 Squadron vanished. No trace of them was ever found. Some investigators have compared it with a triangular area between Bermuda and Florida where boats and planes often get lost.'

'Absolute poppycock, Dr Jones,' said Professor Lindemann, who sat next to him, sucking his pipe. 'You have been reading too many of these American science fiction magazines. Yes there are problems using conventional compasses in the Sahara, but that is because many of the mountain ranges contain magnetic rock. And metal in vehicle bodywork can also affect compasses. That is the reason the LRDG and the SAS prefer to use Bagnold solar compasses. What are you going to suggest next? Little green men from Mars!'

Everyone except Jones laughed. The young scientific advisor's face reddened. Even the usually lugubrious Attlee chuckled. 'A fair point Professor, but I think Major Mayne has more to worry about than magnetic anomalies. If the Germans and Italians discover the convoy then they will do everything they can to stop it. Major Mayne may have a battle on his hands and there is nothing we can do to help him. He will need to use all his fighting skills to survive. And as a religious man I pray that God is on his side.'

# Chapter 7

## Surrender or Die!

**South of Tobruk. 21 June 1942. 01.07 hrs**

Six Chevrolet trucks thundered south at thirty- five miles
per hour, headlight beams illuminating the red – striped
white wooden marker posts at the side of the road. In the
back of Truck Four, Lee felt a welcome blast of cool air
drying his sweaty back, armpits and face. In June, the
Libyan desert was one of the hottest places in in the world
with daytime temperatures of up to 120 degrees Fahrenheit
in the shade. At night it was less warm, particularly well
inland where the temperature approached freezing point,
so the trucks carried sleeping bags and warm clothing.
Now that they were well clear of the port, on the road to
Siwa Oasis, they had switched their headlights on again as
the risk of air attack had diminished. In any case, with
recent advances on the battlefield, any German or Italian
pilot would be unable to tell if the convoy was friend or
foe and so would be reluctant to attack.

In Truck One, Mayne also enjoyed the cool blast in the
front passenger seat. Some soldiers loved the desert, others
hated it. Scorching sun by day and cold at night. Flies
everywhere when you ate. Plus mosquitoes. Vehicle
bodywork that burned your skin if you touched it. And
insect bites that could turn into infected desert sores.
Tinned foods and hard tack biscuits for every meal,
washed down with tea made with Carnation milk. Sand as
fine as talcum powder that got everywhere. In your ears,
eyes, nose, mouth, hair and even under your foreskin. It
contaminated food, clogged carburettors and guns.

And there was never enough water. The standard
British Army ration was eight pints per man per day,
including one pint for shaving, washing and teeth-

brushing. Yet it was not enough — you were always thirsty, and soldiers often dreamt of drinking several pints of cold beer in a country pub.

Still, there were compensations. Deep in the desert, far from the coastal towns, the sky was clear and the stars bright. There was no air pollution from coal fires as there was in Britain. So at night, the Bagnold sun compass was replaced with astral navigation using a theodolite.

There was also an absence of noise. The sound of silence. And a freshness to the air, unlike sooty British cities. Yes, you could come to like the desert if people weren't shooting at you, thought Mayne. Maybe some decades from now, people would come here on holiday.

'Vehicles ahead, Major,' said Private Cornwell, who stood in the back of the lead truck manning a fifty-calibre Browning machine gun covered in a canvas shroud to keep out sand. Cornwell's revelation snapped Mayne out of his reverie.

As the six vehicles slowed down, Cornwell pulled off the gun's cover and yanked back the cocking lever. A belt of ammunition was already loaded.

Mayne slid up his scratched sand goggles to see better as the Chevys approached the obstruction. Their headlights illuminated the scene. Three sand-coloured vehicles straddled the road. A Bedford QL three-tonner, a Humber Heavy Utility Car and a Ford WOT 3 four -wheel drive Truck. All had British Army markings.

A stocky, moustachioed military policeman with a red-topped peaked cap and MP armband stepped out from the Humber and held up his right hand to indicate that the six Chevys should stop. The trucks halted with a squeal of drum brakes and a cloud of dust, engines ticking over noisily.

'Where do you think you're going?' asked the MP. 'We've got orders to blow this bridge over the wadi. In a few hours the Germans and Italians will be driving up this road. You must turn round and head back to Tobruk.'

Mayne studied the MP. He was wearing a clean, well -

pressed uniform. It smelled of soap powder and starch. His brown leather shoes were immaculately polished. Experienced North African veterans always wore suede Desert Boots. Some LRDG troops even wore sandals. And his immaculate belt and webbing had been whitened with Blanco. He was carrying a 0.38 Webley revolver in a canvas holster attached to his Sam Browne belt.

'Just off the boat are you sonny? You may be following orders but so am I. I'm Major Mayne of the Special Air Service and I'm leading a combined force of SAS and LRDG personnel on a mission of vital importance to the war effort.'

'What exactly is this mission? I wasn't informed about this. Our orders are to blow the bridge and turn back any vehicles.' The MP pulled his pistol from its holster and pointed it at Mayne.

'Sorry Major, you will turn back your column, *immediately*. My men are authorised to use force if necessary.' Mayne studied the Webley with disdain and then pointed at the big, gleaming, fifty - calibre machine gun behind him.

'Know what that is, Lieutenant? It's an American Browning M2, fifty- calibre. The Yanks call it the 'Ma Deuce.' The most powerful machine gun in the world. It weighs eighty - four pounds with a barrel nearly four feet long. Fires a bullet as big as your little finger. Just one round will rip the head clean off your shoulders and propel it into that wadi over there. And that beauty can fire six hundred shells a minute. We have two of them, plus several Brens and twin Vickers Ks. And we have a twenty millimetre Breda auto- cannon in Truck Five. My men are loyal, so if you shoot me they will wipe out your squad in the time it would take me to pick my nose. Now, I could contact London via Cairo and get confirmed authorization for this mission from Mr Attlee, or even Churchill, but it would take far too long and I don't want to break radio silence. Take my word for it, it will be a lot easier to kill you and your men and turn your vehicles into Swiss cheese. Our mission is so important that the lives of some sappers and MPs are unimportant. None of my men will face court martial for killing a few British soldiers who tried to stop us. I won't tolerate *any* obstruction. Millions of lives could depend on our operation succeeding. And, by the way, I outrank you.'

The lieutenant's face drained of colour and his gun started to shake.' You leave me no alternative, Major.'

The MP holstered his pistol and turned towards his squad of men.

'Get all our vehicles off the road. This convoy must get through. Once it has passed we will blow the bridge.'

The three sappers' vehicles reversed onto the sand beside the road and the six Chevys moved forward.

'Fucking bureaucrat,' muttered Mayne to his driver, Private Baker. 'These people are worse than the Nazis with their fucking forms and their toilet paper and their committee meetings and their standard procedures. After the war that guy will probably get a job in local government.'

Back in Truck Four , Lee chuckled to himself. He had heard the exchange and admired Mayne's assertiveness . In a few years, when the war was over, he was going to work for Britain's proposed new National Health Service and he expected they would employ a lot of idiots — just like that MP — in administrative posts.

The convoy resumed its journey south. Lee dozed off. Though he was sitting on a hard wooden bench seat, being bounced around by the crude leaf - spring suspension, he found the rocking motion soothing.

Up front in the lead truck, Mayne craved sleep. Right now he wished he was lying between clean, fresh Egyptian cotton sheets in the best room in Shepheard's Hotel in Cairo but he knew he had to stay awake and alert for any dangers. Then he heard it. A familiar thump, thump, thump coming from the offside front wing. The vehicle slowed down with the increase in rolling resistance and Baker gently applied the drum brakes and brought the vehicle to a halt.

'Everyone out,' barked Mayne as he inspected the damage with a torch. Only a flat tyre, but fixing it in total darkness would be difficult. 'Davy, where are you?' screamed Mayne. 'This is a job for you.'

Davy Atkins, the patrol's vehicle mechanic, was travelling in Truck Three as an M2 Browning gunner. Before the war he had worked in a garage and could fix tyres faster than anyone in the LRDG. He jumped over the side of his truck and headed toward the lead vehicle.

Davy inspected the damage. 'Normally this would be a straightforward job, Major. The only problem is that it's pitch black and it will be hard to for me to find the puncture in the inner tube. I will have to change the wheel and patch the hole in the inner tube when it's light tomorrow.'

'OK, but be as quick as you can,' answered Mayne , as he lit a cigarette with a match and took a deep draw. 'We can't afford to get behind schedule.'

Truck Two drove left off the road onto the sand and then turned round until its headlights were illuminating the nearside front wing of Truck One. Davy located the bottle jack, fitted it in place behind the front wheel and slowly raised the bodywork.

Ten minutes later, Davy had almost finished the job. He had replaced the wheel and was tightening the wheel nuts with a socket wrench when Cornwell yelled a warning .' Two vehicles approaching from the south with headlights on.'

Mayne turned his head. Two pairs of lights grew larger and brighter as they approached. He estimated there were only eight hundred yards away. But were they British, Commonwealth, German or Italian? Mayne made a snap decision.

'Everyone back to your vehicles,' he shouted to the crowd of soldiers who had gathered round the lead vehicle. Except you, Davy. Finish the job. And all men, put on your Afrika Korps caps. And get your guns ready!'

The vehicles drew closer. Even though it was dark,

Mayne recognised the distinctive shape of a German Sd. Kfz.222 four - wheeled armoured car followed by a Volkswagen Type 82 *Kubelwagen* scout car, containing four soldiers. Mayne didn't want a firefight so early in the mission. He might take casualties and lose vehicles and the precious Enigma machine could be destroyed. He would bluff it out.

Both German vehicles halted. An officer got out of the *Kubelwagen*. His driver kept the four-cylinder rear – mounted, air - cooled engine ticking over. Mayne felt a lump in his throat but had prepared for this scenario as Cornwell spoke German and Baker was fluent in Italian. Mayne himself knew a little German.

'I am Hauptmann Lutz. What is going on here?' asked the officer. ' This road must be kept clear as we will be advancing into Tobruk at first light.'

'We're fixing a flat tyre,' answered Cornwell, in perfect German with a Hamburg accent, as he stood in the back of the lead truck beside the fifty-calibre gun. 'Once it's done we'll be on our way.'

The German officer took out his notebook and a pencil. 'We weren't informed of any movements on this road. What unit are you from?'

'We're Brandenburgers,' answered Cornwell. 'On our way to our forward operating base.'

Lutz stroked his chin. That made sense. He had heard of the Brandenburgers. They were the closest thing the Afrika Korps had to the LRDG and SAS. Lutz took out a pocket torch and pointed it at the lead truck. 'I see you are using captured vehicles. Stripped-down Canadian Chevrolet trucks.'

'We captured them last week near Gazala. They belonged to the Long Range Desert Group. Very good in sand and excellent American six -cylinder petrol engines. If that one-balled house painter Hitler would only send us more vehicles we wouldn't have to use Allied ones. He's too busy porking that tart Eva Braun to think of logistics, Hauptmann!'

Lutz laughed and looked again at the vehicles. Their British Army markings had been painted out and white Afrika Korps palm tree-and-swastika logos had been applied to the wooden sides of the truck bodies.

'Everything seems in order. You may proceed.'

Lutz got back into his *Kubelwagen* and the two vehicles drove off, heading north. Mayne turned round to find Lee standing beside him.

'Mind if I join you in the lead truck, Major? I reckon it will be cooler and I don't want to miss any of the action.'

Mayne nodded as Davy tightened the last wheel nut and removed the jack.

Five minutes later, the truck convoy was on its way south. Mayne sat in the front passenger seat and smoked while Lee perched on the sideways-facing bench behind him. Mayne was silent so Lee started a conversation.

'It's hard to believe isn't it? If Hitler hadn't come to power we would be a doctor and a lawyer in civilian practice. Now we're taking part in one of the most important missions of the war. Civvie Street will seem so dull once this is all over. What do you see yourself doing once this is all over, Paddy?'

Mayne stubbed out his cigarette before answering. 'To be honest I'm not sure. Life in the Army can be quite dull during peacetime so I will probably resign my commission and go back to being a solicitor in Ulster. How about you?'

'I'm thinking of becoming a pathologist. It's the one branch of Medicine where the patients don't answer you back! I won the pathology prize at medical school. On the other hand I may just end up as a G.P. in the West of Scotland dishing out painkillers to people with sore backs.'

Mayne laughed as the convoy continued south, the sky gradually lightening in the east. At 05.18 hrs. the sun rose above the horizon, brilliant beams of golden light bathing the vehicles. Ten minutes later, a small aircraft appeared in the southern sky. It flew slowly, propelled by a low-power Argus in-line engine and had a distinctive appearance.

Large high-set wings supported by struts. A glasshouse canopy and long spindly fixed undercarriage legs. There were no wheel spats and it didn't have a radial engine so it wasn't a British Lysander. And there were large black crosses under the wings and on the fuselage sides. Mayne recognised it as a German Fieseler *Storch* reconnaissance plane.

As the *Storch* got nearer, all the British soldiers donned their *Afrika Korps* caps once more and waved at the pilot, who circled around the convoy twice, keeping out of effective machine gun range. Then the aircraft waggled its wings and headed west. They had been spotted, but did the pilot think they were friend or foe? They would soon find out.

Twenty minutes later Cornwell yelled a warning.

'Vehicles ahead!'

Several German armoured cars, lorries and half-tracks blocked the road. Soldiers spilled out from the vehicles and stood on the sand clutching MP40 sub machine- guns and Mauser bolt-action rifles. Baker slowed down as Mayne considered his options. He looked behind and saw another group of German vehicles moving onto the road about half-a-mile away. They had to get off the road but in which direction? East or west?

He glanced to his right and saw several German half-tracks and armoured cars cresting a rise and heading straight for them. Over to his left, despite the rising sun, he could just glimpse two Italian Autoblinda 41 armoured cars and three Lancia trucks heading towards them. They couldn't go forwards, backwards, right or left without running into enemy forces. They would be forced to surrender …or die!

# Chapter 8

# Combat!

The six Chevys halted, their engines ticking over. In the leading German Sd.Kfz.251half - track on the right, Oberst Schmitt smiled with satisfaction. So much for Allied propaganda. The Long Range Desert Group and the Special Air Service were not supermen after all. Faced with overwhelming odds, they would surrender without a fight. They were really no braver than the Italians.

Oberst Schmitt spoke into a carbon field microphone. His amplified voice boomed out across the desert from the horn speaker mounted on the left side of his half-track.

'You are surrounded. You have no chance of completing your mission. Lay down your arms and surrender with honour and you will be treated well. General Rommel admires the bravery of British Forces and has given his personal assurance that your men will be treated in accordance with the provisions of the Geneva Convention.

'You are outnumbered. We have armoured vehicles. To fight on would be pointless. The Afrika Korps wishes to avoid needless bloodshed.'

But Mayne was no ordinary soldier and had no intention of surrendering. He had already anticipated this potential situation in his final briefing to the patrol before leaving Tobruk, and was about to implement the agreed escape plan. He picked up a Very pistol, squeezed the trigger and fired a red flare into the sky. All the men aboard the British trucks knew exactly what they had to do.

The engines of the six Chevys revved hard and within seconds, all the British trucks made a ninety degree left turn to the east and accelerated directly towards the Italian vehicles. With great skill the drivers steered their vehicles through the gaps between the Italian lorries and armoured cars.

The Germans reacted quickly but their gunners had a near- impossible task. Their eyes were now blinded by the rising sun in the east and the backlit clouds of dust thrown up by the Chevys. It was hard to tell friend from foe. One Sd. Kfz. 222 armoured car fired a few rounds of 20mm blindly in the direction of the fleeing British trucks but the heavy shells smacked into the thin frontal armour plate of an Italian Autoblinda 41, killing the driver and immobilizing the vehicle.

The Italian troops in the back of the Lancias panicked at the sight of the fearless, bearded warriors of the LRDG and SAS travelling alongside them in the opposite direction, all guns blazing. Private Mills in Truck Six threw a primed hand grenade into the back of one of the Lancias. Four seconds later it exploded, killing five soldiers and wounding seven more.

Within thirty seconds, the Chevys had got past the Italian vehicles and, as planned, the six trucks moved into line abreast formation. Now they could all shoot to the rear, bringing to bear their massive combined fire power. In total the British force had two heavy fifty - calibre M2 machine guns plus four twin Vickers K guns and several Brens , Lee – Enfield 0.303 inch rifles and Thompson 0.45 sub-machine guns plus a couple of Boys 0.55 inch anti-tank rifles and a 20mm Breda autocannon.

Private Tompkins, manning the 20 mm Breda cannon in Truck Five, put a few rounds into the rear of each of the Autoblindas, setting them on fire, and then fired several bursts at the more distant German armour. The Afrika Korps halftracks and armoured cars were also riddled with fifty-calibre rounds from Trucks One and Four. Even at medium range, the heavy slugs could pierce the thin armour of the German vehicles while the relentless stream of bullets spewed out by the thousand - rounds -a- minute Vickers Ks tore the soft -skinned vehicles to pieces, killed and wounded many soldiers and set their engines on fire.

One in three of the bullets fired by the Vickers Ks were Buckingham incendiary rounds which could explode petrol cans and several German soldiers jumped off their armoured vehicles with their uniforms on fire.

The Chevys disappeared over the rise of an escarpment leaving a huge cloud of dust behind them which was backlit by the rising sun and impossible to see through. Oberst Schmitt ordered the remnants of his pursuit force to halt. He was coughing because of the thick , black , acrid oily smoke from burning tyres. A disgusting roast pork smell of scorched flesh hung in the air. Numerous vehicles lay blackened and abandoned, riddled with bullet -holes, their crews dead or badly wounded. Bodies lay everywhere, some burned to a crisp and others lacking limbs or heads. Bullets whizzed through the air in every direction as ammunition boxes caught fire. Dying soldiers screamed in pain and called for their mothers.

A German medical orderly stitched a bullet wound in Schmitt's left arm. He had run out of local anaesthetic so offered the German officer some brandy. Schmitt swigged it down and felt the welcome warmth in his throat and a flush in his face as he spoke to one of his junior officers, Hauptmann Brandt.

'The officer leading the British force is someone who cannot be underestimated. It seems that everything we have heard about the SAS and the LRDG is correct. They are fearless soldiers who have developed their own unique tactics to maximise their strengths and our weaknesses. A unit of regular soldiers would have surrendered when confronted by a superior force such as ours. I am in no doubt about that.

'We *will* catch them. But we need a larger force. Get in touch with our radio direction finding unit. I want a new fix on the enemy column. And I want some armour. Not light armour like half-tracks or armoured cars, but Panzers. The best ones we have in the North African theatre. The new Panzer IV Ausf. G models with long - barrelled 75mm guns if you can get them. Their frontal armour is too thick to be penetrated by a 20mm round. And I want the Storch spotter plane up again as soon as it is refuelled.

'We failed to catch them this time because we were complacent. But we won't make that mistake again. Even the SAS and LRDG will surrender when confronted with tanks. They are not supermen. It is only a matter of time. And as for that British officer, I want his balls to use as paper- weights.'

# Chapter 9

# Despair

**The White House, Washington D.C.**

**21 June, 1942, 10.00 p.m. Eastern Standard Time**

Winston Spencer Churchill slumped in a brown leather armchair, head held forward in his hands, elbows on his knees. His mouth was downturned and tears welled in his eyes. The news was just as he had feared. Tobruk had fallen. Now, people would be pointing the finger of blame at *him*. There might even be a vote of no confidence in the House of Commons over his handling of the war. Churchill turned to his old friend, the American President Franklin D. Roosevelt, who was sitting beside him in his wheelchair in the Oval Office.

'Thirty-five thousand British and Commonwealth troops captured,' said Churchill. 'Tens of thousands of tons of war supplies too, including guns, ammunition, trucks, food and fuel. It is one of the lowest points of my life, Franklin. Will we ever stop Rommel? Even the British Eighth Army think he is unbeatable. Is he really a superman? He never seems to make errors and punishes us severely for our own mistakes. And he always seems to know our moves before we make them.'

'Well I think we both know why that is, Winston,' answered Roosevelt. 'And we have taken steps to eliminate the leak. Our military attaché in Egypt, Major Bonner Fellers, is now using a different code to send his reports back to us. And in any case he will be recalled back to the USA soon.

Churchill knew exactly what Roosevelt was talking about. In September 1941 the Italian Secret Service had broken into the American Embassy in Rome and stolen the

55

US Diplomatic Code. As a result, Rommel had read translations of the reports Fellers had sent to General George Marshall in the USA, which had informed him of British intentions. Among other things, this had enabled Axis Forces to decimate two Malta-bound supply convoys, an episode which had nearly lead to the loss of the island. They had also known British moves in the Western Desert which had allowed them to win the Battle of Gazala and capture Tobruk.

'It is good that the leak has been stopped although it was too late to save Tobruk,' said Churchill. 'All these men captured. All that equipment and stores lost. The Royal Navy and the RAF are sinking many of the supply ships bound for North Africa but with all the war booty Rommel has captured at Tobruk, especially petrol, he can now advance on Cairo and the Suez Canal and maybe even beyond that to Palestine. Once he has captured the whole of the Middle East, he can link up with other German forces advancing south from the Soviet Union and take the oilfields in Iran. At which point the war will effectively have been won by the Germans.'

Churchill slumped back in his armchair, his face a picture of misery. He looked old, pale and wrinkled as he sipped a brandy. Roosevelt had never seen his old friend look so down. Where was that same jaunty fellow he had seen on the deck of HMS *Prince of Wales* the previous August?

Roosevelt looked up at the portrait of Abraham Lincoln in its ornate gold frame, which hung above the fireplace. What would that great American president have said in such a situation?

'Things may be bad, Winston but they are not hopeless. Is there anything we can do to help? I have an idea to put to you. At the moment we have no need for tanks in the Pacific theatre. I could send General Patton to Egypt with a complete armoured division, including two hundred and fifty of our latest M4 Sherman tanks, plus supporting vehicles. You've probably heard of the M4. It's got a

75mm main gun just like the earlier M3 Lee which you Brits call the Grant. Unlike in the Lee though, the 75mm is in a fully rotating turret. The Sherman also has sloping front armour and a very reliable engine. Patton, who is an expert on armoured warfare, assures me that it is more than a match for any German tank in North Africa including the latest version of the Panzer IV. If you give me the go – ahead, then we can have American boots on the ground in North Africa within a couple of months.'

'That is very generous of you,' answered Churchill but I think my Eighth Army commanders would prefer you just to send the equipment and we will provide our own crews. As I have often said, just give us the tools and we will finish the job.'

'We have another new armoured vehicle that may interest you,' said Roosevelt as he passed a large black- and -white photo to Churchill.

'It is a self-propelled 105mm gun called the M7 which is based on the chassis of the M3 Lee. As well as the howitzer it has a defensive machine gun at the top of this cylindrical structure at the front.'

Churchill's face lit up. 'That machine- gun position looks just like a pulpit. The British like to give names to tanks and armoured vehicles so we will probably call it a Priest or something.'

Roosevelt laughed. 'We can send you a hundred of those in addition to the two hundred and fifty M4s. I can also despatch US Army Air Force squadrons to North Africa. At the moment we only have a token presence there, but we could send you B-24 Liberator and B-25 Mitchell bombers, P-40 Warhawk fighters, plus the new twin-engine Lockheed P-38 Lightning fighters which are faster than your Mark V Spitfires and have a greater range. These could fight alongside your own RAF Desert Air Force.'

Churchill beamed, his face growing pinker as his depression lifted. Will all the military hardware that was being sent to North Africa, then how could Egypt fall? The

Allies could re-establish air superiority in the desert and then Rommel would be in serious trouble. The further he advanced east, the longer his supply lines would become and the more vulnerable they would be to interdiction. The best tank in the world would be no use to him if it ran out of fuel.

With his mood lifted, Churchill remembered something else.

'There is another matter I wanted to tell you about. As you know we have had some success in cracking the German Enigma code which is used by their Armed Forces. Thirteen months ago the destroyer HMS *Bulldog* captured an intact Enigma machine from a damaged U – boat before it sank. This enabled us to break the code. Unfortunately the Germans have added further rotors and changed the plug- board settings, which means we are now in the dark once more.

'However, our forces in Libya recently captured an intact machine from a German radio truck which had broken down. A unit of our Special Forces evacuated it from Tobruk just before the port fell and it is due to be picked up at Al-Balad airstrip tomorrow evening.'

While he spoke, Churchill picked up a large world atlas which lay on Roosevelt's desk and indicated Al-Balad, which lay just north of the Qattara Depression.

'Al-Balad, how very interesting,' said Roosevelt. Then his face darkened. 'That must be less than ten miles from Makan Alshayatin. Have your men been warned?'

'No, it was decided it would be better to say nothing. As you know, the armed forces of both our nations were involved in the original operation back in 1937. Our scientists assured us that everything had been buried deep underground and concreted over. Then we replaced thousands of tons of sand. No activity has been reported in the area for years and our scientists believe the craft and its occupants have entered a state of suspended animation again.

'The Free French occupied a fort there until recently

without any incidents being reported. I should really have told General De Gaulle about what happened in 1937 but he is such a *prima donna* that he would have gone berserk, claiming that France should have been involved in the original operation in 1937.'

'Quite so,' said Roosevelt. 'Sometimes I think winning the war would be easier if we had De Gaulle as an enemy rather than an ally. The French might have wanted to excavate the site to recover advanced technology but our own scientists felt this was too risky as it could cause a…reactivation. As long as the site remains sealed off then we expect the area to be safe.'

Churchill nodded in agreement. Mayne's commando force would not be informed about the potential danger in the area they were heading to, in case it caused a panic. If they had known what had happened five years earlier they would have reason to be worried. Because *Makan Alshayatin* was Arabic for *Place of the Devils*.

# Chapter 10

## No Hiding Place

The Luftwaffe Fieseler Storch reconnaissance aircraft circled the wadi at an altitude of five hundred feet, its beige camouflage paint illuminated by the brilliant midday sun. On the rocky ground below, six Chevrolet trucks lay hidden, expertly concealed by Mayne and his men. The vehicles were covered with camouflage nets adorned with local scrub. All the vehicles lacked glass. Mirrors and windows had been removed during their conversion to patrol trucks, and anything that might shine in the sun had been put under tarpaulins. Even sunlight reflecting off a pair of goggles could give their position away.

Mayne looked up through the holes in the camouflage netting and felt his shirt sticking to his back. Salty sweat ran down his forehead and into his eyes, making them sting. There was a smell of body odour, bad breath and musty camouflage nets. The aircraft was making its fourth circuit of the area. Had the pilot seen something?

Beside him the patrol's mechanic, Davy Atkins, lay still. He knew that that the slow-flying *Storch* would be an easy target for the patrol's two Browning fifty-calibre machine guns. Even the Vickers Ks could bring it down at that range. But they might miss and alert the pilot. And even if they did shoot down the aircraft, flames and smoke and the sound of the firing would alert the Germans who were probably only a few miles away.

After making a fifth orbit of the area, the *Storch* flew away to the north. The patrol relaxed. Soldiers emerged from under camo nets and opened boxes of rations.

'OK, that's the excitement over,' said Mayne. 'Let's have some food while we can. But no cooking as the smoke might be seen. Cold rations only.'

Lunch was tinned Fray Bentos bully beef and Peek

Frean biscuits followed by canned pears, all washed down with warm, brackish water. But to the members of the patrol, who hadn't eaten since leaving Tobruk the previous evening, it was like a slap-up dinner at the Ritz.

Mayne consulted his watch as he chewed some bully beef, which had already melted in the hot sunlight. It was only 13.07 hrs. After the unexpected encounter with Axis forces at dawn, they had put as much distance between themselves and the Germans as possible. They had made numerous changes of course and had traversed some areas of hard gravel desert – what Arabs called the *serir* - where their tracks wouldn't show.

Lee joined Mayne under the camo net and they both munched some biscuits and melted bully beef scooped from tins as they chatted.

'Well that was an exciting few hours,' said Lee, his mouth half- full of food. He wiped some crumbs from his moustache. 'I can't believe we got away unscathed. We were very lucky.'

'According to conventional military doctrine, we should have surrendered. But the SAS believe that sudden, aggressive action will often confuse an enemy who is expecting you to do something different. We were lucky though. A few bullets struck the Chevys but, apart from a few cuts and bruises, we didn't take any casualties. We may not be so lucky next time though.'

'So what's the plan?'

'This wadi has already been subjected to an aerial reconnaissance which found nothing so they are not likely to be back soon. I suggest we lie up here for a few hours and try and get some sleep. We will do it in shifts with two men on sentry duty at all times. Then early this evening, we will make our way to Al-Balad and lie up again until the Bombay arrives tomorrow night. After that we can get back to Alexandria by any route we choose. And we can cause a little mischief on the way.' Mayne smirked as he thought of a whole squadron of German bombers being riddled by machine-gun fire and blown apart by Lewes bombs. He had already destroyed more Axis aircraft than the RAF's top fighter ace, Squadron Leader Marmaduke 'Pat' Pattle. On a recent mission, Mayne had wrecked forty-seven bombers. When he ran out of bombs he disabled a few planes by tearing out their instrument panels with his bare hands.

'That sounds like a good plan,' said Lee. 'The only problem is that the Germans know we are in the area and will be looking for us. And I get the feeling that they won't give up that easily.'

*******

Just seventeen miles away, a German Opel Blitz radio van stood baking in the desert sun, windows and rear doors open in a futile attempt to keep the interior cool. A German *Landser* wearing a pair of brown Bakelite headphones slowly turned a varnished wooden wheel which rotated the roof- mounted aerial, as he studied a moving-coil meter which measured signal strength. The instrument's needle did not move.

'Nothing,' he said as he turned to his *Leutnant*. 'I was getting a good signal this morning just before we sprung the ambush but then we lost them when they moved out of range.'

'So if there is no signal, does that mean we have lost them for good?' asked the officer.

'Not necessarily. It's possible that the makeshift transmitter built by our agent has been damaged in some way. It could have been hit by a stray bullet during the ambush or a thermionic valve may have broken if the vehicle went over rough ground. The power supply wire may have come loose. There is another possibility, though. This part of the desert is close to the Qattara Depression so it is below sea level and there are a number of wadis— dried up river beds—which are lower still. If the vehicle was hidden deep in a wadi then we might not pick up the transmission.'

'That seems logical. I suggest you keep monitoring that frequency in case the transmission starts again. I will position another couple of vans to the east and west. If the signal resumes we will ambush them again – and this time there will be no escape!'

A few miles away from the radio van, several German half-tracks, armoured cars, trucks and *Kubelwagens* had stopped at an oasis to replenish their water supplies. The leader of the column, Oberst Schmitt, was sitting in the back of one of the half-tracks, which was equipped with a powerful tactical radio. He took off his headphones and put them down next to the radio. The news was good. The 21$^{st}$ Panzer Division had agreed to supply him with six Panzer IV tanks along with supporting infantry and a fuel truck for a period of four days. The Panzers were the latest Ausf. G models with long- barrelled 75mm guns and two 7.9 mm machine – guns. Once they had a fix on the position of the British column, they would move to crush it and find out what they were up to. If the British soldiers refused to capitulate immediately, they would all be killed. After all, the Panzer IV was the best tank in North Africa. Perhaps even the world. The British force had no weapons that could knock it out as its frontal armour was too thick to pierced by even a 20mm round. The British would all die if they refused to surrender! Schmitt wanted revenge and he was going to get it.

# Chapter 11

## To Sleep, Perchance to Dream

*It is 1937. I am sitting in the University Cafe in Byres Road. It smells of cake, coffee beans, freshly baked bread and Italian cheese.*

*The café opened in 1921 and is fitted out in an Art Deco style with mahogany panelling on the walls up to shoulder height, many ornate mirrors and comfortable customer seating in several booths upholstered in red leather. Above the panelling is dark red and cream striped wallpaper and an ornate plaster cornice.*

*I am savouring their speciality dish, a large knickerbocker glory. Cold, sweet, home-made Italian ice cream that melts in my mouth and leaves a delicious aftertaste. Thick cream and diced fruit. Cherries and wafers on top, served in a long, tall glass and eaten with an elongated spoon. To follow, an espresso coffee in a tiny, pre-heated china cup with matching saucer, served black with brown sugar with a small biscuit on the side. I love the sound the coffee machine makes as Dino, the proprietor, prepares this delicious beverage. The hiss of high - pressure steam and the screeching sound as the cup fills with hot, dark liquid. Most Scottish people prefer tea but I've developed a liking for real Italian coffee. If I am especially thirsty I might also have a tall glass of Barr's Iron Brew, or maybe a ginger beer. With ice. Lots of ice. So cold that dew forms on the outside of the glass. Some of my fellow medical students enjoy drinking beer at the nearby Aragon bar, just across the road from Glasgow's Western Infirmary, but I prefer soft drinks. As I sip my coffee, a gramophone plays 'Vivere' by the Italian singer Daniele Serra. The mahogany counter is crowded with large glass jars filled with amaretti biscuits and Italian confectionery.*

*Dino scowls as he studies the latest edition of the Daily Express. 'Mamma Mia! That fat oaf Mussolini has already taken over my country and in 1935 he invaded Abyssinia. Mark my words, he will cause a lot of problems, Mr Lee. Within a few years he will start a war in North Africa. And Hitler will become involved. What will happen to me then? Will I be interned? I love the British and especially the Scottish. I don't want all this!'*

*'I'm sure The League of Nations will sort everything out,' I say as I sip my coffee. 'And our Prime Minister, Neville Chamberlain, won't allow war to break out. Wait and see!'*

*'Something else I wanted to ask you, Mr Lee. I had an idea for a new dish.'*

*Dino plucks a Mars bar from beneath the counter and holds it high in the air. 'The Scottish like fried food and they also love confectionery. Supposing I deep-fried a Mars bar. Do you think my Scots customers would like it? What do you think, as a medical man?'*

*'Scots love fried foods and have an unusually sweet tooth, as you have indicated,' I say. 'But I think a deep-fried Mars Bar would be just about the most unhealthy food ever devised. I can feel my coronary arteries furring up just thinking about it!'*

*On the pavement outside, scores of Glaswegians clad in waterproofs and carrying brollies make their way home from work. A typical summer's day in the west of Scotland. Some head for Hillhead Subway station, others patiently wait for the Glasgow Corporation electric trams with their garish orange and green paintwork. After finishing my coffee, I plan to spend the evening in Glasgow University Reading Room where I will try to learn the structure of the inguinal canal from a copy of Gray's Anatomy. The Reading Room in University Avenue has always fascinated me. On winter nights when it is lit up, its circular construction with domed top looks like a saucer-shaped alien spacecraft. Tomorrow I will visit the Anatomy Museum to look at the preserved human brain which sits in a tank of formalin.*

'Wake up Captain, time for food.'

It was Sergeant Binns. Lee awoke with a jolt and studied his surroundings. He was lying in a hollow that he had scooped out in the sand. The sun was just above the horizon and cast long shadows on the sand and rock of the wadi. Despite the late hour, his battledress top was still soaked in sweat. Flies and mosquitoes buzzed around him. His mouth felt dry and tasted bad. There was no ice cream in the desert and the Italians in North Africa weren't friendly café owners. Lee stroked his chin and felt stubble. Then he remembered that he had last washed, shaved and brushed his teeth the morning he had arrived in Tobruk. Just thirty-six hours earlier, but it seemed like longer as so much had happened.

Binns offered Lee a plate of melted corned beef and biscuits and a tin mug filled with tepid water.

'No hot food yet sir, but there's pudding to follow. Tinned peaches with Carnation milk.'

Binns smacked his lips in anticipation of this culinary delight while Lee sipped his water and chewed a biscuit. Mayne had already eaten and was cleaning his M1 Thompson forty-five calibre machine gun with a rag. Lee was familiar with this weapon as he had fired one when he was in the Home Guard in 1940. The Americans had shipped a lot of them to Britain in 1940 when invasion seemed imminent. It had been designed towards the end of the Great War as a 'trench sweeper' and fired a low-velocity, forty-five calibre pistol round. It was popular with commando units but was heavy, and expensive, costing Britain 209 dollars per weapon. For these reasons, Britain was now manufacturing tens of thousands of cheaper, simpler 9mm Sten Guns. The Thompson had also gained notoriety as a 'mobster's gun' in the USA and had been used in the infamous St Valentine's Day massacre in 1929. Indeed, a photo of Churchill carrying the weapon had been used in Nazi propaganda posters. According to Goebbels, it proved the British Prime Minister was a gangster.

'Any chance I could have a shave and wash and brush my teeth before we move off?,' asked Lee. 'Personal hygiene is important, even in the desert.'

'A shave? Brushing your teeth? Washing? What planet are you on, laddie? Out in the desert, water is a scarce commodity. We don't waste it on things like that,' said Mayne. 'What on earth did they teach you at Catterick?'

'When I was getting my induction into 131 Field Ambulance in Alexandria I was told that every man would be allocated eight pints of water a day, including one pint for washing, tooth brushing and shaving.'

'Well that may be so, but the Long Range Desert Group and the SAS takes the view that every drop of water is precious,' said Mayne. 'That's why we have condenser cans and hoses attached to the vehicle radiators. I suggest you grow a beard while you are on this mission. It will also help to protect your face from the sun, sand and wind. The LRDG have learned how to use sand for cleaning skin. Dirty pots, pans and dishes are done the same way.

'Clothes can be washed with petrol rather than water and hung out to dry in the hot sun as water is scarcer than petrol in the desert, but we don't see any need for ablutions during a short mission. As for toothpaste, we suggest you don't use it at all on patrol. The SAS have discovered that sentries can smell toothpaste from a great distance in the desert. So your breath is going to stink until we get back to base. Don't worry, I won't be giving you a French kiss any time soon!'

Mayne chuckled while Lee shuddered. He had always believed in a high standard of personal hygiene but he would have to make compromises for the sake of the mission. There would be no Izal medicated toilet paper for his backside, just old newspapers.

All around him, soldiers were enjoying their evening meal. Many were eschewing plates and eating food directly from cans using forks. Tins of sardines, herrings, soya link sausages and the dreaded Mc Connachie's M& V (meat and vegetables),which was more palatable with some added curry powder. And canned Canadian bacon, which was just a lump of grease when eaten straight from the tin.

After dinner, some of the soldiers made deep holes in the sand with their entrenching tools so they could take a dump and ensure their faeces were well buried to avoid detection. In decades to come, with the advent of trained sniffer dogs and tracking technology, Special Forces would be compelled to bag up their faeces and take them with them-and also pee into jerricans — but during the Second World War this was not practised.

Mayne allowed his men to have a cigarette and then all the butts and empty food cans were buried in a deep hole which was filled in. At 21.30 hrs the vehicles' petrol tanks were topped up from the flimsies and all the Chevys started their engines. Except for Truck Six. Private Wyatt couldn't get it started as the battery appeared to be almost flat — the starter motor was barely turning over. Mayne shouted over to Truck Three where Davy Atkins was manning the fifty-calibre machine gun.

'Davy, get over to Truck Six and find out what's wrong. And make it snappy!'

Davy opened the bonnet and spent a few minutes checking the engine with his multi-meter.

'It's a flat battery all right. I'll need to do some investigative work to find out the cause.'

'We don't have time. Just start the engine with a hand crank and we'll be on our way.'

Davy pulled out a hand crank from the truck's wooden toolbox and inserted it into a hole in the centre of the front bumper. Private Wyatt turned on the ignition and put the gearstick in neutral as Davy worked the hand crank. It was something he had done hundreds of times as a mechanic before the war. At the third attempt, the six-cylinder engine sprung into life.

A moment later, all six Chevys gunned their engines and moved out of the wadi in a cloud of dust and exhaust smoke after Mayne had made one final check of the area to make sure that they had left nothing behind. The vehicles climbed up a steep incline and then moved onto the flat desert, heading in a north- easterly direction.

*******

Twenty-five miles due west of the British column, Afrika Korps radio operator Landser Brandt twiddled the dial of his radio as he sat in the back of his Opel Blitz direction-finding van. The rear doors were wide open to give him some ventilation. He searched through the airwaves and listened to a broadcast of the popular song *Lili Marlene*,sung by Lale Anderson and transmitted from Radio Belgrade. Somehow, all the static and fading seemed to increase the song's allure. Brandt adjusted the fine tuning knob to get maximum signal strength on his meter. He knew the Tommies also liked the song as the lyrics appealed to soldiers of all nations. There was a rumour that the Allies were going to issue an English - language version of the tune, sung by Marlene Dietrich. Goebbels had attempted to have the original song banned, but Rommel had objected as he felt it raised morale.

After a couple more minutes of music, there was the news from Berlin. Although Brandt was a loyal German, he had grown to distrust the utterances of Joseph Goebbels, which he knew were often fabricated. He would find something else to listen to.

Brandt searched through the wavebands and discovered a strange transmission. It was a constant audio tone. Brandt turned the varnished wooden wheel which rotated the roof-mounted, direction -finding aerial. The signal was coming from a location east of his position. Brandt made a brief transmission to his tactical HQ and reported his findings. It was the mystery signal they had all been told to look out for. Within ten minutes, two other vans had got a bearing on the signal. Five minutes later, the reports had been collated and a triangulation had been performed.

69

*******

In a nearby oasis, Hauptmann Lutz studied a large map of the Western Desert on the wall of his tactical HQ which was inside a large Leyland Retriever 6 x 4 motor caravan that had been captured from the British at Dunkirk. The new triangulation showed the current location of the signal was just east of a large wadi below sea level, north of the Qattara Depression. That would explain why they had lost contact. But now the enemy column was travelling on level ground they could be tracked. The triangulated location kept changing, showing that the convoy was moving at speed. It looked as though they were heading for the disused airstrip at Al-Balad. If that is where they were going they were in for a shock. Lutz spoke to his tactical radio operator and prepared a brief message. He would arrange for the British force to be intercepted at Al-Balad. But why were they going there? The British hadn't based any aircraft there for months. Was an RAF aircraft going to land there? If that was so, he would need some fighter planes. He would speak to the Luftwaffe. If they couldn't help he would contact the *Regia Aeronautica*.

Even if they weren't needed to down an enemy aircraft, fighter planes would be useful for strafing the trucks. Yes, the British were going to have a nasty surprise indeed.

# Chapter 12

## Ice Boy

Hans Peiper loathed the British. And the Italians. And the Jews. And North Africa. Just six months earlier he had been in Russia, fighting Stalin's armies. That suited him fine because he hated the Russians too. And he enjoyed the cold.

He had always been that way. At least, as far back as he could remember. When he was growing up in Cologne, he loved the frequent winter snowfalls. The sensation of soft, virgin snow under his feet making that curious squelching sound when he walked to school. When it snowed, he loved to eat breakfast in the garden while seated in a wooden chair. A traditional German morning meal of black bread, cold ham and boiled eggs, eaten off a china plate as snowflakes landed in his hair. His parents were horrified as they feared he might get frostbite or hypothermia but Hans seemed to like low temperatures. They made him feel good.

There was nothing Hans liked more than skiing and sledging. And he hated the warm summers in Cologne. All these months of sweating and avoiding the burning sun. His love of cold was known to his classmates and he was known as the *Eisjunge*, the 'ice boy.'

His rich parents worried about his strange tendencies and took him to several distinguished doctors. But none of them could explain why he liked the cold, and even seemed to thrive on it. One physician thought he might have a condition known as hyperthyroidism, an overactive thyroid gland which sped up his metabolic rate, making him feel warm even when the weather was cold, but all the tests were normal. Hans was just weird and it was all in his mind.

He also had difficulties with social interactions. And no

friends. When he was eight, he poked a classmate in the left eye with a bamboo stick after some taunting. The boy suffered a detached retina. Surgeons were unable to repair the damage and the eye was left blind and divergent. Hans showed no remorse for his actions.

'It was his fault, he made fun of me,' he told his mother.

Hans was examined again by doctors but they didn't know what to make of him. In these days psychiatry was in its infancy and psychopathic personality disorders were not recognised as such.

His strange behaviour continued. He enjoyed killing small animals and then dissecting them to find out how they worked. Soon he had a collection of rotting animals which he secretly kept as trophies in the cellar of the family home. Then one day, the smell in the house got so bad that his father, Otto investigated further and checked out the basement. He was shocked by what he found. All the decaying carcasses ended up in a paraffin-fuelled blaze in the back garden and Hans was thrashed on his bottom with a carpet slipper.

Then in 1935, when Hans was seventeen, he heard Adolf Hitler speaking on the radio. What he said made a lot of sense to the young, impressionable boy. All Germany's problems were caused by the Jews. They had caused the Wall Street Crash and the Great Depression. They had started the Great War in 1914 and lobbied hard to ensure the USA entered the war in 1917. The sinking of the liner *Lusitania* in 1915 had been a Jewish plot to force American to side with Britain. And they had been behind the harsh conditions of the 1919 Treaty of Versailles which had made Germany militarily impotent.

But now things were changing, and Germany would become the most powerful country in the world. It would build the greatest military machine in history, armed with the best weapons that German industry could create. Panzer III and IV tanks. Junkers Ju 87 Stuka dive bombers. Messerschmitt Bf 109 fighters and Heinkel He

111 and Dornier Do 17 bombers. All enemies of the state would be ruthlessly annihilated. Anyone who was not physically perfect or of an inferior race would be exterminated.

The British and French were weak and decadent while the Americans were a nation of lazy gangsters, controlled by the Jews,who were only interested in an easy life. Above all, Germany needed *Lebensraum* (' living room') and that could only be achieved by pushing east and taking control of parts of Poland and Czechoslovakia that had really belonged to Germany in the first place.

Hans had never felt so stirred by an oration. Hitler spoke the truth and his views appealed to him on so many levels because the young man needed *order* in his life, and only Hitler could give it. *Hans had to be in control* and Nazi ideology met his needs perfectly. The next day, Hans bought a copy of Hitler's book *Mein Kampf* and read it from cover to cover. He thought it was a masterpiece and agreed with every word that Hitler had written. Soon he had made his own pencilled notes about its main points, including lengthy quotations. He carried them everywhere and when he had a spare moment, he read them. He particularly liked reading them aloud. Soon he had committed the entire book to memory and it became his personal mantra. *The mantra of a madman.*

In 1936 Hans joined the Nazi Brownshirts and two years later, he was inducted into the SS, just in time to take part in the infamous *Kristallnacht* when great damage was caused to Jewish property. He enjoyed kicking and punching defenceless Jewish people, confiscating their property and belongings and smashing windows. It would only be a matter of time before he would be allowed to kill them. For the first time in his life, *Hans was in control. It was all about control.*

The following year, the Wehrmacht attacked Poland, and on Sunday 3 September the British Prime Minister Neville Chamberlain declared war on Germany. Hans was part of a Waffen SS unit which followed the troops into

Poland and became involved in atrocities against civilians.

In May 1940, Hans found himself in France fighting the remains of the British Expeditionary Force, which was trapped in the port of Dunkirk. By this time he had been promoted to *Feldwebel* and was leading an attack on a defensive position by a canal which was manned by soldiers of the 51st Highland Division. Hans admired the fighting skills of the brave Scottish soldiers who had four Bren guns and two Vickers Maxim 0.303s. After four hours of combat, the British soldiers ran out of ammunition and displayed a white flag to indicate that they wished to surrender. What happened next was recorded as one of the worst atrocities of the French campaign.

Hans' unit expected the British soldiers to be disarmed and taken to a rear area for processing and interrogation, after which they would be sent to a POW camp in Germany. Instead, Hans ordered his men to herd the prisoners into a barn. The captives were all blindfolded, their hands tied and they were then killed by several long bursts from an MG34 machine- gun which had been set up on a tripod. Then Hans ordered his men to drench the corpses in petrol and set them alight. All his men would have nightmares for years to come about what they had been asked to do, but not Hans. He was laughing. As the smell of burning flesh assailed his nostrils, he pulled out his pencilled notes about *Mein Kampf* and read an extract out loud. Somehow, the twisted views of Adolf Hitler were being used to justify this atrocity.

The flames had just begun to die down when a grey Mercedes 230 staff car with pennants mounted on its front wings skidded to a halt outside the barn, followed by an Opel Blitz truck filled with soldiers. The driver opened the rear door of the Mercedes and a very distinguished looking officer with a long grey coat and peaked cap stepped out.

Hans recognised him at once. It was General Erwin Rommel, one of the stars of the French campaign.

'What's going on here?' said Rommel. 'Who is behind

this?'

Rommel's driver looked through the doors of the smouldering barn and saw eighteen blackened corpses. The smell of burned flesh hung in the air. It was too much for him to take and he vomited on the ground.

'A group of Tommies put up a fight but we sorted them out. They will never be a threat to Germany again. The Führer will be pleased,' said Peiper. Rommel grabbed Peiper by the lapels of his uniform jacket and shouted into his face, spraying spittle on his cheeks.

'You barbarian! Enemy soldiers who have laid down their arms must be treated in accordance with the provisions of the Geneva Convention. They should be given food, water and medical attention and taken to a place of safety in a rear area as soon as possible. Shooting them and burning them to death is a war crime.'

Peiper looked at Rommel with a fixed grin on his face. His teeth gleamed, his eyes wide open with dilated pupils. The facial expression of a madman.

'Germany has never signed the Geneva Convention,' said Peiper.

'That is correct but the Wehrmacht scrupulously obeys its provisions. We are men of honour not animals. What's your name?'

'Feldwebel Hans Peiper, sir.'

Rommel pulled a 9mm Luger pistol from his holster and pressed the muzzle against Peiper's forehead.

'I should shoot you right now, Peiper, but then I would be just as bad as your SS friends.'

Rommel turned to the twelve soldiers who had dismounted from the Opel Blitz. All carried MP40 machine pistols. 'Arrest all these men and take them to a rear area and from there to a military prison. I want a full investigation into what happened here. Everyone involved will be court - martialled.'

But it wasn't to be as simple as this. Word of the massacre reached Hitler himself who was now faced with a dilemma. He still wanted a negotiated peace with Britain and if the UK Government learned of the atrocity and publicised it, it would stiffen resistance and harden attitudes. Any peace proposals would be rejected. So a decision was made to cover up the killings.

Hans was tried in secret in a military court and found guilty of unlawful killings. He was sentenced to death, although this was later reduced to five years in prison following representations from the head of the SS, Heinrich Himmler, who didn't understand what all the fuss was about.

The following spring, Germany faced a manpower crisis. Millions of troops would be required for Operation Barbarossa, the planned invasion of the USSR. Even before that, Germany intended to invade Greece, Yugoslavia, Albania and Crete. In order to make up numbers, thousands of soldiers were released from military prisons, including Hans Peiper. General Rommel learned of this decision and was furious as he had taken a special interest in Peiper. To keep Rommel happy, Peiper was demoted to *Landser* and transferred to the regular army where he could be kept on a short leash.

Himmler was angry because he didn't think Peiper had ever done anything wrong. Neither did Hitler, but he was aware that Rommel had become one of the greatest generals in the German Army. His brilliant tactical decision to use 88mm Flak 36 guns to defeat the thickly-armoured British Matilda II tanks at the Battle of Arras in 1940 had won him many fans.

In the spring of 1942, German troop reinforcements were sent to North Africa and Rommel used his influence to ensure that these included Peiper. He had read his personnel file and knew that he loved cold and hated the heat, so Libya would be a punishment for him. Even if the Afrika Korps captured Egypt and made it to the port of Alexandria, there would be no chance that Hans would ever be ice cold in Alex.

# Chapter 13

## Desert Rendezvous

**Al Balad Forward Airfield**
**22 June 1942, 19.10 hrs**

Mayne lit a Capstan cigarette with his Zippo lighter and glanced at his watch before scanning the sky again. The Bombay was late. It should have been here at 19.00 hrs. All around him, his men sipped water from canteens and ate food from cans as they waited for the transport aircraft to arrive.

Al-Balad was classed as an advanced landing ground, which meant that it had no facilities. It lacked a barrack block, hangars or a watch tower. There was no cookhouse and no showers. Not even any running water. Just a windsock, a wooden hut full of dead flies and a makeshift runway made from flattened sand. An old Hawker Hurricane fighter lay at one side of the airstrip. It had been stripped of useful parts some months before and abandoned. The engine and propeller were missing and it had two flat tyres and peeling camouflage paint which had been sand-blasted by the wind and bleached by the sun. There were numerous bullet holes in the fabric covering of the rear fuselage.

Then Mayne heard it. It was faint at first but grew in intensity. The distinctive sound of twin Bristol Pegasus air-cooled radial engines. Mayne looked to the north-east and saw a black dot approaching. As it got closer, he could see that it was a high-winged transport with a fixed undercarriage, twin tailfins and two round engines. It was a Bombay.

'You're late, you lazy RAF bastards, but we forgive you,' screamed Binns. All the men waved their arms and laughed with joy as they realised that in a matter of moments the highly important package would be on its way back to Cairo and the most vital part of their mission would be over. The Bombay made a slow flypast from east to west, dipping its port wing so the men could see the RAF roundels. The pilot gave a V for Victory sign through the open side window as the golden evening sun reflected off the windshield. Then the aircraft made a slow orbit of the aerodrome at low level so the pilot could see which way the windsock was pointing. There was a gentle breeze blowing from the south-west so the pilot decided to land into the wind from a north-easterly direction.

The Bombay pulled up and circled the airfield again at a distance of about a mile so it could line up with the sand runway. As it was on its final approach with flaps down, Davy Atkins noticed that it had company. Two biplane fighters.

'The RAF have sent a fighter escort, Major. Two Gladiators.'

Mayne was puzzled. As a prolific destroyer of enemy aircraft, he knew all the current Allied and Axis types. The British Gloster Gladiator biplane fighter had indeed seen a lot of action in the Western Desert but he was sure they had all been replaced by more modern Hawker Hurricanes and Curtiss P- 40B Tomahawks.

Mayne lifted up his binoculars. The two mystery fighters had V-shaped struts, open cockpits, yellow cowlings and wheel spats. They were Italian Fiat CR-42 *Falcos*.

'Enemy aircraft! Man all guns!' screamed Mayne. 'And start engines.'

There wasn't time to raise the Bombay on the radio so Mayne lifted up a Very pistol and fired a red flare in its direction to warn it. But it was too late. The pilot of the Bombay pushed the two throttle levers forward to give maximum power, stamped on the rudder pedals and turned the control yoke to put the transport into a tight turn to port but—just as he did so—the twin machine -guns in the cowling of the leading CR.42 spat flame and a torrent of heavy 12.7 mm rounds struck the Bombay's port engine nacelle. Black smoke poured from the engine and then bright orange flames streamed behind the British aircraft. The second Fiat delivered the *coup de grace* by firing a long burst into the starboard engine.

With both engines ablaze, the Bombay struck the desert floor, smashing its fixed undercarriage, and cartwheeled along the sand, leaving a trail of burning fuel in its wake. A pall of black smoke rose into the sky. Mayne knew there was no point in searching for survivors. Anyone who wasn't killed in the initial impact would have been incinerated in the subsequent blaze.

Elated by their achievements, the two Italian pilots climbed high above the airfield and each did a victory roll. But the Italian pilots weren't finished yet and, after finishing their brief aerobatics, they dived towards the six British trucks. They had shot down the Bombay and now they would destroy as many British vehicles as possible.

'Move!' shouted Mayne to Binns. Using hand signals, he instructed all the trucks to get up to maximum speed, head to the centre of the airfield and then split up so they were all going in different directions. That would make the Italian pilots' task much harder. When the trucks were bunched together, they were dead meat. But travelling individually at speed going in different directions they would be much more difficult to hit.

Mayne had once found himself in a jeep under attack from a strafing Messerschmitt Bf 109F the morning after an airfield raid, but his driver had thwarted the assault by making several sudden changes of course. The Fiat CR.42 was harder to beat in this way because it flew much slower, with a top speed of just 274 miles per hour, and was agile. It could turn on a sixpence.

As the two Italian fighters bore down on the six British trucks, all the LRDG gunners opened up with their Vickers Ks, fifty-calibre Brownings and the single 20mm Breda cannon. All the other soldiers joined in by firing their personal weapons. But it was hard to hit a moving aircraft from a truck that was itself travelling at speed over bumpy ground.

One of the Italian pilots picked out Truck Five, which had developed a puncture in its rear offside wheel and was slowing down and unable to manoeuvre. The pilot fired a two - second burst into the rear of the truck which ignited the 'flimsy' petrol cans. The 20mm Breda gunner in the rear of the truck, Private Tompkins, screamed as burning fuel incinerated his feet and a 12.7mm round hit him in the abdomen. Just before he died, he pulled the firing trigger of his gun and sent a stream of heavy 20mm shells towards the biplane. One of the rounds struck the crankcase of the Fiat's engine, stopping it immediately and causing an oil leak which coated the plane's windshield with a sticky black goo. Unable to see where he was going, the Italian pilot ploughed into the truck and both machines were consumed by an orange fireball. The truck's tyres caught fire, and clouds of black smoke rose high in the sky, accompanied by the acrid smell of burning rubber.

The other Fiat pilot was so shaken by what had happened to his colleague that he forgot to carry out evasive manoeuvres to dodge gunfire. As he flew slowly past Mayne's truck, his aircraft took a few hits from 0. 303 and fifty-calibre rounds which caused a petrol leak. Unsure if he would make it back to base, the pilot climbed above the effective range of small-arms fire, and headed west trailing black smoke.

Mayne fired a yellow flare, the pre-arranged signal for all trucks to regroup. Ten minutes later, the five remaining Chevys stopped around the windsock. Mayne stood in the back of Truck One and addressed his men, as the low sun illuminated them with a golden light.

'The mission has gone tits up. As someone once said, no plan survives contact with the enemy. The Bombay has been destroyed and we've lost a truck and three men. Plus our heaviest weapon, the 20mm Breda cannon. But we *can* complete our mission. We still have the package and five vehicles. We are running low on fuel, food, water and ammunition. But we can top up our supplies at any one of a number of LRDG dumps which exist all over the Western Desert. The nearest one is at the old fort at Makan Alshayatin. It was occupied by Free French Forces until two weeks ago. We will head there immediately and once we have restocked we will make a beeline for Alexandria, using the network of tracks which run across the Great Sand Sea. If all goes to plan, we will deliver the package ourselves, just a few days later than planned.'

Mayne intended to give his men more details of their route but most of them weren't paying attention. They were pointing to the west where clouds of dust showed that a number of vehicles were heading towards them, just a few miles from their current position. Mayne lifted his binoculars and scanned the horizon. It was vehicles all right and they included six tanks. Panzer IVs by the look of them. The most feared tank in North Africa. And the British force didn't possess a single weapon which could knock them out.

# Chapter 14

## Out of the Frying Pan

Five Chevy trucks raced north -east across the hard desert floor, sending up clouds of dust. Behind them there was a red glow in the western sky as the sun set behind the dunes. The vehicles' bodies were still scalding hot but soon it would become chilly.

Lee sat behind Mayne on a hard, sideways-facing , uncomfortable wooden bench and had to shout into his left ear to be heard above the din of the six -cylinder engine and the wind noise.

'Why are we heading north-east? I thought Makan Alshayatin was to the south -east?'

'To fool Jerry,' answered Mayne. 'We'll stay on this course until it is dark then we will make a ninety - degree right turn towards the fort. Jerry won't know we need supplies and will assume we are heading directly towards Alexandria. He will probably get spotter planes up at first light but they will be looking for us in the wrong part of the desert.'

'What if the Panzers catch up with us before we make the turn?' asked a worried Lee.

'Provided we don't get any punctures we can outrun them….and the Germans aren't keen on driving their tanks across the desert at night. The risk of an accident is too great. And if they get a broken track they won't be able to fix it in the dark.'

*******

Ten miles behind them, darkness was falling. The commander of the Panzer force, Oberst Seidel, knew he could only continue the chase for another thirty minutes before it became impossible to see anything. He would have to stop for the night. His men would need food and water and a few hours of sleep. As soon as dawn broke, his tanks would refuel from a petrol truck and resume the chase. He had a direction-finding vehicle with him and a second had been positioned twenty kilometres to the north. They were both getting a good signal so could keep track of the British vehicles. Whatever way they went they would be located.

Thirty minutes later, it was pitch black. Seidel ordered all vehicles to stop. It would be too risky to continue the pursuit in the dark and the six Panzer IVs were considered too valuable to risk being lost or damaged. The 7th Panzer Division had agreed they could be loaned for a maximum of four days and then returned to frontline duties, as they would be needed for the forthcoming assault on Egypt. Seidel had been reassured that they would not be damaged as the British force had no significant anti-tank capability. The Boys anti-tank rifles and heavy machine guns they possessed could penetrate the thin armour of a half-track or armoured car, but their rounds would bounce off the frontal plate of a Panzer IV.

The crews of the six tanks stopped their engines and opened all hatches to let in cooler air. Then they climbed out of their vehicles and dropped onto the warm sand. Some of them opened cans of sardines and tinned sausages, which they wolfed down using a fork. Others drank water. One soldier had obtained some tinned bread, which had originally been produced for U-boat crews. It was an acquired taste and nothing like the fresh rye bread Seidel had eaten in his native Hamburg.

Hamburg. How he wished he was back there right now. He could just imagine himself holding a litre *Stein* of Bavarian beer. A glass so cold that dew formed on it, with a foaming head that dribbled down the side. And the exquisite taste as he swallowed the cold, malty liquid. He wondered if there might be a bar in Alexandria that served beer as cold as that?

Just twenty-one miles from the German position, the British force had also stopped for the night. While escaping from airfield raids, Mayne had sometimes been driven at high speed across the desert in darkness in one of the new American Willys MB four-wheel drive jeeps. In general though, both the British and Axis armies preferred to avoid travelling at night in the desert as it was considered too risky. It could be as dark as a coal mine and people had even got lost and unable to find their way back to their foxhole after going for a dump.

'A brief supper, then sleep,' said Mayne as he addressed his men. 'Two men to remain on sentry duty at all times. McAleese and McTavish, you take the first shift. Change over every two hours. That way we can all get some kip. At 05.30 hours we will have a quick breakfast, then head to the old fort at Makan Alshayatin to restock and refuel. Next stop Alexandria.'

Binns handed Lee his supper – a can of McConnachie's M&V. Since he had arrived in North Africa, this was one of the most common tinned foods he had eaten, and he had become tired of it. He had eaten it boiled, fried, made into rissoles and jazzed up with curry powder. After the war was over he hoped this awful product would be banned …or maybe even shipped to the Russians as revenge for their treatment of his parents, who had been forced to flee the country some decades earlier. After the war, if he ever married and his wife put a plate of McConnachie's M &V in front of him, it would be considered grounds for divorce! He had heard that the Americans had started shipping over vast quantities of a new canned food called SPAM (short for spiced ham) which tasted better than corned beef. What a pity he wouldn't be able to eat it because of his religion!

Lee finished his last mouthful of M&V without throwing up, swigged down some water from his canteen, and crawled under Truck One with his blanket. He closed his eyes and within a minute he was sound asleep and snoring loudly.

*Lee always had vivid dreams when he was in the desert, and this one was particularly odd. It was set in an English café. All the customers were Vikings. Then a table and two chairs descended from the ceiling on wires, with two additional patrons. A middle-aged married couple. The man was thin with fair hair and a little moustache, and his wife looked like a man in drag. A wall calendar showed the year was 1970.*

*The couple were arguing about what to have for breakfast. The problem was that every dish contained Spam and the wife didn't like it. The wife said she didn't want any Spam but the husband was adamant he wanted nothing else. Then some Vikings in the corner started to sing a song about the virtues of Spam.*

*Then the dream shifted to the year 2000, as evidenced by a desk calendar. A bespectacled young man sat at an office desk. In front of him was what looked like an EMI 405-line television receiver and a keyboard like that on an Enigma machine. The man was cursing about receiving a lot of 'spam'. But what did tinned processed meat have to do with electronic devices? Lee couldn't understand.*

'Breakfast sir!'

It was Binns. He held a tin plate with some food on it.

Lee awoke with a jolt. Above him was the chassis of a truck. A little oil was dripping from the differential. The silencer was rusty.

Lee rubbed his eyes. 'What have you got for me today, Binns?'

'Bacon, sausage, fried egg, black pudding, mushroom, tomato and baked beans.'

'You must be pulling my leg , Binns.'

'I'm afraid I am sir. Tinned bully beef, biscuits and water. We're still on cold rations as the Major doesn't want us to make any smoke.'

Lee accepted the plate.

'Well as long as it doesn't have any Spam in it then I

am quite happy.'

'What's Spam?' asked Binns.

'You'll find out before too long. It's a new pork luncheon meat that the Yanks will be shipping to us in the near future.'

Lee got out from under the truck and ate a forkful of bully beef which he washed down with a tin mug of warm water. It had a metallic taste. How he missed the cool, clear soft water that came out of the tap in the West of Scotland.

The sun rose above the eastern horizon, illuminating the desert with a golden light. Lee was amazed by the complex, three-dimensional shapes of the dunes which had been sculpted by centuries of winds and erosion. And the wide variety of colours of the sand was something that people who had never been to Egypt could not appreciate. Some sand was beige, other areas looked brown, pink, butter yellow or almost white. Earlier in the war, the LRDG had found that the best colour for desert camouflage was actually pink and many of their vehicles were painted this shade.

Mayne had been up before anyone else and did a quick check of the vehicles.

'As soon as you have all finished your breakfast, take a dump, have a pee and bury all food cans.'

Fifteen minutes later, all the soldiers had boarded their vehicles and engines were started. Except for Truck Six, the radio truck, which had a flat battery again. Davy started it with the hand crank but expressed his concerns to Mayne.

'The radio truck has got an electrical problem. It could be a dud battery but it was a brand new vehicle before we set out on the mission. I would really like to check the vehicle over with the multimeter, Major.'

'We don't have time. The Germans could arrive any moment. We need to get moving. You can look at it later.'

Five minutes later, the column was heading south- east along a desert track towards the old fort at Makin

Alshayatin. It was only ten miles away.

Before too long a slow-flying, high-winged reconnaissance aircraft with a spindly undercarriage appeared in the western sky. It was another German Fieseler *Storch*. As was standard practice in the LRDG , the British soldiers donned their Afrika Korps caps and waved at the pilot as he circled just out of gun range, the morning sun glinting off his perspex canopy.

Mayne thumped his left hand on the bonnet of the Chevy. They had found them. Again! How did the Germans always manage to locate them? But this time he had no Plan B. He had to get to the fort to replenish their supplies. Then they could make a run for Alexandria and hope they didn't catch them. But supposing the Germans had now guessed where they were going and planned to head them off?

The track descended into a rocky wadi. The drivers slowed down, taking great care not to puncture the tyres on sharp rocks. After another fifteen minutes they had cleared the dried-up river bed and were ascending the far side towards level, sandy ground. As Mayne's truck picked up speed, he saw a familiar, boxy shape blocking their way. It was a tank. With a large rectangular turret mounting a big gun. Mayne estimated that it must be a 75mm weapon. The only tank the British had which mounted a 75mm was the Grant . And that had the gun in a side-sponson. It must be a German tank. The dreaded Panzer IV. And the British force didn't have a single weapon which could pierce its armour.

# Chapter 15

## Standoff

Mayne ordered his vehicles to stop while he considered his options. The sand-coloured Panzer stood a hundred yards away, straddling the road, but had not reacted to the arrival of the British trucks. Its turret remained motionless, its main gun pointed straight ahead. Of course, in North Africa, vehicle recognition was always a problem , as both sides used captured equipment.

Mayne jumped out of the lead truck, binoculars round his neck and stood on the sand. He removed his sand goggles, wiped the sweat from his forehead with his *shemagh* and then put it back on.

'Davy, where are you, I need your help!'

Davy Atkins, the patrol's mechanic, was a complete nerd when it came to vehicles, including tanks. He had been a petrol-head before the war and read all the current motor journals. It was said that he could identify any Allied or Axis vehicle from a hundred paces. Mayne handed his binoculars to Davy, who took a couple of minutes to scrutinize the tank.

'It's the correct shape for a Panzer IV all right, but it's got armoured skirts above the main wheels and two cylindrical fuel tanks at the rear, mounted either side of the engine deck. No German tank has these features. It's got six main wheels, not eight, which would suggest it's a Panzer III and not a IV. However, the first and last main wheels are bigger than the others and the main wheels are mounted in two groups of three with a gap between them. Only one tank in the world has that arrangement – a British Valentine.

'Obviously it's possible that the tank is a captured example being used by the Germans, but the Jerries always put huge black crosses on the side of captured armoured vehicles to make sure their own troops don't attack them. And German tanks usually have a three-digit code number painted on the side of the turret. This doesn't have either of these features. Also, there's a name painted on the side of the turret in black capital letters. It reads *Honeychile*. Who or what is *Honeychile*? Our crews like to paint names on the sides of their tanks. So do the Yanks. But I've never seen the Germans or Italians do it. No, I would say it's a British Valentine Infantry Tank and the crew are friendlies. The only thing that looks unusual is the turret and gun, both bigger than anything I have ever seen on that model of tank. The Valentine usually carries a 40mm QF two-pounder gun in a small turret, although there is a new version with a six-pounder QF about to come off the production lines.'

Mayne grinned. Davy's almost obsessive knowledge of vehicles came in handy now and again.

'Thank you, Sherlock Holmes. Now I think we should take a closer look at this tin can. Davy, you'd better come along ….and you as well Binns… and you, Captain Lee. There may be wounded soldiers in the tank. We'll take some weapons with us just in case.'

Mayne handed Thompson sub-machine guns to Binns and Davy while he and Lee took out their Webley 0.38 service revolvers from their holsters. It took only two minutes for the four soldiers to walk the hundred yards to the Valentine, but it was an ordeal in the scorching sun. Lee could feel his kneecaps burning in the morning heat. He wished he had acquired some long trousers as planned instead of the standard Eighth Army shorts.

As the four soldiers approached the tank, they heard Vera Lynn singing *A Nightingale Sang in Berkeley Square*. The crew was listening to the BBC Overseas Service on the vehicle's radio. All hatches were open. The soldiers walked round the front of the Valentine and discovered a hive of activity on the far side. Three crew members—the driver, gunner and loader —were stripped to the waist as they sweated in the sun, repairing a broken track link, while the tank commander lubricated the bogies with a grease gun.

The tank commander looked up with a start and dropped his grease gun. He wore a standard British tanker's battledress top, trousers and boots, with a black beret, and had heavy stubble on his chin. On his left shoulder was a curved fabric badge with the word *Canada*.

Mayne saluted. 'Major Paddy Mayne, Special Air Service. I am leading a column of LRDG and SAS personnel back to Alexandria.'

The tank commander saluted back. 'Sergeant Jake Crerar. Montreal Tank Regiment.'

'You're Canadian. I didn't know Canada had any forces in the Middle East,' said Mayne.

'Officially we don't. But a small detachment of Canadian tanks—just six Valentines—was sent to the Western Desert to gain combat experience, as we recently started building these vehicles in our own factories. We were on our way to Gazala when we heard our forces had lost the battle. The only thing we could do was head back to Alexandria using the tracks that run across the Western Desert. We were originally travelling on the back of a Scammell Tank Transporter but it broke down. The crew of the Scammell decided to stay with their vehicle and await rescue.'

Crerar took a swig of water from his canteen before continuing.

'So we chose to complete the journey ourselves. We're heading for the old fort at Makan Alshayatin where we're going to top up our fuel and water from the supply dump there before resuming our journey to Alexandria.'

'Makan Alshayatin, that's where we're going,' said Mayne.

'Any chance we could tag along? If you get into a fight then a Valentine can give you a nice edge, Major,' said Crerar, as he reached up and tapped the barrel of the main gun with his left hand.

'I understood Valentines only had a two-pounder gun,'

replied Mayne. 'That 's useless against the latest German tanks. The Eighth Army calls it the *doorknocker* – it wakes up the enemy but doesn't kill them. And its HE round doesn't contain much explosive, which you need for dealing with infantry and anti- tank guns. And even the new six-pounder Valentine lacks an HE round at present. And a Valentine has a maximum speed of only fifteen miles per hour.'

'Ah, but this is not a standard Valentine, Major. We call it the Super Valentine. An old Mark One which has been heavily modified by the RAOC workshops in Alexandria to test new technologies. The turret has been enlarged and the useless two-pounder replaced by an American M3 75mm cannon taken from a knocked-out Grant. As well as firing a very effective M48 high explosive shell, it can shoot the new American M61 armour- piercing round.'

Crerar picked up a large shell with a shiny brass casing which was lying beside the tank. It sparkled in the sunlight.

'Most of the new M4 Shermans coming off the production lines are being supplied with the much less effective M72 round, on the direct orders of the American General Lesley McNair. So the majority of the far superior M61 rounds are being shipped to the Russians. But, through my contacts, I acquired a few crates of these beauties. We tested one against a captured, engineless Panzer IV hulk on a range in the desert near Alexandria. Even at a distance of five hundred yards it penetrated the frontal armour, went right through the tank, made a hole in the rear plate and then knocked out a Panzer III which was sitting behind it. Believe me, one of these shells will ruin your day. It travels at a velocity of two thousand and twenty four feet per second and can penetrate eighty-one millimetres of armour at a range of 500 metres. We also have a very useful BESA 7.92mm machine gun in the mantlet next to the main gun. It' s based on a pre-war Czech design and very handy for defeating infantry attacks. And the frontal armour has been beefed up by adding an extra 35mm of plate. That gives a total frontal thickness of 100mm. The gun mantlet has received the same upgrade. Most of the German tank and anti-tank guns can't penetrate that thickness of armour.'

'What about an 88mm,though?' asked Davy. 'Suppose we come against one of these?'

'Even the Super Valentine can be knocked out by an 88,' replied Crerar. 'There is no tank in the world that can stand up to one of those monsters. You would need armour six inches thick. And if you put six inches of armour all round a tank it would be so heavy it wouldn't be able to move.

'However, the 88 has some drawbacks. It's a big, heavy gun with a high profile that's hard to move and takes a long time to set up. It's only useful in fixed positions. At the moment the Germans don't have a tank large enough to carry it, though that may change.'

'OK, you've made some good points,' said Mayne. 'But you still have a slow tank there…and that enlarged turret, 75mm gun and extra armour will have increased the weight of your vehicle and reduced your performance further.'

'Ah, but we have got that covered that as well, Major. The fitters in Alexandria have worked on the engine to take its output from a hundred and seventy five horsepower to nearly three hundred.'

Crerar opened the hinged engine access doors at the rear of the tank. Amidst all the pipes and hoses and wires was a gleaming metal contraption with the words *Amherst Villiers* written on it in raised letters. Davy's eyes lit up.

'That's right, it's an Amherst Villiers mechanically-driven supercharger. The same device that was fitted to the famous 1931 Blower Bentley. You'll recall how that machine went like a rocket. We've also replaced the carburettor with the Daimler - Benz fuel injection system from a crashed Messerschmitt Bf109F. And finally, we have made use of these.'

92

Crerar held out his hand to reveal several round metal objects which looked like throat lozenges.

'Wondering what they are, Major? They are Fuel Catalyst Pellets. You add them to the fuel tank and they cause a chemical reaction which effectively boosts the octane rating of the fuel, increasing the performance of the engine. They were developed by a British scientist called Henry Broquet specifically for use by Mark II Hawker Hurricanes on the Russian Front. The Merlin XX on the Hurricane II really needs 100 octane fuel, but standard Russian petrol is like donkey's piss – 80 octane at best. These little devices have solved the problem. In combination, all these engine upgrades have increased the top speed to twenty-eight miles an hour. Only the Crusader tank has a better cross-country speed because of its Christie suspension, but it has paper-thin armour and is very unreliable. So can we join the party?'

'I guess so,' said Mayne. ' After the war you should become a car salesman. By the way why is your tank called Honeychile?'

'That's the name of my fianceé. I am marrying her when the war's over. We're going to have our honeymoon in Jamaica.'

By this time the crew of the Valentine had finished their repair of the right- hand track and were putting their tools back in the boxes which were mounted on the deck of the tank. Crerar climbed up onto the Valentine and entered the commander's hatch on top of the turret. He remained standing in the hatch so he could see the surrounding terrain and spoke to his crew using a carbon field microphone which was connected to the tank's intercom system.

'Driver, start engine. Prepare to move out.' An electric starter motor whirred and then a cloud of white exhaust smoke billowed out from the rear of the vehicle as the powerful engine revved up.

Mayne, Lee, Binns and Davy boarded the Chevys and all the vehicles' engines coughed into life— apart from the radio truck which had a flat battery yet again. Once more, Davy had had to start it with the hand -crank.

An hour later, the convoy of five trucks, lead by the single Valentine, neared the fort at Makan Alshayatin. It was perfectly positioned to dominate the surrounding ground as it was situated on top of a low sandy hillock which itself was on a salient of hard rock which extended south into the Qattara Depression – a unique area of salt marshes shaped like a teardrop which extended for hundreds of miles in every direction. The Depression was four hundred feet below sea level and effectively impassable to tanks and military vehicles because of the treacherous quicksand which could swallow up lorries, and even individual soldiers. One geologist had compared it to a soggy rice pudding with a thin crust on the top.

The unique topography of the area meant that the two-storey sandstone fort was in a perfect defensive position. Its thick walls could resist bullets and light artillery fire, while its position on a thumb-shaped area of hard rock which projected south into the Qattara Depression meant that it could not be assaulted from behind or from the side. Any attackers would have to approach from the front to avoid sinking into the salt marshes.

Mayne lifted up his binoculars and scanned the area. A French tricolour was still flying from the flagpole but the fort looked deserted. No sentries were on duty. There were a few sandbagged machine-gun emplacements in front of the fort but all weapons had been removed.

'The fort was built by the Royal Engineers in 1855,' said Mayne to Lee who was sitting beside him in the lead Chevy. 'The most recent occupants were a Free French detachment but they left for Alexandria two weeks ago to be re-trained on new weapons. They had instructions to leave behind much of their stores for use by the LRDG and SAS.'

Mayne shifted his binoculars to an area two hundred yards to the east of the fort. He couldn't believe what he was seeing.

'How on earth did *these* get there?' he muttered.

There were about fifty wrecked vehicles. Some were burned out, others had been abandoned and were sitting with flat tyres. There was also the remains of a crashed single-engine aircraft with RAF roundels . What was it doing here, so far from the nearest battlefield? No fighting had taken place in this area since hostilities had broken out with the Italians in 1940. Both sides tended to avoid the Qattara Depression because it was so treacherous. Before they left for Alexandria he would have a look at these mystery vehicles.

Mayne put down his binoculars and spoke to Binns who was standing beside him.

'OK Binns, get the front doors of the fort open and we'll drive the trucks into the courtyard. I want the building searched for anything that might be of use to us, particularly petrol, water, food and ammunition.'

Five minutes later all the trucks were inside the compound while the Valentine remained outside, its gun pointing to the north, ready to repel any attack. As Mayne got out of the truck , Davy appeared clutching a black model 40 Avometer.

'As we have a little time before we depart I would like permission to do an auto-electrical check on Truck Six to find out why the battery keeps going flat, Major.'

'Very well, but make it fast. I want to be out of here as soon as possible.'

Davy's comments interested Lee.

'If you don't mind Major, I would like to give Davy a hand. I was very interested in electronics before the war and used to build radios.'

The two men walked over to Truck Six, and Davy began his investigation by checking the battery fitted on the nearside running board. There was another on the other side of the vehicle. The Avometer's needle showed both batteries were delivering six volts. Then he turned a rotary dial on his meter to measure current, disconnected the negative lead from the nearside battery and connected the meter between the negative battery terminal and the lead.

'Now that's very strange,' said Davy. 'All lights are off and the radio is not switched on yet the meter is showing a current drain of four amps.'

Lee's eyes lit up. 'I have heard of this problem in auto-electrics. It is called parasitic drain. A short- circuit in the vehicle's electrical wiring causes it to drain the battery even when everything is switched off. Let's take a look under the bonnet.'

Davy unlatched the bonnet and lifted it up but every-thing seemed in order, all wires in their correct positions. Nothing wrong there. Then the two men walked round to the rear of the truck and unlatched the tailgate.

Lee noticed it at once. A small wooden box painted a sand colour with black stencil lettering reading 'Radio Amp No 17.'

'What's this?' he asked Davy as he pointed at the box.

'I dunno. I presume it is a Radio Amplifier which increases the power of the Number 11 set. The fitters are adding new equipment all the time.'

'Why would you need a Radio Amplifier for a Number 11 set?' asked Lee. 'Before the war Ralph Bagnold managed to send radio signals over huge distances in the desert from one of these sets. On one occasion he achieved a range of a thousand miles. I think we should take a look inside this box. Pass me a screwdriver.'

The top of the box was held on with four woodscrews which had been covered with paint. Lee scraped off the paint with the tip of the screwdriver, removed the top and discovered an assortment of electronic components.

There were three thermionic valves containing glowing red filaments, several resistors and a jumble of wires. But most significantly, there was a tuning coil and a variable capacitor. These components were not required for a radio amplifier but they were essential parts of a radio transmitter.

'Well I'll be damned,' said Lee. 'A radio transmitter which has been switched on all the time. The Germans must have located our position using direction finding equipment. That would explain why they have always managed to find us. And why the batteries keep going flat.'

Lee looked up to find Mayne standing by the truck.

'Thank you, Captain Lee. Now I'm going to make sure no more signals are sent. Mayne picked up a short magazine 0.303 inch Lee Enfield rifle from the back of the truck and was about to smash the three valves with the butt of the gun when Lee stopped him.

'No, Major. I know you like to smash things and blow them up, but these electronic components may be useful if we need to fix our own radio set. All we have to do is disconnect the power supply and the signals will stop,' said Lee. A moment later Lee had loosened two screws in a Bakelite connection box and pulled out a pair of cotton-covered wires. Immediately the red glow inside the valves ceased as the power was cut to the heating filaments.

*******

Ten miles away in the back of an Opel Blitz radio truck, an Abwehr radio operator turned to his Feldwebel.'The signal has stopped. The British must have found the transmitter.'

'That is disappointing but it is not a disaster. We already have a triangulation on their most recent position at the old British fort. If we move quickly we will catch them before they leave. They will take at least an hour to restock their vehicles. And this time we have six Panzers in our hunter force. The British force is doomed!'

# Chapter 16

# The Tanks are Coming!

Mayne sat on a rickety wooden chair in front of a worn oak table in one of the rooms in the ground floor of the fort. Sunlight streamed through the open wooden shutters of the glassless windows. The interior walls had been crudely painted with a white distemper and were covered with graffiti, some of which was in French. The room smelled of garlic and cigarette butts. The fort lacked gas or an electricity generator and had no running water, although there was a deep well in the courtyard and a crude latrine block at the rear. Mayne puffed at a cigarette and sipped water from his canteen while he studied a map. A knock at the door interrupted his inner thoughts.

Binns entered, a little out of puff.

'We've completed our search of the building, sir. As expected, there are ample stocks of rations, water, petrol and medical supplies. As for ammunition, there are crates of 0.303 bullets and forty – five calibre rounds and grenades — Mills bombs to be precise — plus a few British anti-tank mines. Unfortunately there's no fifty-calibre ammunition, or 0.55 rounds for our Boys anti-tank rifles. There are also two old, rusty French Chaucut machine-guns and boxes of 7.5mm ammunition for them. And about fifty empty wine bottles. The French do like their *vino* don't they sir! The lads were wondering if they left because they'd run out of wine and cheese!'

'OK Binns, load up the Chevys,' said Mayne as he stubbed out his cigarette. 'We'll take as much of everything as we can carry and top up our petrol tanks before we leave. You'd better ask the tank crew what they want. They can carry a lot on the rear deck and they've also got two auxiliary tanks that can be filled with either petrol or water. I want us to be out of here and on our way within an hour. Keep two men on the parapets as lookouts.'

Mayne folded the map and walked into the courtyard. There was one thing he had to do before they left and that was check out the wrecked vehicles that lay to the east of the fort. They were within walking distance so there was no point in taking one of the trucks.

Davy Atkins was checking the oil level in one of the Chevys with a dipstick when Mayne tapped him on the shoulder.

'Come on Davy, I need your expert opinion!'

Ten minutes later, the two soldiers stood in the middle of a vehicle graveyard. Light and heavy trucks, BSA and Harley-Davidson motorcycles, tracked Carden-Lloyd Carriers, Vickers Light tanks and even some old Great War vintage Rolls-Royce armoured cars with their turret - mounted Vickers 0.303 machine guns.

Some of the vehicles were blackened and burned, while others had just been abandoned and were sitting with flat tyres. Mayne counted fifty-three vehicles, including five cement mixer trucks. *Why would anyone need cement mixers in the middle of the desert?* he thought.

To the north of the vehicles lay a crashed aircraft with wide wings, a long fuselage and a single radial engine with a bent propeller. The starboard wing had been scorched by fire, revealing an aluminium criss- cross structure which was the same as that used in the Vickers Wellington bomber. Mayne recalled it was known as a geodetic structure and was based on a method of airship construction devised by the aircraft designer Barnes Wallis. The plane must be an RAF Vickers Wellesley, a light bomber type which had been based in Egypt in the mid – thirties, but was now regarded as obsolete.

'There's obviously been a battle here at some point,' said Davy. 'But something is not quite right. There are no bullet holes in any of the vehicles so what caused them to catch fire? And there have never been any major battles in this part of the desert because the regular forces of both sides keep their distance because of the treacherous nature of the Qattara Depression.

'There's another thing that bothers me. All this equipment is old kit. Vickers light tanks. Rolls-Royce armoured cars. A Wellesley bomber. And take a look at some of these trucks. They have U.S. Army written on them but they are of Great War vintage. There are even a couple of Ford Model T pickups fitted with the old, water-cooled version of the M2 fifty-calibre gun.

'I know the Yanks were using old equipment until 1940, when they started producing modern trucks such as the GMC six - wheeled truck which the U.S. Army calls the Deuce-and-a-Half. And as far as I know, the Yanks have never sent any troops to North Africa since they entered the war, although that may change in the near future.

'And take a look at the condition of these vehicles. There's not much rust but that is normal in the desert because the air is so dry. But a lot of the paint has been worn off by numerous sandstorms. No, I would say all these vehicles have been sitting out here for about five years. So what happened? And why are there some American army vehicles?

'I don't know,' said Mayne. 'It doesn't make any sense.'

The two men trudged back to the fort. SAS Private McTavish, on sentry duty , shouted from the parapets. 'Unidentified column of vehicles approaching from the north-west. Estimated range seven miles.'

Mayne and Davy raced through the doors of the fort and climbed up the stone steps to the parapet. The Major raised his Zeiss binoculars and confirmed what McTavish had seen. A large plume of dust was rising in the sky and there was the vague shape of a number of vehicles approaching. The image shimmered in a heat haze. They were too far away to be clearly identified but, even at this distance, sunlight was reflecting off multiple windscreens so Mayne knew they must have some trucks.

'They are coming from the north-west but we can still escape towards Alexandria which is to the north-east,' said Mayne.

'No we can't,' said McTavish. 'Look over there!' He pointed to another plume of dust to the north -east.

Mayne realized they were trapped. He couldn't go north-west or north-east because he would be heading directly towards an alert attacking force. If he went due north he could be caught between the jaws of a pincer movement by the two forces. He couldn't go south because of the Qattara Depression and due east was out because of a steep escarpment which couldn't be climbed by a Chevy truck, or a Valentine tank come to that. Going west would get them out of trouble but it would take them in the wrong direction and they might be captured by advancing enemy forces. There was therefore only one option left to him – stay in the fort and fight!

He shouted down to Binns. 'How long till the trucks are ready to go?'

'About ten minutes, sir. All the stores are loaded. We're just topping up all the petrol tanks.'

'There's been a change of plan! We're not leaving! We're going to stand and fight. Dismount all the weapons from the vehicles and install them in defensive positions. Put all the Vickers Ks and the Brens along the first floor parapet. The fifties can fire from the ground floor windows, as can the two Boys anti-tank rifles.'

Mayne tore down the steps and out of the front doors of the fort. The next job was to set up a good defensive position for *Honeychile*. It was essential that this asset was kept in the battle as long as possible. But how was he going to do this? He had no idea.

\*\*\*\*\*\*\*

Several miles away, Hans Peiper sat in the back of an Sd. Kfz. 251 half-track and smiled to himself. He hated North Africa. The heat. The dust. The local population. But today he was going to get a chance to kill some British soldiers. He wanted revenge because he blamed the British for his demotion. And if he found a British soldier who also happened to be Jewish then so much the better. He would take him out of sight and slowly torture him to death for information. There would be no Geneva Convention or cosy POW camp for him. Peiper licked his lips. Today Hans was in control, again. He was looking forward to the next few hours.

# Chapter 17

## Hammer and Anvil

**23 June, 1942 07.17 hrs**

Mayne ran towards the Valentine as the low sun rose in the morning sky. Things were not looking good but he admired the Germans' tactical skill. They were delivering a classic 'hammer-and-anvil' attack. Two mechanised units on courses at ninety degrees to one another which converged at the point of the attack – the fort. He wished he had a few 25-pounder field guns at his disposal. All he had was one tank and a few machine- guns. That would have to do. He shouted up to Crerar who was standing in the commander's hatch.

'We're not leaving! An enemy attack is imminent and we're going to stand and fight! The first thing we need to do is get your vehicle into a better defensive position where it will be hard to spot. I want you to reverse *Honeychile* up that slope on the west side of the fort. Some of my men will help your crew to dig away some of the sand so you can get your vehicle into a hull-down position with only the turret showing. We don't have a field telephone so I will communicate with you using our Number 11 set in our radio truck.'

'OK, you're on. Driver, get the tank started,' said Crerar as he spoke into the carbon mike.

Mayne's plan was to position *Honeychile* at the top of the slope in a small dug-out, so that only the turret was visible above the sand. This could then be covered with camouflage netting and local scrub, making it hard to spot. The Germans didn't know they had a tank. Mayne wanted to keep it a surprise for as long as possible. As the Valentine slowly reversed up the hill, Mayne spoke to Binns who was standing beside him:

'How many anti-tank mines have we got?'

'Just seven sir.'

'I would have preferred fifty. Lay them out in a fan pattern a hundred and fifty yards from the fort. And mark their positions with small stones so we can remove them if we have to. There's another job for you. Take some Nobel 808 plastic explosive, a can of petrol and a time pencil and create an incendiary bomb over there, well to the east of the fort,' said Mayne, pointing with his right hand. 'That will provide a useful distraction when the time comes. And allocate four men to help the tank crew dig out the sand to create a hull-down position.'

'Very good sir.'

The fort was a hive of activity as soldiers removed all the machine-guns from the Chevys and mounted them in defensive positions on both floors. Mayne's force had two fifty-calibre machine -guns and a pair of Boys anti -tank rifles at ground level. On the first floor of the fort he had four twin Vickers K guns and four Brens plus a few Lee – Enfield rifles and Thompson sub - machine guns. He also had an ample supply of grenades.

As his men scurried about, preparing the defences, Mayne climbed up to the first floor of the fort and looked through his binoculars once more. The enemy force which was approaching from the north-west was the nearer of the two columns, and Mayne could now make out details of the vehicles. The force was led by three tanks. At this range, Mayne could not make out whether these were Panzer IIIs or IVs but either model was bad news. The Germans had learned from their earlier mistakes and had deployed their vehicles to give maximum protection to their infantry. The three tanks were at the front in line abreast formation. Behind them were the lightly armoured vehicles consisting of Sd. Kfz.222 four – wheeled armoured cars and Sd. Kfz. 251 half-tracks. At the rear were the infantry, who were travelling in soft-skinned lorries.

He guessed the other column approaching from the north-east would be deployed in a similar fashion. That meant they would probably be facing a total of six tanks with only one of their own. Yet in any battle, what really mattered was tactics. The French had plenty of tanks in 1940 and they were actually superior to their German opponents. But their tactics were poor and they were commanded by a lot of senile generals who had no idea about the principles of fast-moving modern warfare.

Binns was still busy setting up an improvised bomb outside the fort so Mayne spoke to Private McTavish, who was manning a twin Vickers K gun.

'We'll be facing armour. Our main anti-tank weapon is the Super Valentine with its 75mm but we will need more than that. There are plenty of empty wine bottles lying around the fort so take a few men and prepare as many petrol bombs as you can. And make up a few satchel charges with the plastic explosive.'

Lee climbed up the steps and arrived on the parapet, slightly out of breath. 'Anything I can do to help out, Major?'

'Once the shooting starts you will be needed to attend to casualties. That's your primary role on this mission.'

'I know Major, but we will soon be facing a superior force. You only have fifteen men, including both of us. You need as many men as possible who can shoot. I can fire many types of weapon as I was in the Home Guard for a few months. I even became an instructor on the Bren Gun. Under the terms of the Geneva Convention, my primary duty is medical care of combatants of both sides. But I am also entitled to fire a weapon in self-defence and I think that would cover our current situation.'

Mayne sighed. 'Very well, I'll let you have a Thompson. Just remember, it doesn't have much of a range and isn't very accurate. And it's heavy. Wait till the enemy is close, very close. And fire in short, controlled bursts to avoid overheating the barrel. Just two or three rounds at a time.'

Mayne handed Lee a Thompson and the young Scottish medical officer descended the steps with a smile on his face. He looked as though he had just been given a Hornby electric train set for his birthday.

As Lee took up a defensive position on the ground floor of the fort, Mayne gazed through his binoculars again. He estimated that it would be just ten minutes before the tanks got within firing range of the fort. On the sand outside, Binns had finished making his improvised bomb which consisted of a can of petrol with a lump of Nobel 808 plastic explosive stuck on the top. Binns partly buried the bomb in the sand, inserted a time pencil with a fifteen - minute fuse into the plastic, and then crimped the top with pliers. This broke a vial of cupric chloride which would slowly dissolve a fine wire holding back a spring. When the wire was burned all the way through, the spring would fire a detonator, setting off the explosive. Binns checked the time of the crimping with his watch and ran back into the fort. Two soldiers closed the heavy wooden doors and bolted them shut.

In the Super Valentine to the west of the building, Crerar stood in the commander's hatch and waited for the three Panzers approaching from the north-west to come within range of his 75mm weapon. His gunner, Sutherland, was observing the scene through his brass sighting telescope. He already had an M61 armour-piercing round in the breech, ready to fire. In just moments a battle would start that would have a decisive influence on the outcome of the war. Sutherland rotated the turret slightly until the crosshairs of his sight were centred on the most westerly Panzer and prepared to fire.

# Chapter 18

## Battle Royale

A single drop of sweat dripped off Sutherland's right eyebrow and landed on the brass sighting telescope to the left of the main gun. The tank gunner wiped the eyepiece clean with a soft cloth and resumed his gaze. The sight's cross hairs were centred on the advancing Panzer which was furthest to his left, part of the column which was approaching from the north-west. When he got the command, he would fire.

Up in the commander's hatch, Crerar also studied the approaching Germans. The range was about a thousand yards. An M61 round would probably penetrate the frontal armour of a Panzer IV even at that distance but there would be a far greater chance of a 'kill' if he let them get closer. The other German column approaching from the north-east was about three thousand yards away, so could be ignored for the moment.

On the parapet of the fort, Mayne examined the two columns of approaching Germans through his binoculars and shouted down to his soldiers:

'Hold your fire, men. No – one is to shoot until the Jerries are within effective range. Don't waste ammunition. Even our fifty-calibres are ineffective at this distance.'

Binns studied his watch. In six minutes the bomb would explode. He hoped he had timed it right to provide a distraction at the crucial moment. The Valentine crew had been told to expect an explosion at that time. The only problem was that the chemical reaction in a time pencil could be affected by the ambient temperature, so it might detonate earlier or later than expected.

Less than fifty yards away, in the fighting compartment of the Valentine, Sutherland baked alive. Sweat ran down his back and legs and soaked his socks. It was hot enough in a tank with the hatches open in a Canadian summer. In the scorching sun of Egypt in June, every square inch of the tank's bodywork could burn skin. How he wished the Super Valentine had been fitted with the new American invention of air- conditioning. He had been told that one cinema in Cairo had installed it. How he would like to be there right now, sipping an ice-cold orange juice and watching the latest Humphrey Bogart movie.

Crerar estimated the range of the nearest German column once more. About seven hundred yards. He spoke into his carbon field mike:

'Open fire five seconds after the bomb goes off!'

A minute later, there was a loud bang to the east of the fort. An orange fireball rose into the sky, followed by a large plume of oily, black smoke. Aboard the German vehicles approaching from the north- west, there was a moment of confusion. Had someone in the other column opened fire on the fort at long range? All eyes looked east and three tank turrets rotated in that direction.

At that exact moment, when all the Germans were looking the wrong way, the Super Valentine shot its first round. There was a loud crump and a brief muzzle flash as the 75mm M3 gun fired. The entire tank rocked on its suspension as the powerful weapon recoiled.The high-velocity M61 round whizzed through the hot desert air, skimmed over the top of the left- hand Panzer and narrowly missed the commander who was standing in the turret. It hit the front of an Sd. Kfz 251 half- track which was travelling directly behind it, making a loud metallic clang. The front end of the German vehicle caved in and erupted into flames. Burning petrol spilled onto the sand and several soldiers bailed out the half-track, their uniforms blazing.

But Crerar was not pleased. The Panzers were the greater threat. They had to be taken out first.

'For Christ's sake get those Panzers before they hit us!' he screamed into the microphone.

The loader, Kelly slammed another M61 round into the breech and Sutherland fired a second time. Again, the powerful round shot through the sky and flew above the turret of the Panzer, hitting a Volkswagen Type 82 Kubelwagen at the rear of the column. The flimsy vehicle disintegrated, all the occupants killed by the sheer kinetic energy of the projectile.

Crerar slammed his hand on the top of the tank, burning it in the process. He grabbed the mike again.

'Can you not hit that fucking target? What's wrong with you man?'

'I had the tank in the centre of my sight. Right in my crosshairs. The sight must have been knocked out of alignment during our bumpy journey across the desert.'

Kelly loaded a third M61 round. This time Sutherland aimed ten degrees low and fired. Bang! The gun barrel recoiled as the heavy round sped through the sky and smacked into the front of the enemy tank. The munition penetrated the front glacis plate and cut the driver in two. It then went through the fighting compartment of the tank and lodged in the engine at the rear. The Panzer stopped, black smoke pouring from the ventilation grilles on its rear deck.

'That's more like it. Fire at will,' said Crerar.

Another M61 round was already on its way towards the second Panzer. It struck the gun mantlet, causing a hole three inches in diameter and killing the gunner, commander and driver who were all hit by flying pieces of metal. The only surviving crew member—the loader — opened a hatch on the right side of the turret and bailed out as the tank was consumed by flames.

The crew of the third Panzer, number 031, started to panic. Where was all this defensive fire coming from? Did the British have anti-tank guns hidden in the fort? Maybe even the new six-pounder ,which could knock out any German tank? It had only been in service for a few weeks but had already acquired an awesome reputation for punching above its weight. The German tank crews were terrified of it. The Panzer commander ordered his driver to make a sharp right turn and get up to full speed. His plan was to approach the fort from the west which, he expected, would be out of the line of fire of any emplaced anti-tank guns.

'What the hell is that Kraut doing?' said Crerar. 'Why couldn't he just stay on that course and be blown to kingdom come?'

Now the crew of the Super Valentine were faced with a tank moving fast from right to left which would be harder to hit. Down below in the turret, Kelly slammed another M61 round into the breech. Sutherland knew that he was now faced with a difficult target. But he had done a lot of hunting back in his native Canada before the war and knew the solution was to aim ahead of the target. Just like hunting wild birds and animals. He also now understood how much vertical compensation to allow for the misaligned sight. And a Panzer IV's side armour was only 30mm thick.

Sutherland did a quick mental calculation. He estimated that the Panzer was travelling at 25 miles an hour at a range of 500 yards. It had a length of about twenty feet so, knowing the velocity of an M61 round, he was certain that if he aimed one tank length ahead of the target he should hit it.

Sutherland slewed the turret round until the crosshairs were ahead of the Panzer. He aimed low to take account of the vertical misalignment he had already discovered and pulled the trigger. The breech of the big M3 gun shot back into the fighting compartment with the recoil and Sutherland's view was momentarily obscured by white smoke from the muzzle blast. After a minute he could see clearly and saw that the Panzer had taken a direct hit on the side of the engine compartment. A hole three inches in diameter had appeared in the side plating and Sutherland could see bright orange flames beyond it. Within seconds, the twelve-cylinder Maybach petrol engine was ablaze and emitting clouds of thick, black smoke. The crew bailed out. The battle had only been going on for ten minutes but already the Germans had lost half their tanks.

Up in the commander's hatch, Crerar smiled.

'Well done, men. The other German column is still beyond effective firing range so let's take out some of that light armour. Load with HE. These armoured cars and half-tracks have thin plating so there's no need to use our precious M61 shells.'

Kelly selected an HE (High Explosive) shell from the ready-use rack and loaded it into the gun. Sutherland fired and a couple of seconds later an Sd. Kfz.251 half-track burst into flames. For the next ten minutes the process was repeated until four half-tracks and three Sd.Kfz. 222 four - wheeled armoured cars were ablaze. Some of the German gunners returned fire but they had nothing heavier than a 20mm cannon, whose shells could not penetrate the Valentine's thick hide.

By this time the German column was only three hundred yards away and the crew of *Honeychile* finished the job with short bursts from their single, mantlet-mounted BESA machine-gun. All the soldiers in the fort opened fire as well with the two M2 fifty-calibres and Boys rifles and multiple Vickers Ks and Brens, smashing truck windscreens, puncturing radiators and bursting tyres. Soon the desert was littered with the black carcasses of burning vehicles. Two German Opel Blitz trucks survived the assault and did U- turns to escape the torrent of fire. The Germans attempted to fire back, but the British soldiers were well protected by the fort's thick stone and added sandbags.

On the parapet of the fort, Binns punched the air with delight.

'They're retreating, Major, they're falling back. They're not Nazi supermen. They can be beaten.'

But Mayne wasn't celebrating because the soldiers defending the fort had another problem to deal with. The second German convoy which was approaching from the north-east was now only eight hundred yards away. The first column had been taken by surprise as they weren't expecting a tank, it was well dug-in and camouflaged, and they had been distracted by Binn's exploding bomb.

The tank crews in the second column had seen the smoke and muzzle flashes of *Honeychile's* gun, and started plastering the area around the tank with high-explosive to spoil its aim. Aboard the Canadian tank, Crerar knew the time had come to reverse out of danger and find a different firing position. He spoke into his mike:

'Driver, reverse as fast as you can. We'll go round the back of the fort and take up a new firing position to the east of the building.'

Private Colt, who was sitting in the driving compartment at the front of the tank, put the gearstick into reverse and accelerated hard. The powerful engine spewed out copious amounts of white exhaust smoke as the tank moved backwards over the crest of the sandy hill and then retreated down the slope on the far side. Once he was on level ground, Colt did a sharp right turn and drove the tank at walking pace along the narrow, hard, rocky strip which lay behind the fort, taking great care to avoid plunging into the salt marsh which was to his right.

After he had gone past the fort, he turned left and ascended the sandy hillock which lay to the east. He understood Crerar's plan. He was using what the Americans called a 'shoot and scoot' technique, in which he would take up a new position at the top of the hill, fire off a couple of rounds and then quickly reverse back down the slope to avoid the return fire. This time they wouldn't have the luxury of a 'hull-down' dug-out position and camouflage netting but if they were quick they might get away with it.

Kelly loaded an M61 round into the breech as the Valentine ascended the hillock. They would have only a few seconds to acquire a target and shoot before they attracted return fire. One advantage the tank had over its German counterparts was that the Super Valentine upgrade had included a facility to depress the gun up to twenty degrees below the horizontal, enabling it to fire from the reverse side of slopes.

Sutherland saw three approaching Panzer IVs in his sight and slewed the turret slightly to get the middle one centred in his crosshairs. He fired and a second later saw the armour-piercing round strike the tank where the turret joined the hull. The turret was completely ripped off and landed in the sand behind the vehicle. A half-track crashed into it and men jumped off the vehicle.

The other two Panzers could only see a turret projecting above the top of the hillock. It was a small target but they fired anyway with the rounds they already had loaded, which were high-explosive. Seconds later, the HE rounds exploded on either side of the Valentine, showering it with dust. Sutherland couldn't see clearly and aimed as best he could. He fired, and two seconds later an M61 round struck the right-hand track of the most westerly Panzer. The track came off the tank which came to an abrupt halt. Sutherland had scored a 'mobility kill' as the tank was now stationary although still able to fire its gun.

The third Panzer fired again, and this time the shell scored a direct hit on the front glacis plate of the Valentine, causing a mighty concussion that reverberated throughout the tank. It gouged out a large chunk of metal, causing a concave depression on the front of the tank. But it did not penetrate into the driver's compartment. Crerar knew that the extra 35mm of armour plate had made all the difference. All the same it was time to move. Another hit in the same area might crack the armour.

'Driver, reverse!' he screamed into the mike. His plan was to reverse back down the slope and then pop up at a different location. With the element of surprise, he might get off a couple of rounds at the third Panzer before he was spotted.

Colt expertly reversed the Valentine down the slope and then turned the vehicle left. His plan was to drive along the narrow, flat ,rocky strip behind the fort before ascending the slope on the west side. He had gone only a few yards when he heard a loud bang coming from the right hand side of the tank. A few seconds later the tank slewed to the right and came to a halt. He knew what must have happened. A track link had broken. It could be fixed, but not in a hurry.

Up on the parapets of the fort, Mayne received a radio message which had been sent from the Valentine. They had a broken track link and were stuck behind the fort. Consequently they would be out of the battle for a while.

Mayne lifted his binoculars and studied the scene. One Panzer IV in the force approaching from the north- east had been destroyed. A second had been immobilized but could still fire its gun from long range. A third was unharmed and was heading straight for them. It had a powerful 75mm gun and two machine guns. They had no weapons that could defeat a heavily armoured Panzer IV. For the first time in his Army career, Paddy Mayne had no idea what he was going to do.

# Chapter 19

## For You The War Is Over

Mayne stood on the parapets and watched through his binoculars as the Panzer IV approached. With its 75mm main gun, two 7.92mm machine guns, thick frontal armour and good mobility, it was the best tank in the German arsenal. Now one of them was heading towards the fort and the British force didn't have a single weapon that could knock it out. The two M2 fifty-calibre machine guns and the pair of Boys anti-tank rifles they possessed could penetrate almost an inch of armour plate at close range but that wouldn't be enough to pierce the frontal armour of a Mark IV.

Mayne lowered his binoculars and noticed that Lee was now beside him. He carried a Thompson sub- machine gun and had acquired a standard British Army webbing kit which included pouches for spare magazines and grenades.

'A penny for your thoughts, Major.'

'I was just wondering what the food will be like in German POW camps. I hear they get Red Cross food parcels which include some Swiss chocolate and the new Spam,' answered Mayne.

'I hear Spam is delicious though you get tired of it after a while.'

But Mayne wasn't thinking about Spam. He had noticed pairs of small stones arranged in a crescent pattern a hundred and fifty yards from the fort. They were barely noticeable markers for the buried anti-tank mines. He switched his gaze to the approaching Panzer and observed that, if it held its present course, it would pass midway between two buried mines. An idea formed in his head. He shouted to Binns, who was down in the courtyard preparing petrol bombs.

'Binns, ask a couple of men to bring up the two – inch

mortar and some bombs. We'll need both HE and smoke.'

A couple of minutes later, Binns arrived on the parapet, rather breathless from carrying the mortar tube up the steps. Behind him were Privates Johnson and Perkins, with a wooden crate containing mortar bombs and the baseplate. Binns hurriedly fitted the tube onto the baseplate while Mayne kept the enemy tank under observation.

'I want you to fire a few HE bombs at the tank,' said Mayne. 'But aim to miss. The rounds won't penetrate the armour but we may persuade the driver to alter course. Direct your fire to the right of the tank.'

Binns lined up the mortar barrel with the target using the white stripe that was painted on the tube. A crude aiming system, but it worked. Johnson dropped the first round down the barrel. It fell to the bottom and engaged a trigger mechanism which exploded the propellant charge, sending the bomb flying through the air in a high arc. Ten seconds later, it exploded fifty yards to the right of the tank, sending up a cloud of beige dust. But the Panzer continued on its previous course.

'Adjust your aim,' ordered Mayne. 'We need the bombs closer.'

Binns corrected the orientation of the barrel and twenty seconds later, another bomb was on its way. It exploded twelve yards from the tank, which maintained its course.

Ten seconds later, a third bomb detonated just four feet to the right of the tank, showering it with sand and small rocks. The armour was not penetrated but the crew felt the shock wave reverberate through the fighting compartment. The driver wondered if they were under attack from a British six -pounder gun and veered to his right to get out of the line of fire. A moment later the Panzer ran over an anti-tank mine which detonated with a loud bang and sent fragments of red-hot metal in all directions. The tank was enveloped in a cloud of smoke and dust.

Mayne watched the smoke clear and smiled with satisfaction. The right-hand track was broken and now lay motionless on the sand in front of the vehicle. The Panzer had been immobilised. Now he would deliver the *coup de grace*. But first he had to eliminate the tank's ability to fire back.

'All Vickers and Bren gunners. Open fire on the Panzer,' shouted Mayne.

Multiple 0.303 rounds pinged off the thick armour of the tank, chipping the paint finish. None of them could penetrate the Panzer's thick hide but they would force the crew to close all hatches and fight 'buttoned up', limiting their visibility.

'We've immobilised them. Now we're going to blind them,' muttered Mayne, before shouting down to the two fifty-calibre gunners at ground level :

'Cornell, aim at the driver's vision slit on the front of the hull . Davy, fire at the gunner's sighting telescope on the mantlet.'

Both were small targets but the M2 could fire six hundred rounds a minute and it would take only one hit to craze the armoured glass, impairing visibility. Both heavy machine -guns opened up on their targets and bullets sparkled as they impacted on the armour plate.

*******

Fifteen hundred yards away from the fort, Oberst Seidel stood in front of his now stationary column and watched events unfold with a sense of dismay. He had started off with six tanks and now had just two, which were both immobilised. How had the British managed it?

Did they have some of the new six-pounder anti-tank guns hidden in the fort? The wounded Hauptmann Lutz had seen the column at first-hand and was certain they were not towing any anti-tank guns behind their trucks. Perhaps the Free French garrison had left some artillery behind when they had departed? But,as far as he knew from intelligence reports, the French did not yet have this new gun which had arrived in North Africa only a few weeks before.

One of his men, who had been looking through binoculars, had caught a fleeting glimpse of a tank appearing above the sandy hillock to the east of the fort. He was sure it was a British Valentine but that couldn't be right. Everyone knew the Valentine had only a puny two-pounder gun that couldn't pierce the frontal armour of a Mark IV. There were reliable reports that an improved version with a six-pounder cannon was now being manufactured, but it wasn't expected to arrive in North Africa for a few months.

Seidel looked through the binoculars once more. A Panzer IV, turret number 007, stood about 150 yards in front of the fort with its right - hand track broken. As Seidel wondered if it would be possible to retrieve the damaged tank, the doors of the fort opened and a Chevy truck drove out.

Driving in a wide arc, the Chevy turned west and then circled north of the tank, just as Perkins fired two smoke rounds from the mortar on the parapets. They exploded a hundred yards beyond the tank, preventing the distant Germans from seeing what was happening and opening fire. Mayne instructed his driver to get within a few yards of the rear of the tank while Binns handed him one of the makeshift petrol bombs which consisted of an empty wine bottle filled with petrol and a bit of rag as a fuse. Mayne lit the bomb using a Zippo lighter while Binns ignited another using a match.

The two soldiers chucked the pair of flaming bombs at their target, the rear engine deck of the tank, followed a moment later by two more. Orange flames rose from the rear of the tank as burning petrol dripped into the engine compartment through the ventilation grilles, where it destroyed the insulation on electrical cables, including the crucial spark plug leads. Rubber drive belts caught fire. Two minutes later, the engine stopped due to a short circuit in the ignition system. Acrid black smoke from burning rubber seeped into the main fighting compartment of the tank, causing the crew to cough violently. They couldn't see and were unable to breathe.

The Germans decided they had had enough, opened all hatches and bailed out of the tank only to find Binns and Mayne pointing Thompson sub - machine guns at them.

'Hände-Hoche!' said Mayne as he ushered the five tank crew into the back of the Chevy.

*******

Some distance away, Seidel watched in amazement as the white smoke cleared and the Chevy drove through the open doors of the fort, which closed a moment later. The tank crew had been captured. The British had destroyed an immobilized Panzer IV using improvised petrol bombs. Now it lay useless in front of the fort with black smoke pouring from all its open hatches.

Seidel was despondent. Of the six Panzers that had set out on the mission, five had been knocked out. A sixth had been immobilised although its engine still worked, as did its gun and turret. So it could still provide fire support at long range with its 75mm gun.

Between the two original columns he still had about thirty troops, a few lorries and some armoured cars and half-tracks. That would be more than enough to take the fort. But what defences did the British have? If they really had six- pounder guns then they could defeat an armoured attack but they would have problems countering infantry as the six- pounder could fire only armour piercing rounds, not high explosive. On the other hand, the British also had a number of machine- guns.

Seidel was deep in thought when a Landser approached him and saluted. He had some news.

'Message from the radio truck, sir. All the surviving vehicles from the other column are coming to join us. And something else. One of the Panzer crewmen inspected the shell holes in the knocked - out tanks and discovered they have a diameter of 75mm.'

Seidel was stunned at this revelation. The British had a 75mm gun! He knew that the new six-pounder had a calibre of 57mm while the old two - pounder was 40mm. The only 75mm gun in service with the British Eighth Army was the M2 or M3 weapon fitted to the American - made Grant tank which had been in service for only a few weeks. Could they be facing a Grant? But the Grant had a very high profile and the 75mm was mounted on a side-sponson on the right-hand side while the small turret on top had a puny 37mm which had an even worse performance than the two - pounder.

Yet one of his men had caught a glimpse of the enemy tank and was certain it was a Valentine. Was it possible that the British had up-gunned the Valentine with a 75mm? It would explain a lot of things. And where was that tank right now? It must be behind the fort. Why had it not been used to knock out that Panzer IV? It must have been knocked out or immobilised.

Seidel's inner thoughts were interrupted by the sound of several armoured cars, half-tracks and lorries clanking to a halt behind him. The surviving vehicles from the second column had arrived. Now they would assault the fort with everything they had. The last Panzer would pound the British from long range with its 75mm gun, using high explosive shells. Once his men got closer to the British, they could set up a few mortars and MG42 machine-guns. They would capture the fort regardless of casualties, that was certain. The British might have a tank but it looked as though it was out of action. No, the reputation of the Afrika Korps was at stake. *They would capture the fort whatever the cost.*

*******

Back at the fort, Mayne looked at the distant German force with alarm. They were going to attack in strength and although their last Panzer had been immobilised, it could still shell them at long range. *Honeychile* could take it out and repel the attack but it was sitting behind the fort with a broken track which might take hours to fix. *Unless there was a miracle they were all doomed!*

# Chapter 20

# Crack in the World

Seidel took thirty minutes to arrange his force in a good tactical formation. His five half-tracks and three armoured cars were spread out in a line abreast pattern. Some soldiers would travel in the half -tracks while others would march towards the fort on foot beside the vehicles, holding only their personal weapons. The vulnerable lorries, carrying heavier weapons such as mortars, would be kept to the rear, protected from machine- gun fire by the light armour travelling in front.

A thousand yards away, the British soldiers manning the fort heard the sound of multiple petrol engines starting up as they wiped sweat from their brows. In brilliant sunshine, the distant vehicles were just visible through a shimmering heat haze. Clouds of white exhaust smoke rose into the air as the German vehicles approached at walking pace so the infantrymen could keep up with them.

Mayne lowered his binoculars and turned to Davy, who was now manning a Bren gun next to him.

'If only we had Honeychile, we could smash them. How long before its track is fixed?'

'It normally takes two to three hours to repair a broken track,' said Davy. 'And that is in a well-equipped workshop, not a combat zone. It's hard to fix a track when the temperature is a hundred and twenty degrees Fahrenheit in the shade and insects are biting. In theory, repairing a caterpillar track is no different from fixing a broken cycle chain, but they are incredibly heavy things and it is back- breaking work. Very often, tanks that break tracks in the desert are simply abandoned as it's not worth the effort required to fix them.'

'Maybe the crew could do with a little help. Davy , you're the best mechanic in the Eighth Army. See if you can lend them a hand and speed things up a bit. I promise you that if you can fix that track in record time and get Honeychile back in action, you will be mentioned in dispatches. And I'll give you a bottle of whisky as well. I've still got a bottle of Bell's I haven't opened.'

Davy smiled. ' OK Major, I'll see what I can do. But someone will have to man my Bren gun.'

As Davy raced down the steps, Mayne turned to Lee who was standing behind him, clutching a Thompson sub - machine gun.

'Captain Lee, you were an instructor on the Bren gun when you were in the Home Guard in 1940. Perhaps you'd like to fire one in anger. That Thompson you're holding is only of use in a close quarter battle but right now we need to kill as many of the enemy as possible before they get anywhere near the fort.'

'Fair enough Major. My primary duty remains the medical care of our troops and our prisoners but I agree this is an emergency situation.'

Lee put down his Thompson and pressed the butt of the Bren up against his shoulder. It was a good weapon. Well engineered too. Fired five hundred rounds a minute. Based on a pre-war Czech design. Probably the finest light machine-gun in the world.

Meanwhile, the German force continued its inexorable progress towards the fort. A moment later the distant immobilised Panzer opened fire. A brief orange muzzle flash and a puff of white smoke was followed by a screeching sound as a high - explosive round flew through the air and impacted in the sand fifty yards in front of the fort. The gunner corrected his aim and, thirty seconds later another round hit the stonework on the front of the fort and gouged out a huge chunk of masonry. A third projectile followed, which blew a large hole in the fort's front doors.

Just before the Panzer could fire off a fourth round, a smoke bomb launched by Binns from the two -inch mortar on the parapets exploded in front of the advancing German force. Another followed a few seconds later, blocking the

German tank's view.

Mayne shouted over to Binns. 'Keep firing a smoke round every few minutes to blind the Panzer. How many smoke rounds do we have?'

'Only eight left,' said Binns.

Now the German force was only five hundred yards from the fort. The three armoured cars opened fire with their long-barrelled 20mm auto - cannon. The rounds gouged small chunks out of the stonework. Private Johnson –who stood on the parapet –fired a single bullet from his 0.303 Lee Enfield rifle at the attackers without any visible effect.

'Don't waste ammunition,' shouted Mayne. 'Let them get closer! Wait for the order to commence fire!'

The minutes ticked past as the Germans neared. Four hundred yards away. Three hundred yards. Two hundred yards. Now the 7.9mm MG34 machine guns mounted on the armoured vehicles opened fire and rounds bounced off the parapets. Private Johnson died instantly as a bullet hit him in the head. He slumped to one side and his Thompson sub- machine gun clattered on the ground. Still, the British force held their fire. When the Germans were just a hundred and fifty yards away, Mayne screamed the order his men had been waiting for :

'Open fire! Browning and Boys rifle gunners, concentrate on the armoured cars and half-tracks. Everyone else take down the troops.'

Firing at short range, the M2 Browning and Boys rifle gunners aimed at the thin frontal armour of the German vehicles. Red sparks showed they were hitting their mark and two half-tracks stopped, their radiators punctured by bullets. Clouds of scalding steam rose into the air. One armoured car ran over an anti-tank mine which exploded with a loud bang, tearing off the front wheels. The crew bailed out, their clothes on fire, and rolled on the sand to extinguish the flames. The British soldiers manning the fort let out a great cheer.

'Burn in hell you bastards,' screamed Perkins.

The two Boys anti-tank rifles cracked loudly as they fired round after round into the engine compartments of the remaining armoured vehicles. The heavy .55 slugs could smash engine blocks and make fist -sized holes in radiators.

Meanwhile, the Bren and Vickers K gunners were taking down the infantry. The Vickers K could fire between 1,000 and 1,200 rounds a minute but it only had a 100 round drum magazine so was best fired in very short bursts. Lee contributed to the carnage by firing short, well-aimed bursts at individual soldiers from his Bren. He reckoned he had killed at least five enemy troops.

It was a massacre. The German infantry stood in the open with no cover while the British were well protected by the thick stone of the fort and additional sandbags. Mayne estimated that his men had killed about half the attacking force. The remaining Germans sheltered behind the burning hulks of destroyed half-tracks and armoured cars. Only two armoured cars and three half-tracks were still in running order and they were now reversing away from the fort, badly damaged.

But there was a problem. A breeze was blowing away the smoke in front of the distant Panzer and Binns had already fired his last smoke bomb. Then Mayne saw an orange flash from the tip of the Panzer's gun barrel followed by a cloud of white smoke. There was a loud screeching sound which increased in pitch and then the first shell fell in front of the fort, throwing up a huge cloud of sand.

Another shell struck the front of the building, dislodging a huge chunk of stone. A third round followed and this one hit the right-hand side of the parapets, killing three soldiers. Mayne knew that the tank gunner had now zeroed in on their position and could pound the fort with 75mm shells until everyone was killed …or they surrendered. The next shell could kill him and there was nothing he could do about it.

Mayne observed the distant Panzer through his

binoculars. The commander was standing in the main hatch watching the fort through his own binoculars. As Mayne continued to study his opponent, the tank's turret flew into the air and landed in the sand behind the vehicle. Black smoke poured from the hole in the upper hull where the turret had been fitted. The commander had been cut into two pieces at the waist and the rest of the crew burned to death as flames enveloped their vehicle.

Mayne looked to his right and saw the Super Valentine on the crest of the hillock to the east of the fort. White smoke drifted from the muzzle of its hot gun barrel. Its engine was running and Davy was standing beside the tank with a blackened face and grease -covered hands.

'That's a bottle of whisky you owe me Major,' he shouted. ' I reckon that was the fastest track repair in the history of armoured warfare.'

But Crerar wasn't finished yet. Clutching the carbon field mike, he gave orders to Sutherland:

'Gunner, load with HE. Destroy the retreating vehicles!'

Bang! There was a blinding muzzle flash and a cloud of white smoke as the barrel recoiled and the tank swayed on its suspension. An M48 high-explosive round hit the back of a retreating German armoured car, which burst into flames. Sutherland rotated the turret slightly and knocked out a half -track. The next round just missed a second half-track which escaped by ducking into a small depression in the ground.

'Shit,' said Sutherland. He would have to find more targets so he spoke to Crerar using the tank's intercom system:

'What do you want me to hit next?'

'Get the lorries,' said Crerar. 'They're retreating and are at the limit of our effective range but we might just get 'em.'

Kelly loaded an HE shell into the breech and Sutherland fired. The shell exploded fifty yards behind a retreating truck. Sutherland elevated the gun slightly and shot again. The shell scored a direct hit on the truck cab and turned the vehicle into a flaming orange fireball.

Kelly shoved another M48 round into the breech and Sutherland fired at another truck. This round just missed but the blast from the exploding shell overturned the vehicle. A third vehicle ascended a small hillock of sand and disappeared down the other side.

Mayne scanned the battlefield. Several burning half-tracks and armoured cars lay in front of the fort with peeling, blackened paintwork. Some of their deflated tyres were on fire. In the distance, plumes of black smoke showed the locations of knocked - out tanks and lorries. Bodies lay strewn across the desert. Some were burned to a crisp, like steaks that had been left too long under the grill. Other bodies lacked arms, legs or heads and some had been cut in two by fifty-calibre bullets. Within a day there would be the foul odour of rotting flesh but for the moment there was only the disgusting roast pork smell of burned human tissue.

The battle was far from over but Mayne knew he had won a major victory, comparable to the incident at Rorke's Drift in 1879, when 150 British soldiers had repelled an attack by 4,000 Zulu warriors. If the remaining German soldiers regrouped and attacked again they would be wiped out. They had lost all their tanks and most of their light armour while the defenders still had *Honeychile* with its 75mm gun and a highly trained crew.

At the very least they had won a brief respite. This might be an opportunity to have a proper meal and attend to any casualties. Once darkness fell they could attempt to break out and make their way to Alexandria.

Mayne turned to Binns. 'Set up the desert cookers. We're going to have a hot meal. The best we can manage under the circumstances.'

The 'desert cooker' was a uniquely British invention and one reason the Army didn't want to completely dispense with the 'flimsy' petrol cans. One can had its top cut off and was filled with sand which was liberally drenched with petrol and ignited. A second can on top of the first was then used to boil water, make tea or cook tinned food.

All the soldiers enjoyed their meal which comprised bully beef fritters and fried tinned sausages followed by tinned peaches with Carnation milk. Everything was washed down with mugs of strong Army tea with plenty of sugar and more Carnation milk.

As Mayne was finishing his meal, Binns appeared with a basket filled with eggs and dates.

'Where did you get these?' asked Mayne.

'Some Bedouins just appeared at the back door,' answered Binns. 'They're travelling by camel. They offered to trade us a few items in exchange for tobacco and sugar.'

Binns put down the basket and munched on a piece of cake.' They gave me this traditional Arab cake to try out. Not bad! First time I've ever eaten cake in the desert. Where do they get the milk from?'

'It's made with a woman's milk,' answered Mayne. 'Breast milk.'

All of a sudden, Binns looked a little green. Mayne thought he would now have a lifelong aversion to any kind of cake.

'Well I'm all right. I'm drinking some goat's milk which I got from the Bedouins,' said Private McTavish as he greedily slurped down some cool white liquid from an old jam jar. 'It tastes great. But why do the Arabs put these little brown pellets in it! I presume they are little bits of chocolate to make the milk sweeter?'

'It's actually camel shit,'said Mayne. 'The theory is that the bacteria in the dung prevent you from getting dysentery. But the same friendly bugs can still give you rather nasty food poisoning.'

A few yards away, Lee was listening to the conversation as he changed the curved magazine on his Bren gun. He walked over to Binns and McTavish who both had rather sheepish expressions on their faces.

'I think you two will be sticking to Army rations from now on. I remember when I was at medical school…Oh my God, what is happening!'

Lee's oration had been interrupted by a loud cracking sound. Then there was the noise of rocks falling. In front of the fort, a huge fissure five hundred feet long had appeared in the ground between two of the shell craters. Tons of sand fell into the crack, which gradually widened until it was twenty feet across. The burned -out wreck of a German armoured car fell into the chasm. A loud crashing noise followed as it hit solid ground.

White smoke started to issue from the fissure. But it was like no other smoke Lee had ever seen. It hugged the ground and drifted over to the fort. Soon all the soldiers were enveloped in the white mist which was completely odourless. It did not irritate the throat, and it was cold, very cold. Lee could feel himself shivering with cold in the desert. How was that possible as it was still daytime?

Then the white cloud dispersed and Lee wondered what had just happened. Had the shell hits caused a crack in the underlying rock? Perhaps there was a naturally occurring fissure? Lee knew that some parts of the Sahara had hard rock under the sand.

As the soldiers stood gaping at the unexpected spectacle, a single white hand appeared at the near edge of the chasm. Then another. And another. Within a minute, six humanoid figures stood on the near edge of the giant fissure. Each creature had a metal breast plate, which looked like polished aluminium. And a matching skull cap, plus metal shrouds over their legs and arms, rather like a medieval suit of armour. The shrouds had rubberised joints at the elbows and knees to permit limb movement.

And there were wires running down their arms and legs and what looked like electrical junction boxes at different points on their bodies. Numerous spike – shaped projections extended from the circumference of the skull caps. Each of the beings had a transparent visor made of what looked like perspex. And a metallic belt to which various pouches had been attached. Their faces — just visible through the visor — were noticeably pale and waxy, like a corpse's , and the eyes were pure white with opaque corneas. Lee wondered how they could see.

The six creatures stood on the edge of the fissure, facing the fort while one of them took a small silver box with flashing coloured lights out of a belt pouch and consulted it. It was taking some kind of reading. Then three of them walked off to the east, turned north when they reached the limit of the fissure and headed in the direction of the surviving German soldiers. The other three stood motionless for a moment and then headed for the door of the fort, which had a huge hole in it.

Mayne, stunned by what had happened, now came to his senses and screamed an order:

'Treat as hostiles. Open fire!'

Two soldiers confronted the first creature, who was making his way through the hole in the fort's front door, ripping further bits of timber out of the way as if they were balsa wood.

'Stop or we open fire!' shouted Private Jones.

The creature ignored the command and stood in front of the British soldier. Jones pulled the trigger of his Thompson sub – machine gun and unleashed a hail of bullets, which bounced off the figure's breastplate. Two rounds hit the being's upper left arm without any noticeable effect. A moment later, the mysterious entity grabbed the Thompson out of Jones's hands and snapped it in two. Then it put its right hand on top of Jones's head. There was a crackling sound and the soldier convulsed and fell dead, his brain cooked by the powerful electric charge. His bladder and bowel evacuated immediately, leaving a puddle of faeces and urine on the floor of the fort.

The other soldier, Philips, fired a whole box magazine of 0.45 rounds at the creature without any effect. Then he turned and fled up the steps to the parapet on the first floor, hoping Major Mayne would be able to help. All three creatures followed with the first still carrying the small silver box with the multiple flashing lights.

Up on the parapets, Mayne and Lee turned round to see three creatures advancing on them. Lee picked up his Bren gun and, firing from the hip, emptied an entire magazine at them. Mayne took pot-shots with his Webley pistol while Binns and McTavish shot at them with Lee-Enfield 0.303 rifles. Still the creatures kept coming.

The leading creature, who seemed to have some kind of authority over the other two, stood in front of Lee and placed his right hand, palm down on top of the medical officer's head. A moment later an electric shock travelled through Lee's body. His muscles twitched and his eyes closed as he slumped to the floor.

Then two creatures carried Lee's limp body down the steps and out of the front door of the fort, followed by their leader. They made their way to the fissure in front of the building and disappeared over the edge.

On the parapets, a shaken Mayne felt despondent. Was Captain Lee dead? He already knew the creatures could deliver an electric shock, which could kill. And if Lee really was dead why did these strange beings want him?

# Chapter 21

# The Solar System

**4500 years earlier**

A million silver, saucer-shaped spacecraft , each a mile wide ,traversed the solar system, which included the planet Earth. Each craft contained a large, fluid-filled tank holding a single giant organism which looked like a human brain, though much larger, with a diameter of almost 400 feet. Millions of years before, these creatures, the Cerebri, had a humanoid form but they had now evolved to the point where they were pure brain. The creatures now lived in their own life support tanks, their blood supply fed through arteries connected to machines which took the place of the heart and lungs. Under each tank lay a plutonium- fuelled nuclear reactor which could supply almost unlimited amounts of power for 50,000 years. The inner walls of the craft were lined with thousands of white cylinders which contained beings known as Marizans, humanoid life-forms which had been created by 'recycling' aliens captured on various planets.

The million-strong fleet had been on its long journey for several centuries, on a mission to find new planets which could be stripped of their natural resources. In order to conserve energy, the Marizans had been placed in suspended animation using cryo-technology, while the Cerebri creatures which commanded the craft had gone into hibernation mode, akin to a deep sleep.

There was no need for the Cerebri to awaken, because the crafts' computers could complete the mission on automatic pilot. They were incredibly complicated spaceships. The only problem with such advanced technology was that it could sometimes go wrong, even with duplication and triplication of essential systems. And that is exactly what happened one day as the 13$^{th}$ Cerebri spacecraft in the formation developed a fault. It looked quite innocuous, just a blinking red light on a control console, but it signified a reactor problem. It was something that could be fixed—the craft's auto-repair systems could deal with it—but the automatic computer program required that an emergency landing be made on the nearest planet before repairs could begin.

The craft's computers scanned space and discovered that the third planet from the nearest star would be ideal for the purpose. It had a similar gravitational pull to the home planet and was also inhabited by beings who were ideal for conversion to Marizans but had not yet developed advanced technology. First, it would be necessary to land the craft in an area which was largely uninhabited. Before doing so, the computers launched four much smaller saucer craft which landed on the deserted moon that orbited the selected planet.

The mother craft went into orbit around the planet while its sensors scanned all electromagnetic frequencies. It was clear that the inhabitants had not yet developed their own sensor technology and were at a primitive level of development. There were no electromagnetic emissions on any frequency. The huge saucer's computers detected a large land mass which was ideal for their purpose. Towards the north of this zone was a large area several hundred miles across in each direction which was below sea level. It was also uninhabited, so would be an ideal spot to carry out repairs. The computers made a decision and steered the craft into the atmosphere of the planet Earth. The ship's heat-shields glowed a fiery red as the craft plunged towards the surface of the planet.

*******

The slave labourers emerged from their tented camp around the half – completed pyramids at Giza in Egypt and looked up in terror as a large, burning red light crossed the sky. What was it? They had seen shooting stars before but this was much larger. And it was making a screeching sound. Was this a message from the Gods? Was it a sign that they approved of the building of the pyramids? Or maybe that they did not approve?

Millions of Arabs saw the mysterious light cross the sky as it passed over Memphis, the ancient capital of Egypt, and headed south - west. A group of Bedouins riding on camels in the middle of the Great Sand Sea saw it descend towards the northern edge of the area that later became known as the Qattara Depression.

The craft landed on the northernmost edge of the Depression. If the computers had picked a spot a little further north, then it would have rested on hard rock but it was now sitting on a thin crust that overlay a deep salt marsh. Within a minute, the crust broke under the weight of the huge metal saucer and it sank into the soft ground, until it rested motionless on a layer of hard rock a hundred feet below the surface.

For the next few thousand years, the single Cerebri on board the craft continued to hibernate, while the Marizans remained in suspended animation. The computers saw no reason to wake them because they had the situation in hand. They would repair the reactor. Although they succeeded at this task they were unable to extricate the craft from the thick quicksand. Even with all their advanced technology, the saucer was stuck in the mud. The best thing they could have done at this point was wake up the Cerebri and ask for instructions. But due to some faulty programming, they didn't do this. Instead the computers chose to shut themselves down as they couldn't come up with a solution. So the Cerebri and the Marizans remained asleep for thousands of years. Until the day someone woke them up.

# Chapter 22

# Descent Into Hell

It took a lot to faze Major Paddy Mayne. But these were exceptional circumstances. He had won a major battle against superior German forces. Then his whole world had changed. Why had a giant fissure appeared in the desert? What were these strange humanoid creatures that had emerged from it ? And why did they want Captain Lee, who might now be dead?

For a moment Mayne processed the new information. Then he made a decision. He had to mount a rescue mission. Immediately.

He turned to Binns, as his normal composure slowly returned.

'Sergeant Binns, we're going to rescue the Captain, and you're coming with me. We'll also take McAleese and McTavish. They're our two best fighting men.'

McAleese had been a middleweight boxer in Glasgow before the war. One Saturday night in 1938 he had been jumped by four 'hard men' from the Gallowgate as he was leaving the Saracen's Head pub in Glasgow. The four 'heid bangers' ( as McAleese later described them to the police) were all inebriated after drinking several bottles of cheap South African wine. Though they were armed with flick knives and open razors, their drunken state affected their reactions, and McAleese downed all four with well-aimed punches. Three ended up in the casualty department at Glasgow Royal Infirmary where they were treated for facial injuries. The fourth fled in terror. McAleese was arrested but was subsequently released from custody after the Procurator Fiscal accepted his plea of self-defence.

His wiry colleague, McTavish was from the shipbuilding town of Greenock further down the River Clyde and had learned the latest unarmed combat techniques during his previous service in the Commandos. He was an excellent marksman and very skilled in the use of the deadly Sykes-Fairbairn fighting knife. Major Mayne was also a former sportsman, having been a professional rugby player before the war.

'We'll need backpacks and full webbing kit,' said Mayne. 'Every man is to take a Thompson and four spare box magazines. And as many Mills bombs as we can carry. Do we have any smoke grenades?'

'We've used up our entire supply of smoke mortar rounds but we do have a few Number 76 white phosphorus grenades,' answered Binns.

*Bang! Bang! Bang ! Rat- a--tat-a-tat.*

Mayne's conversation with Binns was interrupted by the sound of firing outside. It was the distinctive noise of several German machine-guns. Mayne looked over the parapets and saw three of the strange creatures returning from the German positions. One of them was carrying the limp body of an *Afrika Korps* officer. Twenty yards beyond them, a German soldier in the back of a Volkswagen Kubelwagen, fired a pintle-mounted MG42 belt-fed light machine-gun while two soldiers stood in the sand beside the vehicle, shooting their MP40 machine pistols. The multiple rounds pinged off the creatures' silver body armour without having any noticeable effect.

Two of the monsters descended into the fissure, carrying the body of the German officer, while the third turned back and walked towards the German soldiers. The entity dealt with the nearest squaddie by putting its right hand on top of his head. There was a crack of electricity and a whiff of burnt flesh as the *Landser* convulsed, died and fell on the ground, leaving a damp patch in the sand as his bladder emptied. The creature turned round and walked rapidly towards the other soldier who was panicking as he had just emptied an entire magazine into the being without any result.

'*Donner und Blitzen!* You are a creature from hell,' screamed the soldier.

The German knew his only chance was to get away as fast as possible so he raced towards the Kubelwagen and urged the driver to retreat:

'Move! Get out of here before it kills us both.'

The soldier jumped into the front passenger seat of the Volkswagen as the driver revved its four – cylinder, horizontally – opposed, air-cooled engine and performed a rapid U-turn, before heading back towards the German lines. It looked as though the VW had escaped danger but then the creature pulled a stubby golden pistol from its belt and aimed it at the retreating vehicle. The being pulled a trigger and a thin dart attached to a fine wire shot out of the barrel. The projectile struck the rear of the VW, the wire extending fifty yards back to the muzzle of the pistol. A crackle of electricity reverberated across the desert and then the vehicle's fuel tank exploded. An expanding orange fireball rose up from the scout car, followed by a plume of oily black smoke. The driver, gunner and soldier were incinerated in the blaze and never got a chance to get out. Their bodies looked like blackened shop window mannequins as the petrol-fuelled blaze scorched the vehicle's beige camouflage paint and set fire to the tyres as it slowed down and came to a halt. Satisfied with what it had done, the creature walked back to the fissure and descended into the abyss.

The whole horrifying spectacle was witnessed by the surviving members of the Allied patrol manning the fort, who were aghast at what had just happened. Though three of the 'enemy' had been killed they knew they could be next.

Binns was the first to speak. 'If you don't mind me asking sir, how are we going to rescue Captain Lee if we can't kill these creatures? You've seen how bullets just bounce off their body armour. And they can kill just by touching.'

'I don't know Binns, but we've got to try. We have a tradition in the SAS that we don't leave a man behind on the battlefield. These creatures are obviously evil and a threat to humanity. As well as rescuing the Captain, we need to find out what they are up to. I'm sure they have a weak spot, it's just a question of finding it.'

Ten minutes later, Mayne, Binns, McAleese and McTavish stood in front of the fort, gazing at the giant chasm. All four were wearing full webbing kit, including backpacks. Binns shone a torch into the giant crack. He could see broken rocks and at the bottom there was a flat, smooth passageway like the cement floor of a corridor.

'It beats me how these creatures got out of the chasm and back down again. There are no steps, ladders or handholds.'

'I take your point,' said Mayne. 'We'll need a couple of ropes. Bring one of the Chevys through the front doors of the fort and attach a pair of ropes to the front bumper. The truck can pull us up if we are in a hurry.'

Private Baker started Truck One, and drove through the fort's entrance. Then the four soldiers abseiled down the two ropes, their Thompson sub machine-guns attached to their bodies by carrying straps. It took them only a few moments to reach the bottom of the chasm. Mayne expected that the corridor would be pitch-black, but there were rectangular wall lights along its length. The western end of the passageway was blocked off by a rock fall and the wrecked German armoured car that had fallen into the chasm , so Mayne lead everyone east. After a few yards the tunnel took a sharp right turn, and Mayne estimated they must be heading due south directly under the fort and towards the Qattara Depression.

*******

Just a hundred yards away, Captain Lee opened his eyes. Was he dead or dreaming or was all this really happening? He remembered that a strange humanoid creature wearing silver body armour had placed its right hand on his head. There had been a sensation like an electric shock and then he had lost consciousness. He guessed the creature had used a powerful electric current to induce a brain seizure which had caused him to pass out. Yet the same method had killed Private Miller. He supposed that the unfortunate Private had been subjected to a much higher voltage and amperage which had caused a fatal convulsion. So these creatures could use electricity either to stun or kill.

Obviously they wanted him alive – but why? As Lee's head started to clear, he looked around him. He was in a huge circular room with metal walls, about 500 feet in diameter, and was strapped to a metal chair by clamps attached to his wrists and ankles. There were several such seats in the room and two creatures were busy strapping another man into the one next to him. He wore the beige uniform of an *Afrika Korps* Colonel. Lee guessed he was the commander of the mechanized force which had attacked the fort. He was still only semi-conscious and was muttering a few words in German:

'Let me free, I am a German Officer.'

But the most interesting part of the room lay immediately in front of him. A huge circular liquid- filled glass tank about 400 feet in diameter, which contained what looked like a human brain, only much bigger as it occupied most of the container. Lee noted that it resembled the brains he had seen in the Anatomy Museum at Glasgow University, preserved in tanks of formalin. But this one wasn't dead, it was still alive. Lee could see blood flowing through the many translucent arteries which supplied it. All the various parts of the human cerebral circulation he knew so well were there including the crucial middle cerebral artery and the Circle of Willis at the base of the brain.

And all the various lobes of the human brain were there too. The temporal, parietal and occipital lobes plus the vital frontal lobes, which were the seat of personality. Various wires and tubes stretched from the bottom of the tank to different parts of the brain. The two optic nerves weren't attached to eyes. Instead they were connected by thin black cables to a moving, gold - coloured box with a glass lens, mounted above the tank. Lee thought it was some kind of high-resolution TV camera. He was being observed by a golden eye.

As Lee continued to study his surroundings with professional interest, a robotic voice spoke to him from a box that hung above the tank on a pair of brackets.

'Captain Lee, you are wondering how I can speak to you in your own language. The answer is quite simple. The technology aboard this ship includes a Universal Translator. It enables us to speak to you in your own tongue.'

'What do you want?' replied Lee. 'I am only a Captain in the Royal Army Medical Corps. How can I be of use to you? Your technology is obviously much more advanced than ours.'

The disembodied voice spoke again.

'Our portable sensor boxes have indicated that you are the most intelligent member of your military team. That is valuable to us.'

'But I will never help you. You are evil.'

'You have no choice. We will use our technology to extract all your memories and intelligence. The same thing will happen to your former enemy, Oberst Seidel who is in the next chair. We have detected that he is also of high intelligence.'

'But what will happen to us? How will we be once our memories and intellect are removed?'

'In your own terminology you will be left as an imbecile. But that is of no concern to the Cerebri. You will be recycled to become one of our foot soldiers.'

'You mean these humanoid creatures with the skull caps and body armour?'

'That is correct. We call them Marizans. They are our soldiers and servants and cannot be harmed by your bullets. They are created by recycling the bodies of other species, whether dead or alive.'

'You mean you can reanimate the bodies of dead humans?'

'That is correct. But only within 24 hours of death.'

Lee was gobsmacked at this revelation.

'But how is that possible? Human tissue undergoes irreversible necrosis within hours of death. In the case of the brain, the necrosis starts within just three minutes.'

'We have technology that can reverse the process provided it is done within 24 hours of death. But the Marizans are not truly alive. In your terminology they are nothing more than animated human cadavers. But they have proved invincible in battle. Our race, the Cerebri, were like you once but through a process of evolution over millions of years we have eliminated our physical bodies.'

'But that is inhuman,' replied Lee. 'You will never experience the joy of sexual gratification or the pleasure of a fish supper with plenty of vinegar on a Saturday night.'

'We have no need of these things,' said the alien voice. 'We have developed technology which can directly stimulate our pleasure centres. But we are wasting time. Now the mind extraction process must begin. Resistance is useless. Prepare for a great darkness to envelop your mind.'

Two Marizans stood in front of Lee and placed a large silver metal dome on his head. Curly coloured wires lead from the dome back to a control panel behind the captain, which had two large levers. The Marizans fixed a second dome to Seidel's scalp and plugged in the leads

\*\*\*\*\*\*\*

Just thirty feet away, Mayne and his three soldiers crouched down, hidden behind some control desks. He had heard every word that had been said in the last few minutes and even though he didn't understand all of it, he knew he had to act without delay.

'OK everyone, get ready. Mc Aleese and McTavish, you deal with the two creatures. Binns, help me to free the Captain. And we'll rescue that German officer while we are at it. Now go!'

The four British soldiers sprung out from behind the cabinets and raced towards the two prisoners. McTavish grabbed the right arm of the nearest Marizan and twisted it behind its back, taking care to avoid touching its deadly right hand. He twisted the limb and broke its right humerus, rendering the whole arm useless. The creature was taken by surprise and staggered forwards.

'Here's a wee taste of Glasgow, Jimmy!' said McAleese as he grabbed the disabled Marizan by both shoulders, lifted up its visor, pulled back his head and delivered a classic Glasgow head butt against the creature's nose. Blood sprayed everywhere from the being's shattered nose as the creature collapsed on the floor, stunned by the sudden assault.

'Stop them!' said the disembodied alien voice. 'They must not interfere with our plans.'

The second Marizan turned to face the British soldiers, its right hand already outstretched. Mayne dodged out of the way as McTavish pulled his Sykes-Fairbairn fighting knife from its sheath and plunged it deep into the front of the Marizan's neck, in a weak spot just above the top of the armoured breastplate. As McTavish intended, the deeply penetrating knife blade severed the creature's spinal cord and it collapsed on the ground, paralysed from the neck down.

'Great work men,' said Mayne. 'Now let's release the two officers and get the hell out of here!'

Binns, McAleese and McTavish pulled the metal skull caps off Lee and Seidel and ripped the wires out of the instrument consoles. Lee and Seidel were still weak and dizzy from their induced convulsions and required help just to stagger along the corridor towards the dangling ropes.

A metal power-operated door slid open at the far side of the chamber. Four Marizans came through it. Three of them had their right hands outstretched, ready to kill or stun the intruders while the fourth had its golden pistol in its right hand. The British soldiers lurched along the corridor towards the two dangling ropes….but the four Marizans were gaining on then.

'Smoke ,' ordered Mayne.

All four members of the rescue team chucked Number 76 smoke grenades at the creatures. The far end of the passageway filled with burning white phosphorus smoke which blinded the creatures, but two of them made it through.

'Grenades,' screamed Mayne.

A quartet of Mills bombs flew through the air and exploded at the creatures' feet. One Marizan collapsed as a shower of rocks fell from the ceiling of the passageway and landed on its head. The other pursuing Marizan was unharmed and continued relentlessly towards the rescue force. It was now only ten feet away from the soldiers, far too close to use grenades. Binns fired a burst from his Thompson, but the rounds bounced off the creature's armoured breastplate. As the Marizan was just about to place its right hand on Binns' scalp, the sergeant lifted up the creature's hinged visor and put the gun's muzzle into its mouth.

'Eat this, you devil,' screamed Binns as he pulled the trigger. At point-blank range, several heavy 45-calibre rounds tore off the back of the Marizan's head. Brains and blood splattered on the wall of the corridor and the creature fell onto the floor, its limbs contracting with death spasms.

As the Marizan lay dying in a rapidly expanding pool of blood, McAleese and McTavish tied the ends of one rope round Lee's waist. The other was secured in a similar way to Seidel.

Mayne barked out orders. 'McAleese and Mc Tavish, climb up the ropes and I will follow. Once we are up at the top we will use the Chevy to haul up the two officers. Binns, stay down here and hold off any more of these creatures until we can send a rope back down for you.'

McAleese and McTavish were both experienced mountaineers and climbed the rope at record speed. They were helped out of the chasm by a couple of soldiers who were looking over the edge. Mayne arrived at the top seconds later and ordered Baker to start his Chevy and reverse back towards the fort, pulling up Lee and Seidel as he did so.

At the bottom of the chasm, Binns felt relieved as Lee and Seidel started to rise up towards the surface. But his problems were far from over. Three more Marizans appeared through the smoke. Binns hurled a primed Mills bomb at them, followed by a second. The grenades exploded, ripping the armoured breastplate off the front of one Marizan. Binns took advantage of the creature's temporary weakness and riddled the Marizan with 45-calibre rounds from his Thompson. The creature fell dead but the two others continued relentlessly towards the British sergeant.

One of them attempted to place its right hand on Binns' scalp but the British sergeant dodged out of the way and then pulled the pin out of a Mills bomb which he held in front of him. Four seconds later it exploded, killing him and seriously damaging the Marizan, which fell to the ground. But the other Marizan was undamaged and started to climb up the wall of the chasm directly below Captain Lee, who was slowly ascending on the end of a rope.

Lee had heard the explosions and Binns' screams. As he looked up, he could see the bright light of the surface. The blue desert sky had never looked more welcome. The thick cord tied round his waist was hurting and he had rope burns on his hands but he was still travelling slowly towards safety. To his right, a semi-conscious Seidel was also being hauled to the surface.

After another couple of minutes, Lee clambered over the edge of the fissure and felt three pairs of hands grab his body. But his right ankle was being gripped by something far stronger than a human hand. He looked down to see a Marizan, its body armour gleaming in the desert sunshine. It had opaque white eyes, rotten teeth and terrible body odour.

144

'It's one of these creatures. It's got my leg.'

Mayne grabbed Lee's shoulders and pulled hard to stop him being hauled back down into the chasm. Then he gave some orders to his men.

'Cornwell, bring me a Lee-Enfield rifle.'

Cornwell ran back to Truck One and retrieved a short magazine Lee -Enfield 0.303 rifle which he handed to the Major. Mayne stood beside Lee, held the rifle with both hands and started to smash the heavy wooden butt repeatedly into the right upper arm of the creature. Each blow would have smashed the humerus of a human arm but the creature's body armour was protecting it well.

Lee noticed that the Marizan had wires running down its arms and there was some kind of junction box over the triceps muscle.

'Major, direct your blows against that junction box. I believe it controls the muscles of the arm and it may be a weak point'

Mayne did as Lee had suggested. He hit the box with his rifle butt once. Nothing happened. Then he struck it again. The creature's grip remained as strong as ever. Then he smashed it a third time with all the force he could muster. The box shattered, there was a blue electric flash and the creature's right arm and hand became flaccid. Lee broke free from the creature's grip and crawled onto the sand as the Marizan fell four feet back down the chasm. But it was not dead and started to crawl back up using its good left hand.

'Grenades!' screamed Mayne. Cornwell and Baker each dropped a primed Mills bomb down the chasm. Four seconds later they exploded, blowing the breastplate off the Marizan to reveal a mess of wires. The creature started making a buzzing noise, as though in pain, but it was still alive. Then Davy arrived, clutching a lit petrol bomb and dropped it on top of the creature which was immediately enveloped in flames. Completely ablaze from head to toe, the Marizan lost its grip and fell fifty feet to the bottom of the passageway. The impact broke all four limbs.

'I can't believe how tough these things are,' said Davy. 'Two grenades and a petrol bomb and it was still hard to kill. And that was just one creature. I wouldn't like to fight a whole army of them'

'I know ,' said Mayne,' and unfortunately we may soon be facing hundreds of them!'

# Chapter 23

# First Encounter

## The Fort at Makan Alshayatin
## 3 November 1937, 15.31 hrs

Six camouflaged RAF Vickers Wellesley bombers, escorted by three stubby U.S. Army Air Corps Seversky P-35 fighters in a natural metal finish, approached the fort from the south and lined up on their target, a group of humanoid figures, clad in silver body armour, which were marching across the desert.

Below them was chaos. Palls of thick, black oily smoke rose from fifty abandoned, burning vehicles, both American and British. Carden-Lloyd tracked carriers, Ford Model-T pickups fitted with M2 Browning fifty-calibre water-cooled machine guns, Bedford trucks and several Vickers Light Tanks which had shed their tracks or had their turrets blown off. Dead soldiers lay everywhere.

The wreckage of an experimental drilling rig owned by the Anglo – Iranian Oil Company lay a hundred yards north of the fort. All that was left were twisted, blackened metal girders. Just south of it was a fissure in the ground about a hundred yards long which spewed out a thick, white cold smoke which hugged the ground.

It had all started a week earlier when a group of geologists employed by the Anglo-Iranian Oil Company had started drilling on the north side of the old fort in the hope of finding oil deposits next to the Qattara Depression. Scientists had thought that it was possible. Up to that point it was believed that oil was found only in Persia (or Iran as it was now known) but some geologists had speculated that there was more awaiting discovery in North Africa. That was the reason they had set up the experimental drilling rig.

Nothing much had happened on the first day of drilling. But on the second day, the geologists had discovered a hidden passageway about a hundred feet below the surface. There was nothing unusual in that as ancient burial sites were being found all over the Middle East by construction workers. The scientists had briefly considered if they should stop drilling in order to get an opinion from an archaeologist.

Then things started happening. On the third day, a large fissure about a hundred yards long had developed on either side of the drill hole. It appeared that the excavations had opened up a natural fault line in the underlying rock. A strange white mist which clung to the ground had emerged from the fissure …. and then the creatures had appeared. At first there were only a few of them. Looking vaguely human, and wearing some kind of thin metal armour, they had killed five geologists with electric shocks delivered from their right hands, and dragged then into the chasm. The sixth,who happened to be visiting the latrine some distance away at the time, saw what had happened and fled the scene in a red Ford truck. One of the creatures had fired at him with some kind of gun, but had missed.

The geologist just made it to the nearest settlement—with only a few drops of petrol left in his fuel tank — and raised the alarm. The Egyptian police sent an armed nine - man patrol in three Chevrolet trucks but eight of them were killed by the strange creatures and only one escaped. Eventually the Egyptian military became involved but they had no combat experience and so they asked the British garrison in Egypt for help.

Fortunately for the Egyptians, the British were carrying out joint manoeuvres in the Western Desert with a small US Army detachment which had been sent to the Middle East to gain experience. Both President Roosevelt and General George Marshall felt that another major war was imminent and wanted to test out the US Army's current equipment – including the new M2E2 tank - in desert conditions. Within 24 hours, a fully mechanised force of

10,000 British and American troops, backed up with light armour and tactical air power, was sent to the drilling site with orders to defeat the creatures and seal off the area.

Now that was all in the past as the six Wellesley bombers approached from the south and prepared to make a bombing run on their target – the fifty or so figures which were marching north across the desert, heading for the large cordon of troops which surrounded the area. The leader of the flight of Wellesleys, Squadron Leader Geoff Gordon, couldn't understand why aircraft were being ordered to attack these wandering figures with 250 pound general purpose bombs. Would rifle bullets not do the job? Still it wasn't his remit to question orders, only to carry them out.

As the Wellesleys overflew the creatures, they each released their payload of eight 250 pound bombs. Some of the munitions exploded well clear of the beings, showering them with sand. But other bombs found their mark and blew off limbs, heads and body armour.

Most of the creatures survived and continued their relentless march towards the cordon of troops. As the Wellesleys departed, one of the creatures aimed a golden pistol at the nearest aircraft and fired a small dart attached to a fine wire which struck the engine cowling of the plane. The Bristol Pegasus radial immediately stuttered, poured out black smoke and then stopped. A moment later the pilot belly landed his aircraft in the desert next to the abandoned Allied vehicles.

The five surviving Wellesleys hugged the ground as they flew north - east towards their base. Now the three rotund Seversky P-35 fighters raced towards the marching figures in vic formation. The pilots waited until the creatures were just two hundred yards away and then pressed the gun buttons on their control columns. Each aircraft was armed with one fifty-calibre and one thirty-calibre machine gun in their nose cowlings. The pilots could see that the thirty-calibre rounds had no effect on the creatures—they bounced off the body armour —but the fifty-calibre bullets could amputate heads and limbs if they struck the vulnerable joints in the creatures' armour.

One of the Severskys was hit by a dart gun and flew off to the north at low altitude, its engine smoking. Then it crashed behind a hillock before its pilot had a chance to bail out. A large orange fireball climbed into the sky, followed by a plume of black smoke. The two surviving Severskys made a second pass and fired their remaining ammunition at the creatures before escaping to the north. One of the beings fired a dart gun at the nearest P-35 but the pilot had got wise to this tactic and avoided the projectile by making a sudden, violent evasive manoeuvre to port. The dart reached the limit of its trajectory and fell harmlessly into the desert.

Now the troops—who were arranged in a huge semi-circle north of the fort —gradually moved towards the creatures, lead by thirty M2E2 and twenty Vickers Light Tanks. Accompanying them were twenty US Army armoured bulldozers. The plan was to push the creatures back towards the fissure in the ground, force them to fall into the chasm, and then seal the giant crack using rubble and cement.

Five days earlier the original force – which was then 10,000 strong – had attempted this very same move using ordinary cement. It didn't work. The creatures simply burst through the wet concrete, which took twenty-four hours to harden, and a full month to attain full structural strength.

Then scientists advising the military remembered that the Royal Navy used quick - setting cement for emergency repairs on battle – damaged aircraft carriers and battleships. Twenty cement mixer trucks were rushed from the Royal Naval dockyards at Alexandria to the area of the fort while the troops did their best to hold back the creatures. 1,937 soldiers had been killed in the subsequent battle to secure the area but, after a struggle, the Allied force was on the verge of victory.

Now the cordon of troops advanced towards the fort at

ten miles per hour, lead by armoured bulldozers and tanks. The infantry followed behind in scores of trucks. The commander of the US contingent, General George Patton, looked through his binoculars and estimated that repeated air attacks had killed perhaps twenty of the fifty creatures. But thirty remained, and he knew they were hard to kill. When they got within range, the British and American tanks opened up with their main guns. As was the norm in 1937, the tanks had a weak armament. The M2E2s only had one thirty -calibre and one fifty - calibre machine gun in twin turrets, while the British tanks had a single Vickers 0.5 inch water-cooled machine – gun. Neither model of tank had a powerful cannon.

General Patton cursed the poor armament of his tanks. 'When I get back to Washington I'm going to tell these sons of bitches to fit a decent gun to our tanks,' he muttered. He looked down at the Colt revolver with an ivory handle, which he carried on his belt in a holster, and wondered if he would get a chance to shoot one of the creatures between the eyes. From what he had heard, the creatures shrugged off pistol rounds, but it was worth a try.

Hundreds of tank machine-gun rounds pinged off the creatures' body armour. Most of them had no effect but a few fifty-calibre rounds scored lucky hits on weak points and heads and limbs fell off. Five more creatures lay dead in the sand, but twenty- five remained and they were fighting back with their dart guns.

A few of the armoured vehicles, including one bulldozer, took hits from dart guns and burst into flames but, through sheer weight of numbers, the Allied force pushed the creatures into the chasm. The bulldozers proved crucial. Soon all the creatures lay at the bottom of the fissure, but most were apparently still alive and attempting to climb up the walls. Patton ordered his troops to drop primed grenades on top of them. In the confined space of the chasm, some of the creatures had arms and legs blown off but others attempted to scale the walls.

Then, as planned, US Army tipper lorries reversed up

to the fissure and deposited tons of rubble into it, burying the creatures alive. Then the cement mixers took their place and dumped several tons of grey, glistening quick-drying cement on top of the rubble. The following day, when the cement was rock-hard, thousands of troops covered the area with tons of sand and rolled it flat.

The 1937 battle at the fort had been won at a huge cost in dead and wounded. But no decorations would ever be awarded. It would never appear in any history books. And the troops who took part were told it was all a training exercise, albeit with live ammunition, and the creatures were actors and dummies mocked up by film industry technicians. But Roosevelt and Churchill knew the truth. They would take this secret to their graves.

# Chapter 24

# Electric Zombies

Lee slurped a tin mug of strong Army tea with two teaspoons of sugar and a good dollop of Carnation milk. Though he had a variety of drugs in his medical bag, he had to admit that strong sugary tea cured a variety of ills, which on this occasion included the trauma of nearly having his intellect sucked out of his brain by an alien mind probe. Private Baker prised opened a tin of biscuits and offered them to Lee.

'Take a couple, sir. Or even three. They're good. Made by Peek Frean in Bermondsey, in good old London town since 1857. The same brand that Captain Scott took on his Antarctic expedition.'

On the other side of the old wooden table, Mayne was also drinking tea and eating biscuits in between puffs of his cigarette.

'I started this mission with eighteen men, including myself. Now there are only nine of us left, plus the tank crew. I will have to write a letter to Binns' parents if we get back to Alexandria. I am going to recommend him for a posthumous medal, perhaps even the Victoria Cross. He sacrificed himself to let us escape.'

'Binns was a good man,' said Lee. 'But his sacrifice was not in vain. We have learned a great deal about our enemy.'

Mayne stubbed out his cigarette on an old tin lid and looked at Lee.

'Yes, Paddy, you probably heard everything the Cerebri creature said. But I know considerably more. You see, before you ripped off that metal skull cap, it was on my head for a full minute and I was in telepathic contact with the alien. I know its intentions and capabilities and I believe that mankind is now facing the greatest threat to its existence since the beginning of civilization. Far greater even than that posed by the Germans, the Italians and the Japanese.'

'How's that possible? asked Mayne. 'These Marizan creatures are hard to destroy but they are not indestructible, and the Allies have millions of troops and thousands of tanks and planes. We can overwhelm them by sheer weight of numbers. And don't forget the Soviet Red Army, which is enormous.'

Lee finished chewing his biscuit and put his tin mug on the table.

'We've only encountered a few of these creatures so far but I believe there are thousands aboard that spaceship. Most of them are frozen in suspended animation but in time they will all be revived and put into action. It is my belief that what we have encountered so far is merely a small group of Marizan sentries who were on standby to be defrosted quickly when the fissure in the ground was opened. The ship was in a kind of dormant mode. But that is all changing and as time goes by more creatures will be revived. Our situation will become more perilous by the moment. We might hold off a few of the creatures but we will eventually be overwhelmed by weight of numbers. In addition, the Cerebri have the ability to convert our casualties into further Marizans.'

'But there's only one spaceship,' said Mayne. 'Surely the Desert Air Force can deal with it? We have several squadrons of Halifax and Wellington bombers in Egypt. They can blast the ship to pieces with their 500 – pounders and destroy all the Marizans, plus the Cerebri creature.'

'I doubt that strategy would be effective,' said Lee. 'If the ship's hull is constructed using the same technology as the Marizans' body armour then it will stand up to even a direct hit. Furthermore, the craft is a mile in diameter. Even if our bombs were effective, you can imagine just how many hits would be required to destroy something that big. It would be like firing a peashooter at a blue whale. And there's even worse news. That Cerebri ship was part of a battle fleet a million strong.'

'A million of them! So where are the other ships now?' asked Mayne.

'Going by the information I acquired telepathically, I believe they are in deep space a considerable distance from Earth. But the Cerebri on board the ship underneath the Qattara Depression has already activated an on-board homing beacon, an S.O. S. if you like. That is one thing I picked up from my brief telepathic contact. The rest of the fleet is heading for the Earth and there is nothing we can do to stop them. Unless we can do something about it, the Earth is doomed!'

Mayne thought for a moment before replying.

'Supposing we raided the ship again and killed the Cerebri creature and destroyed the homing beacon. Would that stop the Marizans?'

'It probably would?' said Lee. 'But how would you kill the creature?'

'We could attach a lump of plastic explosive to that glass tank and set it off with a time pencil. That would smash the glass and all the nutrition fluid would run out. That brain creature, the Cerebri would die.'

'Sorry to rain on your parade, Paddy but I suspect the nutrition tank has been built using superior alien technology. It is likely that the glass will resist the blast of the plastic explosive. We would probably stand more of a chance if we could use a shaped- charge warhead.'

Mayne knew all about shaped charges. As far back as the late 19$^{th}$ century it had been known that a lump of explosive which had a cone - shaped cavity lined with thin metal could punch through several inches of armour plate. This scientific phenomenon—known as the Monroe Effect—was the theory behind a number of hand-held anti -tank weapons which were under development, including the British PIAT, the American bazooka and the German Panzerfaust.

'Unfortunately we don't have any shaped charges with us,' said Mayne. 'Their main use is knocking out tanks, which we generally try to avoid rather than fight.'

McAleese and McTavish were standing at the back of the room cleaning their Thompsons with oily rags and had listened avidly to everything that had been said. McAleese spoke.

'Permission to speak freely, Major.'

'Yes McAleese. What is it ?'

'These creatures we just fought. What exactly are they?'

'The Cerebri call them Marizans,' said Lee. 'Although they look like robots , they are actually reanimated human corpses. When I was in the ship I caught glimpses of British and American Army uniforms under their armour, which leads me to believe that they were originally the bodies of soldiers who died in a battle at this site a few years ago.

'The metal body armour which covers much of their bodies is the product of a superior alien technology. It is as thin as card, yet provides the same degree of protection as a couple of inches of conventional armour plate. Their transparent visors can also deflect bullets.'

'But if they are really corpses then how can they move? How can their muscles work? I dinnae understand,' said McAleese.

'That's an interesting question,' said Lee. 'Why do they not suffer from rigor mortis and putrefaction? For some years it has been known that there are parts of the world where dead people come back to life and start walking about. They have been used as slave labour in plantations in Central America and the Caribbean, and are often called zombies. I saw some film of these zombie creatures when I attended a meeting of the Glasgow University Medico Chirurgical society at the Glasgow University Union while I was at Medical School.

'The general consensus of most of the audience members, including several doctors who were present, was that these creatures were not actually dead. Instead they had suffered some kind of brain damage which affected their higher centres. Thus they were able to carry out manual labour but could not speak.

'However, I believe the Marizans are not true zombies. Instead, I think the Cerebri have discovered a way to reanimate dead tissue using electric currents. There is nothing new in this idea. In 1780 the Italian scientist Luigi Galvani discovered that he could make the leg muscles of dead frogs twitch by using electric stimulation. It was a significant scientific discovery and today's galvanometers are named after him.

'Yes, electricity seems to play an important role in the Marizans' functioning. You will have noticed how they use electric shocks to stun and kill. And these deadly dart guns they carry transmit an electric charge along a wire.

'As far as their brains are concerned, I have no idea how the Cerebri have managed to reverse the process of cerebral necrosis. Brain tissue dies through lack of oxygen when the blood supply is cut off for as little as three minutes. One possibility though, is that the Cerebri have wound back time itself so that the brain returns to the state it was in before death. When I was at Glasgow University I recall reading a 1932 paper by Professor Menahem Linovich of the University of Leipzig. Linovich proposed a method by which a temporal displacement field could be created using an advanced form of thermionic valve similar to the cavity magnetron.

'A standard magnetron produces microwave radiation, which can be used in advanced airborne radar systems. But Linovich's modified magnetron emits a temporal displacement field which can send objects backwards and forwards in time. Alternatively, by connecting a tuned oscillator circuit to the Linovich Magnetron, it is possible to make necrotic tissue viable again by returning it to an earlier state. In his paper, Linovich suggested his device could have medical applications such as the reversal of strokes and heart attacks.

'Which leads me to conclude what our next course of action must be. We have to go back into that alien spaceship and capture a Marizan. I want to find out how these things work so we can devise a better way of dealing with them.'

Mayne's eyes nearly popped out of his head when he realised what Lee was proposing.

'You can't be serious,' he said. 'Those things are deadly.'

'Oh, but I am. Despite the risks involved we are going to go back into that alien spacecraft ...and capture a zombie!'

# Chapter 25

## To Catch a Zombie

Major Paddy Mayne stood up and accidentally knocked over his mug of tea which was on the table. Despite Mayne's desert suntan, his face had turned a shade of purple and he shook with rage. His fierce temper was a legend in the SAS.

'I can't believe I'm hearing this,' he shouted in his broad Northern Ireland accent. 'We nearly got killed down there …and lost one of our best soldiers into the bargain. Now you're suggesting we go back into the chasm to capture one of these things. Have you seen how dangerous they are? They only have to touch you to kill you.'

'I appreciate your concerns,' said Lee, as he struggled to maintain his composure. 'But if I could dissect one of these creatures, I might find a weakness that could help us to defeat them. And the time to do it is *now* while there are only a few of them. If we delay, then the Cerebri will have time to bring more of them out of hibernation, and we won't stand a chance. If we go immediately, I believe there will only be a few Marizans. I don't deny there's a risk but we've got to take a chance. Is the SAS motto not *Who Dares Wins*? So we can't delay. No risk assessments. No committee meetings. We go now!'

Mayne looked down at the table as he thought over what Lee had said. An expanding puddle of hot, milky tea was already drying in the stifling desert heat. 'OK, I agree that we must capture one of the creatures,' said Mayne. 'But I will be in charge of the military side of the operation and you will go along with whatever orders I give.'

'Agreed,' answered Lee.

'Assuming we can capture one of these things, then we'll have to bring it to the surface. Have you thought about how we're going to do that?'

'We'll need some kind of net that we can throw over the Marizan. We could use the camouflage nets that we carry in the Chevys. They are not very strong so we'll have to disable the creature – or even kill it – before we wrap it up. Then we can pull it to the surface using a rope attached to the bumper of a Chevy.'

'And all this time, we'll have to fight off any Marizans that turn up. I hardly think they'll just stand by and let us do what we want!' said Mayne.

'I know, Paddy,' answered Lee. 'That's why I will be relying on your excellent combat skills to keep us out of trouble.'

'OK, we'll take McAleese and McTavish again. They're our two best fighters. And I want to have a word with the tank crew. They may be able to help.'

Mayne walked through the open doors of the fort as Private Baker drove his Chevy to the edge of the chasm and re- attached two ropes to the front bumper. The Super Valentine was parked on the reverse slope of the sandy hillock to the east of the building. Crerar stood puffing a cigarette in the commander's hatch on top of the turret, while all the other hatches were open to cool the vehicle as much as possible.

Mayne strolled up the sandy slope to speak to Crerar, who was experiencing a mixture of elation and disappointment. He was proud of his crew for defeating the German attack but saddened that he had been unable to stop the recent raid by the strange silver creatures.

'I've a job for you,' said Mayne. 'We're going back into the chasm to capture one of these creatures. They' re called Marizans, by the way. But this time I want Honeychile positioned to give us fire support when we exit the fissure. I suggest you move your vehicle forward over the crest of the hillock so it's facing downhill. If you then elevate your 75mm gun you should be able to cover the chasm. I suggest you load your main gun with HE and also have a few T30 anti-personnel canister rounds in your ready rack. Don't bother with your BESA machine gun. We already know that rifle - calibre rounds have no effect on the Marizans.'

'OK,will do,' said Crerar, before speaking into his carbon field mike. 'Driver, start up …move forward twelve yards, then stop.' The Valentine's six-cylinder petrol engine coughed into life and it travelled forward, tracks clanking and bogies squealing.

Mayne walked back to the chasm where the other members of his snatch squad stood ready for action. McTavish and McAleese wore backpacks with their Thompson sub- machine guns carried on slings while Lee was packing a long length of black rubber electrical lead attached to a copper rod into his own backpack.

' What's that you've got in your pack?' asked Mayne

'It's the grounding lead and earthing rod for the number 11 radio set from Truck Six. Your radio operator, Private Mills loaned it to me.'

'What do you want that for?' asked Mayne. 'You're not going to be sending radio transmissions once you get into that chasm.'

'I just want to test a private theory, that's all, Paddy.'

'OK men ,no more dilly - dallying, Let's go!'

Only ten minutes had elapsed since the decision had been made to mount the mission. Now the four soldiers climbed over the edge of the chasm and abseiled down the two ropes. Lee had borrowed a pair of leather gloves to protect his hands. He was glad he had some experience of using ropes. He had never liked gym at school but had done a bit of hillwalking and mountaineering in his youth.

Soon, the four soldiers stood in the corridor at the bottom of the chasm. Dust and loose rocks lay everywhere, plus the bodies of three dead Marizans which had been destroyed by grenades. One lacked a head, the other two had missing limbs. Two wall lights had been smashed by the blasts, and small fragments of Mills bombs were embedded in the rock walls of the corridor. The air smelled of burnt amatol.

For a moment, Lee considered whether he could do a post – mortem on one of these damaged creatures. It would certainly avoid all the dangers involved in capturing a live Marizan, who would almost certainly put up a fight and try to electrocute one or more members of the snatch squad.

As he was pondering over this possibility, McAleese shouted a warning.

'Marizan approaching.'

Lee screwed up his eyes to see better in the dim light. One of the humanoid creatures was marching along a section of corridor which was in semi-darkness, as the wall light was broken. The Marizan's eyes glowed a brilliant white in the dark, as though they were a pair of lightbulbs. Lee also noticed that this one had a small speaker box mounted on the left side of its chest armour. A familiar robotic voice issued from the grille :

'Stop. You will surrender and submit yourself for recycling. Recycling is compulsory. It is standard procedure.'

It was the voice of the Cerebri, which was being transmitted from the glass tank.

McTavish pulled out a grenade from his webbing pouch as the Marizan approached, and prepared to withdraw the pin. 'There's only one of them, Major. Two or three grenades should be enough to destroy it.'

'No ,' said Lee. 'We want this one undamaged. Leave this to me.'

Lee stood forward from the other three soldiers and raised his hands. 'We agree to your demands. We surrender. What do you want us to do?'

'Lay down your arms and move forward,' said the robotic voice. 'Resistance is futile. Prepare to be recycled.'

The four soldiers put down their guns and walked towards the Marizan. When they were just a yard away, Mayne dived towards the creature and did a classic rugby tackle, grabbing both of the creature' s legs and making it fall to the ground with a crash. The Marizan was now lying on its back with the full seventeen – stone weight of

Paddy Mayne keeping it down. The creature raised its right hand and attempted to touch Mayne's head but McAleese and McTavish had joined the struggle and both gripped the Marizan's right forearm, keeping it clear of Mayne, while taking great care to avoid touching its hand. Lee pulled the creature's dart gun out of its belt and threw it down the corridor out of reach.

McAleese and McTavish struggled to stop the Marizan's arm from moving. Despite their combined efforts, the creature's right hand was getting closer and closer to Mayne's head.

'Jesus, what does this thing eat for breakfast? A plate of girders?' said McAleese. 'It's got the strength of an ox.'

As the two soldiers attempted to restrain the Marizan, Lee took the earthing lead out of his backpack and shoved the grounding rod into a patch of damp sand at the edge of the corridor floor. Then he uncoiled the black rubber – covered cable attached to the rod and pressed the copper connector at the end against the palm of the Marizan's right hand. Bang! There was a blue flash and the creature went limp.

'What did you do there?' asked Mayne.

'I just confirmed a personal theory. These creatures seem to work by electricity. By earthing its right hand I have shorted its electrical system. You might say I made it blow a fuse.'

'It appears dead or dormant,' said Mayne. 'Will it become alive again?'

'That's something I don't know. It's possible all I have done is blow a circuit breaker. The Cerebri may reset it remotely once it works out what has happened. I suggest we get this thing up to the surface as quickly as possible in case it reactivates.'

It took the four men only a few minutes to wrap up the Marizan in a makeshift body bag made from a camouflage net. Then they tied one of the two dangling ropes to the immobilised creature. The other went around Lee's waist.

'OK, Captain Lee, this time you can go first,' said

Mayne. 'When you get to the top, untie yourself and the Marizan and then drop the ropes back down.'

'Right!' said Lee as he stuffed the Marizan's discarded dart gun into his backpack. He would examine the weapon later.

Mayne gave three firm tugs on the left - hand rope. Up on the surface, Private Baker noticed the pre-arranged signal, started the Chevy and put it into reverse. As the vehicle backed slowly towards the damaged open doors of the fort, Lee and the immobilised Marizan rose up the walls of the chasm.

Down below in the corridor, the three SAS men waited for their turn to escape. Their bodies were tense, their muscles tight. In a few minutes they would ascend to the surface but time seemed to be standing still. Captain Lee and the captive Marizan had started their ascent only a moment earlier but it seemed as though a whole hour had elapsed.

A moment later their fears were realised. Three pairs of glowing eyes appeared in the smoke and darkness at the end of the corridor.

'Grenades,' shouted Mayne. Each soldier threw a primed Mills bombs at the creatures, followed by three more. The six grenades exploded with loud bangs, showering the creatures with metal fragments. One fell dead with its head blown off. Another lost its left arm but continued relentlessly towards the soldiers. The third was apparently undamaged and pulled its golden dart gun from its belt. It pointed it directly at Mayne and fired, but the Major had excellent reflexes and ducked out the way of the high-speed projectile which struck the wall of the corridor, making a blue flash.

Mayne got behind the creature and rugby- tackled it. It crashed to the ground and attempted to fire its dart gun at point-blank range at Mayne's head, but McAleese pulled the weapon from the creature's grasp, turned round and shot the other surviving Marizan, which was lacking its left arm. The dart struck the creature's chest armour but failed to penetrate. It did though, give the Marizan a violent electric shock which stunned it. There was a blue flash and it fell to the ground, banging its head.

Meanwhile, Mayne held the other Marizan on the ground with his body weight while McAleese and McTavish struggled to prevent the creature from using its deadly right hand.

'Where's the earthing lead?' said Mayne.

'Captain Lee put it in his backpack before he ascended to the surface,' said McAleese.

'Not my lucky day,' said Mayne. 'Pass me your Thompson. We'll do this another way.'

Mayne pulled up the hinged, oval transparent visor which protected the Marizan's face and stuck the muzzle of the Thompson's gun barrel into the creature's mouth. Mayne flinched from the smell of rotten teeth and foul breath.

'Eat this , you ugly bastard,' said Mayne as he pulled the trigger. At point – blank range , several heavy forty-five calibre slugs tore off the back of the Marizan's head. Brains and cerebrospinal fluid splattered over the floor of the corridor as the creature died.

A few yards away, the other Marizan began to recover consciousness and started to move its limbs. Mayne gave the creature the same 'treatment' he had just doled out to its companion, blowing off the back of the Marizan's head with a burst from his Thompson fired directly into the zombie's mouth after lifting the visor. Then, getting to their feet, the three soldiers ran to the two dangling ropes which had just been thrown down from the surface as Mayne took command of this situation.

'McTavish, you're our best mountaineer. Climb up the left rope as fast as you can. Mc Aleese, attach the end of the rope round your waist. I'll do the same with the other one.'

Mayne tied the rope round his waist and gave three sharp tugs. Up on the surface, Private Baker reversed the Chevy once more and the three SAS men ascended towards the light at the top of the chasm. Mayne knew the journey to the top would take only two minutes but it seemed like the longest couple of minutes of his life. As he was halfway to the top, three pairs of glowing white dots appeared at the bottom of the chasms. Marizans! Would they never give up?

Mayne was sure he would escape. He had only a minute to go until he reached the surface. But then one of the Marizans started to climb up the walls of the chasm, using spikes which had appeared as if by magic on the end of its fingers and the front of its boots. The Marizan was scrambling up the rock walls faster than Mayne was ascending.

Mayne and McAleese made the surface and several soldiers arrived to untie them and help them get up. Then a Marizan's head popped up above the fissure, its silver skull cap gleaming in the brilliant sunshine. Two soldiers struggled to untie the rope around Mayne's waist as the Marizan reached out with its right hand. It was only a foot away from Mayne's head. Mayne could hear a crackling of electricity as the creature prepared to kill him.

Aboard the Super Valentine, Sutherland had the Marizan in his sights. The creature's chest was centred in the cross hairs of his Barr & Stroud brass sighting telescope. A high explosive round was loaded in the breech of the M3 gun.

'I can cream that fucker with one round,' said Sutherland. 'But I'll kill the Major with the blast. What should I do?'

'Hold your fire,' said Crerar. 'Don't shoot!'

Mayne was about to die. There was nothing anyone could do about it.

# Chapter 26

## Alien Autopsy

For a moment, Crerar hesitated. Then he came to a decision and spoke to his loader, Kelly, using the tank's intercom system.

'Kelly, open fire with your BESA but aim to miss. Shoot to the right of the creature. Don't hit the Major!'

Kelly cocked his weapon and fired a few short bursts from the mantlet – mounted machine gun aimed at the rocks and earth to the right of the Marizan. One round pinged off the creature's left arm. Crerar knew the rifle-calibre bullets would have no effect on the zombie, but he intended to distract it, not kill it.

The Marizan immediately lost interest in Mayne and turned towards what it considered to be the greater threat – the tank. The creature pulled its dart gun out of its belt, aimed it at Crerar and fired just as the Sergeant ducked down inside the turret. The dart flew harmlessly above the commander's hatch and landed some distance away in the desert.

Meanwhile, Mayne, McAleese and McTavish scrambled into Private Baker's Chevy. The young soldier put the truck into reverse gear and backed away from the chasm.

Now, Sutherland had a clear shot at the Marizan and pulled the firing trigger. The mighty M3 gun recoiled, belching smoke and flame from its muzzle, as a powerful high – explosive shell shot out of the barrel and blew the Marizan to pieces. Body parts and metal armour clattered against rock as they fell down the chasm.

Just as the smoke cleared, a further three Marizans appeared above the lip of the fissure. They were well spaced out, to make the gunner's task harder.

Crerar reappeared in the commander's hatch where he

could see what was going on.

'Gunner, target twenty degrees left, shoot!' he barked into the microphone.

Sutherland rotated the turret slightly to the left and fired. The HE shell exploded on the lip of the fissure, blowing off a Marizan's head. Already, Crerar had spotted a second target.

'Gunner, Marizan ten degrees right. Shoot!'

Again, a powerful HE round sped through the hot desert air towards its target. The shell hit the Marizan square in the chest, blowing it to pieces. The third Marizan was at the eastern end of the fissure, aiming a dart gun at the tank. Crerar was unsure if Sutherland could nail it in the next few seconds as the creature was preparing to fire.

*Bang! Bang! Bang! Bang! Bang!*

Crerar was deafened by a loud chatter from the front of the fort as Private Cornwell shot at the Marizan with a fifty-calibre machine -gun. One of the heavy rounds knocked the dart gun out of the Marizan's right hand. Private Cornwell followed up with a short but accurate burst aimed at the vulnerable gap where the Marizan's chest armour met its neck. Several of the heavy slugs bounced off the armour but one found its mark, piercing the creature's spine and severing its spinal cord. Paralysed from the neck down, the creature lost its grip on the walls of the fissure and fell fifty feet to the corridor floor below. A loud metallic clang echoed off the walls of the chasm as the Marizan hit concrete, bits of body armour flying everywhere.

Now five soldiers came out of the fort and each dropped two primed hand grenades into the chasm, followed by flaming petrol bombs. A pall of black smoke rose high into the azure blue desert sky. The Marizan attack had been defeated – but how long would it be before they were back in greater numbers?

\*\*\*\*\*\*\*

Meanwhile, in a room inside the fort, the captured Marizan lay motionless on an old, worn, wooden table as Captain Lee prepared to carry out an autopsy. He was unclear if 'post – mortem' was the correct term as he wasn't sure if the creature was actually alive, dead or merely dormant.

Mayne and McAleese stood by to offer any assistance as Lee prepared his tools. During his training he had witnessed a number of post – mortems being carried out at the Pathology Department at Glasgow Royal Infirmary, so he knew what tools were required. Unfortunately all he had was his basic surgical kit, which included a Swann – Morton scalpel handle and several Number 11 blades. He also had a bone saw which was normally used for amputations. He didn't have a large surgical cutting knife so would have to use one of the soldiers' razor – sharp Sykes-Fairbairn fighting knives

Lee began his inspection of the creature by removing the silver skull cap, which was held on by a couple of spring clips on either side of the head. He turned the cap over and noted that the inner surface was studded with multiple circular metal electrodes, each surrounded by what looked like a black rubber washer, which presumably provided electrical insulation.

Then Lee removed the hinged, transparent plastic visor that protected the face of the creature and was attached to a metal ring around the Marizan's head.

'Fascinating,' said Lee. 'This visor is made of a transparent plastic which is only a few millimetres thick. Yet it shrugs off bullets. Our fighter aircraft have bulletproof windshields – but they are inches thick. I am sure the Royal Aircraft Establishment at Farnborough would love to see this.

'The Marizan's face looks human but has a deathly grey pallor,' continued Lee. 'And the corneas of both eyes are opaque ….. so how does it see clearly? Let me have a look at that skull cap again.'

The skull cap had a metal flange studded with sharp spikes. At the very front was a tiny lens surrounded by a black plastic ring.

'What is it?' asked Mayne.

'I believe it is a television camera, which is augmenting the eyes,' said Lee.

'A television camera. I have heard of this,' said Mayne. 'There was a Scotsman called John Logie Baird who built something called a televisor. But it was big and clunky with electric motors and spinning discs.'

'That is correct,' said Lee. 'But the EMI company has produced their own all-electronic system with 405-line resolution. It is quite conceivable that in decades to come it will be possible to make TV cameras which are tiny. My guess is that this TV camera can pick up light over a much greater frequency range than the human retina, including infra – red, enabling the Marizans to see in the dark.'

The stench from the Marizan's mouth was unbearable. Lee noticed that the teeth were all rotting. The Cerebri obviously didn't believe in sending their workforce for dental check-ups or insisting that they brush their teeth.

'I guess these creatures don't eat. The Cerebri must have found some other way of providing nutrition for their bodies.'

Next, Lee unfastened the clips that were holding on the creature's chest armour to reveal a dirty, faded 1930s – era British Army uniform. He cut away the clothes to reveal the Marizan's bare chest, which was covered with wires of different colours. Many of them passed into holes in the chest. There was a large vertical wound over the sternum which had been secured with metal clips.

Lee cut open this old scar with his scalpel and pulled the chest open. The breastbone was missing and the chest cavity was filled with more wires and tubes.

'This wiring goes to all the muscles and internal organs. Some kind of electro-stimulation is being used to keep all the creatures muscles and organs in working order.'

Lee examined the golden dart gun which he had removed earlier during the Marizan's capture. He thought it looked like a chunky child's toy with its simple design and thick barrel.

'It's light. Very light. And it's got four darts in the barrel with spares on the belt. Each dart is attached to a fine wire at the tail end. I guess that some kind of electric current is sent down the wire to kill or stun. This weapon would be very useful to the SAS, wouldn't it Paddy?'

Mayne nodded.

With the help of McAleese and McTavish, Lee turned the Marizan onto its stomach.

'What have we here?' said Lee. 'I hadn't noticed this before.'

Lee was looking at a black box about nine inches high by four inches wide which was fitted on the Marizan's lower back. On the top was a telescopic aerial about three inches high. Lee pulled on the unit and found it could be easily removed as it was plugged into a socket on the creature's back.

'What is it?' asked Mayne.

'I believe this is a radio receiver which transmits commands to the Marizan. I guess they are all controlled by the Cerebri creature on the ship using voice commands. This unit must convert these voice signals into electronic impulses. I will have a closer look at this later.'

With the assistance of the others, Lee turned the creature onto its back and slit open the abdominal cavity. The intestines had been removed and in their place was a green box attached to two thick electrical cables.

'What is that?' asked Mayne.

'I believe this is what powers the Marizan,' said Lee. 'It is some kind of high - capacity rechargeable battery. Probably far in advance of anything we have on Earth. I am going to disconnect it from the creature as this should prevent it coming to life again.'

Lee snipped through the heavy wires with a pair of diagonal cutters and then cleaned his hands.

'This is all very interesting,' said Mayne. 'But have you found anything that will help us to destroy the creatures?

A weakness that we can exploit?'

'I think their biggest weakness is that radio -control unit on their backs. I believe that if I could …'

Lee was cut off in mid – sentence by a deafening humming noise above the fort. Private Baker rushed into the room.

' Major Mayne, Captain Lee. You have to come and see this. Some very strange – looking aircraft have appeared.'

Mayne and Lee raced up the stairs to the parapets to be greeted by the spectacle of three gleaming, silver, disc-shaped craft orbiting the fort at low – level. Each machine was a hundred feet in diameter and had a saucer – shaped body with a cylindrical crew compartment on top. There was no obvious means of propulsion.

The sunlight reflecting off the craft was dazzling and Mayne had to put on his sunglasses to see them properly.

'What are these craft? ' he said. 'They have no camouflage paint and no markings. Are they British, American ,German or Italian? And how can they stay aloft? They have no wings, no propellers.'

On the ground floor of the fort, Private Baker fired a short burst at the nearest craft from his fifty-calibre Browning gun. The rounds bounced off.

'Cease fire!' shouted Mayne. 'Don't waste ammunition.'

After making another circuit of the fort, the three craft flew north at low speed and then split up. Four telescopic landing legs unfolded under each saucer as they prepared to land. One selected a patch of flat ground to the north-east of the fort, about a mile beyond the German positions Another landed to the north-west behind the wrecked Afrika Korps vehicles. The third landed due west of the fort.

'They are blocking all our possible escape routes,' said Mayne.' Who or what is in these craft? Do they contain more of these Cerebri creatures?'

'I don't think so,' said Lee. 'These craft aren't big enough to hold a complete Cerebri creature in its nutrition tank. There's only one possibility. These flying discs contain Marizan reinforcements.'

'Marizans,' said Mayne. 'But where did they come from?'

'I don't know,' said Lee.

Mayne picked up his binoculars and looked at the nearest craft, which was to the north-east of the fort. A ramp had dropped down from the belly of the saucer and a large squad of Marizans started marching towards the German forces. Their plan was clearly to overwhelm the remaining Afrika Korps soldiers and then take the fort. Obviously, the Marizans in the other two saucers would launch their own attacks, so the British could expect to be overwhelmed.

They had one tank and a few machine-guns but they were running low on ammunition and were heavily outnumbered. Unless a miracle happened they were all going to be killed or captured!

# Chapter 27

## My Enemy's Enemy

Mayne lowered his binoculars and came to a decision.

'I must speak to Oberst Seidel. Immediately!'

Mayne ran down the steps and burst through the old creaking wooden door of the ground-floor room where Seidel and the three captured German soldiers were imprisoned. The German officer sat at a wooden table sipping a tin mug of water while the Afrika Korps squaddies played cards.

'I understand you speak fluent English,' said Mayne.

'Yes,' replied Seidel. 'I studied Civil Engineering at Imperial College in the 1920s. And in the thirties I was the Military Attaché at the German Embassy in London. I returned to my homeland in July 1938.'

'Excellent! Unfortunately I don't have time for chit-chat because an urgent situation has developed. I need your help immediately. You remember these evil creatures we encountered underground? We believe they have come from another world. They are inhuman killers!'

Seidel put down his mug and nodded. 'How could I forget?'

Mayne continued. 'A large force of them has landed to the north-east of this fort. And elsewhere. We believe they intend to kill your men and then attack us here. We need to get all your troops and vehicles to the safety of this fort as quickly as possible. We don't have a minute to lose!'

'Are you proposing some kind of a truce between our forces?'

'Correct! For the moment, we must forget our differences and fight alongside one another to defeat our common enemy. Believe me, these creatures won't discriminate between you and me! We're heavily outnumbered and running low on ammo but if we join forces we have a

174

better chance of repelling the attacks. But we must do it now, without delay. We only have minutes to act!'

Seidel thought for a moment. 'What you say makes sense. You have a saying in your language. I believe it states that my enemy's enemy is my friend. I therefore agree. But what do you want me to do?'

'I want you to come with me. We're going to take a truck to your positions, and I want you to order your men to move to this fort. I'm not asking for a surrender. I don't want your men to lay down their arms. Far from it, I want your troops to bring every vehicle, every gun, every bullet, every grenade they can carry. And we need to do it now!'

Just five minutes later, Truck One was speeding across the desert, leaving a cloud of dust as it headed towards the German positions. Private Baker was driving. Mayne was in the front passenger seat. Seidel sat behind him. A makeshift white flag fluttered from the fifty-calibre pintle mount.

A few hundred yards away, the German soldiers cocked their weapons as they looked nervously at the approaching Marizans. They had already seen what these silver creatures could do, when they had abducted Oberst Seidel. They had also witnessed the Allied force battling them. Even though they were regarded as enemy troops, the Germans still had great admiration for their bravery and fighting skills.

Most of the Germans were observing the approaching Marizans, but one Landser had been ordered to keep a watch on the fort just in case an attack developed from that direction. A shimmering heat haze made it hard to see clearly, but Landser Hartmann could see a cloud of dust to the south-west. He raised his binoculars. Slowly an image appeared through the heat haze. It was one of the LRDG Chevrolets and it was heading straight for them. Was this a surprise attack and if so, why was there only one vehicle? Hartmann turned round and called out to the other soldiers:

'Enemy vehicle approaching from south-west.'

Oberleutnant Rudel turned round in the turret of his Sd.

Kfz.222 four-wheeled armoured car and observed the approaching truck through his own binoculars.

'Don't fire! The truck is flying a white flag. And that looks like Oberst Seidel in the back.'

Three minutes later, the LRDG vehicle skidded to a halt in front of the German positions with a squeal of brakes. Mayne jumped out and saluted Rudel. Seidel scrambled out the back of the truck and also gave a salute. Then he spoke.

'Oberleutnant. You have no chance of repelling an attack by these creatures. I command you to order all our troops to fall back to the fort. I want you to bring every man, every weapon and every vehicle we have. I stress that I am not saying this under duress. We have to join forces with the British to fight the common enemy.'

'But... are you sure that is wise?' said Rudel.

'No buts, Oberleutnant,that is an order from your commanding officer.'

Rudel turned towards his men and screamed as loud as he could

'Board the vehicles and fall back to the fort. The British are giving us sanctuary. Bring all the weapons and ammo we have. And hurry!'

The German troops quickly mounted their vehicles and headed to the fort as fast as they could travel. By this point the Marizans were just a hundred yards away and one fired its dart gun at the rearmost vehicle in the retreating column, a Volkswagen Type 82 Kubelwagen. The projectile struck the rear of the scout car, causing the four-cylinder air-cooled engine to stop and burst into flames. The four soldiers in the vehicle promptly abandoned it and ran towards the fort as fast as their legs could carry them.

Back at the fort, McAleese and McTavish saw a formation of vehicles heading towards them. Experts in vehicle identification, they could see the group of trucks was led by the LRDG Chevy. They also recognised one Opel Blitz lorry plus two captured Bedford OYs which had been adorned with oversized black German crosses. There was some light armour – one Sd. Kfz.222 armoured car and a single Sd. Kfz.251 half-track. Both had a forward-firing 20mm cannon, plus a 7.9mm machine gun. There were no Panzers, as Honeychile had knocked out all six. McTavish estimated there must be at least twenty soldiers in the German force. All the vehicles steered round the eastern edge of the fissure and parked in front of the front while Mayne considered how best to deploy his now-augmented forces.

'There's no room in the courtyard for any more vehicles. Park all the trucks round the back of the fort. All soldiers go inside the building and take up defensive positions on the first floor parapets. The half-track can go on the reverse slope of the hillock to the west of the fort and the armoured car can block the entrance,' he said.

Soon all the vehicles had been deployed as Mayne had instructed and a mixed force of German and Allied troops manned the battlements. Ammo belts were fitted to machine -guns and all eyes looked to the north-east as the Marizans approached. Mayne felt a pain in his gut as he wondered if his newly-augmented force would be enough to repel the imminent assault. He now had about thirty troops defending the fort. But would that be enough?

# Chapter 28

# Fight to the Death

Thirty gleaming Marizans stood motionless, a thousand yards to the north - east of the fort, the brilliant desert sunshine sparkling off their highly polished armour. They were just within effective range of Honeychile's 75mm M3 gun but Crerar resisted the urge to open fire. On the parapets, a mixed force of Allied and German soldiers hunched behind their weapons. The fort's defences now included four of the excellent German MG42 7.92 mm light machine guns which could spew out 1,200 to 1,500 rounds a minute. A few of the Afrika Korps soldiers had bolt – action Mauser K98 7.92 mm rifles, but most carried 9mm MP40 machine pistols which were effective in a close - quarter battle, but useless at long range.

Further Marizans emerged from the other two saucers to the west and north – west. Up on the parapets, Mayne shouted his orders.

'No firing until I give the command. Wait until they are just 500 yards away.'

Seidel quickly translated the orders into German and ordered his own soldiers to do likewise.

A cloud of clinging, white smoke drifted up from the fissure and lay on the desert sand around the chasm. Then a shining, silver football-sized sphere rose vertically from the giant crack until it was hovering fifty feet in the air. It had a round grille on the front and above that was what looked like a camera lens. On top of the sphere was a blinking red light.

'I can take it out with my Bren,' said Davy Atkins, who was lying on his stomach aiming his gun which was resting on sandbags.

'No, wait,' said Mayne.

A familiar electronic voice boomed from the grille on

the front of the sphere and echoed around the fort. The Cerebri was speaking.

*The silver ball is a communication device*, thought Lee, who was standing to the left of Mayne.

'You have fought well for a primitive race,' said the Cerebri. 'But you are all doomed! Marizan reinforcements have arrived and will soon attack the fort.'

'Can you hear me?' shouted Lee.

'Yes ,' said the voice. 'Two - way communication has been established.'

'Where did your reinforcements come from? I thought your battle-fleet was in deep space. And why didn't you revive more of the Marizans in your main ship? Would that not have been simpler?'

'Our small craft containing reinforcements came from your moon. They arrived in your solar system a long time ago, along with our main ship. They went into auto-hibernation mode when our large ship sank into the ground some centuries ago. But I have reactivated them. Further Marizans are being revived in our main ship but this will take some time as a great amount of power is required. However, you will soon be overwhelmed by weight of numbers. A homing beacon has been activated and the entire Marizan fleet —nearly a million ships—is on its way to Earth. Each craft contains 50,000 of our warriors. Earth will be overpowered.'

'So what do you expect us to do?' said Lee. 'What is the purpose of this communication?'

'I offer you the chance to surrender. If you lay down your arms and agree to be recycled into Marizan warriors then much pain and suffering will be avoided. To die is futile. Resistance is useless. Our recycling process is painless. It will be as though you had never existed. You will have the honour of serving the Cerebri.'

'No, we will never agree to that,' said Lee. 'Ending up as a Marizan is a fate worse than death. You will have to fight the entire population of the world. The human race will never agree to being turned into a string of sausages to meet your whims.'

'Resistance is useless,' said the Cerebri. ' If the human race does not capitulate then we will destroy it. Aboard our ships we have weapons that can vaporize an entire city with a single blast. We have the capability to wipe out the entire human race with neutron bombs. Every living thing on Earth will be destroyed. *Every living thing!* We will strip the Earth of all its natural resources and then turn it into a charred husk, devoid of life, orbiting a dead sun. The choice is yours. Serve the Cerebri or you will all die!'

'No we refuse, we will never surrender,' said Lee. 'As our Mr Churchill once said, we will fight you in the beaches, we will fight you in the fields and we will fight you in the landing grounds.'

'It is clear that further discussion is pointless,' said the electronic voice. 'We will attack your positions and many of you will be killed.'

The silver ball descended slowly into the chasm as the three groups of Marizans started marching towards the fort from different directions.

'Peter, you know a lot about science,' said Mayne. 'What was that voice saying about weapons that can destroy an entire city? Do they have large bombs filled with explosive?'

'Oh no, I think it's something far worse than that,' said Lee. 'There are no secrets in science during peacetime. Just before the war began, some scientists claimed that it would be possible to build a bomb that harnessed the power of the atom. It would use heavy radioactive isotopes like uranium and plutonium to create a chain reaction which released a tremendous amount of energy, as predicted by Einstein's classic equation $E$ equals $mc$, squared. I think it's likely that Britain, America, Germany …maybe even Japan, are working on their own nuclear weapons.'

'So what sort of explosive power are we talking about?' asked Mayne.' Equivalent to 500 tons of TNT perhaps?'

'It will be far more powerful than that,' said Lee. 'Even

the smallest atom bomb is likely to have an explosive yield equivalent to 10,000 tons of TNT. And within a decade it may be possible to create bombs with an explosive power equal to ten or twenty million tons of TNT. It would also be theoretically possible to build what is known as a neutron bomb, which kills living tissue using radiation, but leaves buildings intact. This may be what the Cerebri was talking about.'

'Oh my God ! That all sounds fascinating, but also horrifying,' said Mayne. 'From what you have said, I think we should be worried. Very worried indeed.'

*******

On board *Honeychile*, Crerar wiped sweat from his forehead and gave orders to his crew.

'We'll start by plastering them with HE when they get within 500 yards. Then we'll switch to anti - personnel canister rounds.'

'There's just one problem, Sergeant,' said Kelly, the loader. 'We're running low on ammo. We've only got seven rounds of HE left, plus nine canister rounds and three M61 armour - piercing. And we've got just one belt of ammunition left for the BESA.'

'OK, Kelly. Sutherland, aim well. Don't miss. Make every round count!'

Crerar looked through his binoculars. He had a good view of the Marizan forces that were approaching from the north - east, plus the other contingent that were marching from the north –west. He couldn't see the enemy forces that were to his west because his view was blocked by the fort. He could only hope that the German half-track could take them out with its 20mm cannon. It didn't have the range and hitting power of the Super Valentine's 75mm M3 gun but could probably penetrate a Marizan's body armour at close range.

*******

Mayne studied the advancing creatures with professional interest from his vantage point on the parapets. He didn't have an optical rangefinder, so was having to rely on his combat experience to gauge distance. He reckoned the Marizans were 600 yards away. Three minutes later, he estimated he had let them get close enough.

He put his hands on either side of his mouth and screamed an order to all the troops:

'Armoured vehicles, mortars and all machine-gunners and riflemen, open fire. Sub-machine guns hold your fire until the Marizans get within 100 yards.'

Private Mills, in Truck One in the courtyard, repeated the instructions over the Number 11 radio set to ensure Crerar got the message while Seidel translated the order into German and shouted it to his troops.

*Honeychile* fired its main gun immediately, as it had an HE round in its breech. The high explosive round struck the front row of Marizans approaching from the north-east, blowing three of them into the air. They crashed back down onto the desert floor, arms and legs twisted at crazy angles. The shrapnel from the explosion would have killed a dozen human troops but the Marizans' armour protected them well and only two others were destroyed.

*Honeychile* fired twice more and destroyed another five Marizans. Then Sutherland rotated the turret left and shot three HE rounds at the creatures advancing from the north-west. Many of them were blown into the air by the explosions but some got up, apparently undamaged. Sutherland rotated the turret again and fired his last HE shell at the group approaching from the north-east.

'That's us out of HE,' said Kelly.

'OK, Sutherland. Load with canister anti - personnel rounds.'

'Loaded. Ready to fire.'

'OK Kelly, fire three rounds at the group to the north - east then give the north- west group the same treatment.'

While Crerar and his crew blasted away at the advancing warriors, Mayne directed the other weapons.

Rifle and machine-gun bullets pinged harmlessly off the Marizans' body armour.

'Don't fire at their chests,' screamed Mayne. 'Aim at the vulnerable spot where their head joins their body. There's no armour there and you've got a good chance of severing their spine!'

Despite the heavy defensive fire, the Marizans continued their relentless advance towards the fort. Up on the parapets, the German troops were launching 3.5 kg bombs from their two 80mm *Granatwerfer 34* mortars as fast as they could drop them down the barrel. But it took almost a direct hit to take out a Marizan , as the soft sand cushioned the explosions and metal fragments from the exploding mortar bombs were only lethal at very close range.

The 20mm cannon on board the two German armoured vehicles were proving more effective. Even a single round could penetrate the breastplate of a Marizan at short range. The British force's fifty-calibre machine guns could not pierce the armour but could decapitate the creatures if aimed correctly. But the big problem was ammunition. It was running low. Right now Mayne wished the RAF could parachute a few containers of supplies onto the fort, but that was never going to happen.

Now the surviving Marizans were just a hundred yards from the fort. Almost simultaneously, they pulled out their deadly dart guns and aimed them straight ahead. Their first target was the German half-track to the west of the building. Seven Marizans approached the vehicle from different directions to make the gunner's task harder. The 20mm cannon on board the half-track opened fire, destroying two creatures. A third was hit in the neck by a long burst of machine -gun fire at close range from the vehicle's 7.9mm MG34 machine gun. But the four surviving Marizans fired their dart guns simultaneously. Four slender darts streaked through the desert air, each trailing a fine wire behind it. Each projectile hit the bodywork of the vehicle at different points, causing a blue flash. The entire crew died from electrocution. Then the punctured petrol tank exploded with a loud *whoof.* The air filled with the smell of burning flesh and rubber as the tracked armoured vehicle became a funeral pyre. Black smoke billowed into the desert sky.

Another group of Marizans converged on the four - wheeled German armoured car which blocked the entrance to the fort. Two Marizans fell dead, their chest armour pierced by 20mm rounds. Then a third, which had some kind of pack strapped to its chest, ran forward and crawled under the vehicle.

Mayne wondered what this creature was up to. A moment later he had his answer as the pack exploded, wrecking the armoured car and blowing off its wheels. The petrol tank burst into flames and the crew—who had already been riddled with shrapnel —were incinerated. The shock wave from the explosion reverberated throughout the fort and three soldiers fell from the parapets and landed in the courtyard below. One of the three, Landser Peiper survived although he sustained a fracture of his left wrist and lacerated his forearm.

Mayne was shocked that the Cerebri was willing to use its Marizan warriors as expendable suicide bombers.He had heard that the Japanese were using similar tactics in the Far East to destroy Allied tanks.

Meanwhile, the sole surviving armoured vehicle, *Honeychile*, had expended all its HE and anti-personnel rounds and was firing its last M61 armour – piercing shells. These were highly effective against Marizans—as they blew a dinner - plate sized hole in their chests—but required an expenditure of one round per creature, as they lacked any kind of explosive blast effect.

'Just two rounds left,' said Kelly.

'OK. Make 'em count!' answered Crerar.

Five Marizans stood in front of the Super Valentine in a wide arc. Sutherland destroyed two of them with direct hits from M61 rounds. A third was decapitated by a long burst of BESA fire from the mantlet gun. The two surviving Marizans approached the Super Valentine from different sides and aimed their dart guns at their target – the cylindrical auxiliary fuel tanks mounted on either side of the rear engine deck. Both darts sped through the air with a whooshing sound and struck the tanks, which promptly exploded. *Honeychile's* rear deck was enveloped in orange flames and black, suffocating smoke entered the fighting compartment.

'All crew bail out,' said Crerar. It was the only option left because there was no way of extinguishing the fire and the tank had no ammunition left.

The driver was first out, using the hatch above his head, but was immediately attacked by a Marizan who killed the crewman by touching him with its deadly right hand. Crerar, Sutherland and Kelly bailed out through the commander's hatch on top of the turret but, as they ran towards the fort, they were all hit in the back by multiple Marizan darts. The three soldiers dropped dead, killed by electrocution.

Now all the surviving Marizans had reached the base of the fort and fired their dart guns into the open windows on the ground floor, killing a few soldiers. It was not a one-sided battle, as three of the creatures were decapitated by short bursts of fifty- calibre machine – gun fire at short range. Mayne looked down in frustration. He could have ordered his men to drop grenades on them from the parapets, but the resulting blasts and metal fragments might injure or kill his own men who were manning the guns on the ground floor.

Some Marizans attempted to climb the front of the fort, but the near - vertical walls proved too smooth to get a grip. Others were trying to get in through the front entrance, but their way was completely blocked by the red – hot, blazing hulk of the German armoured car.

As Mayne wondered whether they were going to be overrun, the silver ball emerged from the chasm and once again rose into the desert sky. Its electronic voice could be heard over the sound of ammunition 'cooking off' in the wrecked armoured vehicles :

'All Marizans,relocate to position X24. Await further instructions'

Responding to this command, all the Marizans turned round and marched in unison to a point about 600 yards to the north - west of the fort. Then they stood motionless in line, facing Mayne's troops.

'What's happening?' said Private Mills. 'Have they given up or what?'

'I don't think so,' said Lee. 'They've killed and injured a lot of our men and destroyed our armour support but they've been unable to capture the fort. My guess is that they are awaiting delivery of heavier weapons that will enable them to knock down the walls.'

'Tell me something, Peter,' said Mayne as he put down his binoculars. 'How do you know so much? I know you're qualified in medicine but you seem to know an awful lot about science. Even the science of the future.'

Lee laughed. 'I 've always been a bit of a know – all. It used to annoy my teachers at school. And it's all because I read a lot of books and journals. One of my favourite pastimes used to be spending a whole Saturday at the Mitchell Library in Charing Cross, Glasgow. I would read books on all kinds of things. And I keep up with the latest developments in technology by reading journals like *The Scientific American* and *Popular Mechanics*.'

'That's very interesting,' said Mayne. 'You know something, after the war is over, I'm going to read a few books myself.'

Lee chuckled.

'So what should we do now, Peter? Should we just wait for the Marizans to attack?'

'I think we should take advantage of this brief respite to have a meal and use the latrines. I will attend to the wounded and then join you all for some food.'

'Good idea. I will keep two men on the parapets on sentry duty at all times and the rest of us can eat. I can't remember the last time I had a proper meal.'

'Quite so,' said Lee. 'We need to keep up our strength because one thing is certain …the Marizans will attack again and I have no idea what is going to happen when they do.'

# Chapter 29

# Revelations

Lee was surprised at the small number of casualties he had to treat. This was because no-one had survived electrocution by a Marizan, and the entire crews of all three armoured vehicles were now dead. There were just three soldiers in need of medical attention, who had all fallen from the parapets onto the courtyard during the last Marizan attack. Two had landed on a pile of soft sand and had sustained only minor lacerations, which Lee had sutured under local anaesthetic.

The third casualty, Landser Peiper, had badly injured his left arm which had multiple lacerations. Despite the prompt application of field dressings, he had lost some blood. His left wrist was also broken, with the characteristic 'dinner fork' deformity of a Colles fracture, which involved the lower end of the radius. Lee knew he would have to reset his smashed wrist into the correct anatomical position. Some kind of anaesthetic would be needed. He would then apply a splint. Ideally, he should apply a plaster cast but he had no plaster bandages or plaster of Paris powder in his medical kit, so he would have to make do with whatever was at hand. The role of medical officer in an LRDG patrol involved a lot of 'bush medicine.'

Lee palpated Peiper's right radial artery at his wrist and noted a fast pulse with a sinus rhythm. The German Landser was staring at him with a fanatical gleam in his eyes.

'Do you speak any English?' asked Lee.

'Yes, I learned it at school.'

'We have to reset the bones of your broken left wrist. We don't have the facilities to give you a general anaesthetic, but I can perform a local anaesthetic block on your left forearm which will enable me to reset the broken bones, which will then be splinted. In addition, I can give you an intravenous injection of a sedative which will make you drowsy and comfortable during the procedure.'

Lee took off Peiper's battledress shirt so he could examine his chest and listen to his heart and lungs with his stethoscope. As he was carrying out his examination he noticed that the young soldier had an SS tattoo on his upper left arm and a puckered scar the size of a penny over his right kidney.

'You have noticed the lesion on my back. I've had it as long as I can remember,' said Peiper.

Lee knew that some birthmarks could look like scars but he was sure this was an old burn injury which had probably happened in childhood.

'I hate being in North Africa,' said Peiper.'I loathe the heat. Why couldn't they have sent me to Russia, where it snows a lot? I love cold weather. I used to be in Waffen SS you know. I wish I was in Russia right now with the SS, rounding up Jews and sending them to concentration camps. That would be my dream job – the extreme cold, and being unpleasant to inferior, non – Aryan races.'

*How very interesting*, thought Lee. This young man hates the heat and loves the cold. And he doesn't like Jews. And he has an unexplained burn scar on his right loin, which he thinks is a birthmark. *I wonder if there is a connection here?*

'We'll get you fixed up as soon as we can,' said Lee. 'But first I 'm going to have some food as I'm feeling dizzy from hunger. I want you to abstain from eating and drinking until after you have had your treatment, in case it makes you sick.'

Four petrol – fuelled 'desert cookers,' employing used 'flimsy' four – gallon petrol tins, had been set up in the courtyard and the British and German troops were sharing their rations, which were mainly canned foods. As time was short, the squaddies were making 'pot mess,' which was a mixture of whatever was available. The British put in opened cans of potatoes, corned beef, steak and kidney and meat stew, while the Germans contributed *Ebswurst*, plus a rather unloved Italian tinned meat which was dubbed *Anisus Mussolini* (Mussolini's ass). One Landser stirred a large can filled with steaming hot pork goulash stew with peas. To men who hadn't eaten for a long time, everything smelled delicious.

All the food was eaten off metal plates and mess tins which were cleaned with sand after use as water was scarce. For pudding, there were tinned pears and Carnation milk. The Germans enjoyed the British tea with lots of sugar and Carnation milk, as they were used to horrible – tasting *Ersatz* coffee made from burned acorns. Real coffee was very scarce in Germany and North Africa in the Second World War.

Lee proffered an empty mess tin to one of the cooks. 'I'll take whatever you've got. But make sure you don't give me any pork or bacon.' Sitting nearby on a pile of sandbags, his desire for foods free of pork was noted by Peiper, who was a fanatical devotee of the racial policies of the Nazi Party.

To finish, the troops ate some chocolate. The Germans handed round Manner chocolate and also some *Scho-Ka-Kola*,chocolate loaded with caffeine.

'This stuff is not bad,' said Lee as he stood beside Mayne. 'It raises your blood sugar and also gives you the same caffeine hit as two cups of strong coffee. It would be an ideal ration for your SAS night missions. I believe the Germans have also developed special chocolate containing the drug Pervitin. It is an amphetamine but much stronger than our own Benzedrine tablets. The only snag is that it is highly addictive and can cause a lot of health problems, such as skin sores and rotten teeth.'

Finally, the German troops handed round Oberst cigarettes which were provided in their own ration packs, along with Jupiter matches. The courtyard smelled of burning tobacco.

'You like our cigarettes,Tommy. We grow our own

tobacco in Germany you know,' said one German soldier.

'Isn't it strange?' said Mayne. 'A few hours ago, we were all trying to kill each other and now we're fighting together, against a common enemy, as though we'd always been friends. German soldiers aren't really different from our own boys. Long and short. Thin and fat. The same hopes and fears, the same desires. It makes me wonder if we should really be sorting out our problems by killing one another. And all this coming from a man who is personally responsible for the deaths of scores of German and Italian troops. I have killed a few with my fighting knife. I was so close I could see the fear in their eyes and smell their bad breath, their sweat and their blood.'

'I know what you mean,' said Lee, 'There is a saying that people are really the same all over the world. It's just that the German people have been held hostage by the most evil regime the world has ever seen. The same might be said for the Japanese, who are under the control of a vicious military dictatorship, and an Emperor who just does what the Generals and Admirals tell him to do.'

*******

On the other side of the courtyard, Peiper had a very different perspective on things as he spoke to his commanding officer.

'Oberst Seidel, I must protest at the conduct of our men. It is bad enough that we fight alongside our foes, the British. But now we're fraternizing with them. This is bad for morale. In the SS we were always taught to hate our enemies, to show them no mercy in combat.'

'Point taken, Peiper. But I have no personal hatred for the British. It is just that their aims conflict with our own. General Rommel has spoken of his admiration for the fighting skills of British troops. He also respects the New Zealand and Australian soldiers who have played a vital part in the battles in North Africa. And the British LRDG and SAS units have achieved spectacular results despite their relatively small numbers. Major Mayne himself has destroyed more of our aircraft than the RAF's greatest fighter aces.'

'You mention General Rommel,' said Peiper. 'Yes, I have met him and I believe he is not a true supporter of Hitler. Good soldier, yes, and a brilliant tactician but I have doubts about his loyalty to our Führer. He has refused to implement the Reich's racial policies and has ignored orders to kill Jews wherever they are found. I believe he may prove to be more of a liability than an asset in the long-term. It would not surprise me if he was in league with others who are under suspicion, such as Admiral Canaris.'

'That is enough, Peiper,' answered Seidel. 'You are not in the SS any more. You are part of the Afrika Korps and you will obey orders from your commanding officer, is that clear? There are no SS units in North Africa. Neither are there Gestapo personnel. That is why we have managed to fight a clean war without any atrocities. We treat enemy prisoners of war according to the provisions of the Geneva Convention. They receive the same rations as our own troops and medical attention if they need it. The British do the same to their prisoners. We don't want the Gestapo and SS arriving and cluttering up the battlefield with their torture chambers.'

Peiper's face fell. The conversation had not gone as he had hoped.

'There is one more matter I wish to discuss with you, Sir. The British Medical Officer, the one called Captain Lee. I believe he is a member of a non – Aryan race. A Jew. His facial features look Jewish and I noticed that he refused to eat pork.'

'But Lee is not a Jewish name,' said Seidel.

'That is true. But as Himmler has pointed out, many of the Jews who have joined the British Armed Forces have changed their names in case they are captured. I believe this Captain Lee is Jewish and I do not wish to be treated by him.'

192

'Landser Peiper, you have a fractured wrist which is deformed. If you do not get this treated you could end up with a permanent disability. As your commanding officer, I order you to be treated by Captain Lee. Our own medical officer was killed earlier in this mission. There is no – one else who can mend your wrist.'

' But…'

'No buts! That is an order, Landser Peiper. You will submit to whatever treatment the British Captain recommends or else you will face a charge.'

'Yes, Sir!'

*******

On the other side of the courtyard, Lee sipped a mug of hot, sugary tea and ate a few pieces of Scho-Ka-Kola as the patrol's radio – man, Private Mills approached him. Mills saluted.

'Yes what is it, Mills?'

'Sorry to bother you sir. I know you have to set a fracture but I've got something interesting to tell you. Major Mayne mentioned that you used to build radios and have an interest in electronics.'

'That' s correct Mills, so what do you want to tell me?'

'Well it's that control unit you took from the Marizan's back during the post – mortem. Me and Davy Atkins managed to prise it open and we found it contains a number of British radio components.'

'How extraordinary! Any ideas on how that came about?'

'Well ,we now know that there was a battle here some years ago. I guess some of our vehicles may have been captured by the Marizans and taken to their ship for examination. They may even have fallen down the chasm. We know the Cerebri are keen on recycling anything they can get their hands on so I think it's possible they used components from British Army radio sets to create Marizan control units. Perhaps because they were short of

193

their own parts.'

'That's a very interesting deduction, Mills. But is it of any practical value?'

'Well you see sir. I'm not the brightest tack in the toolbox, but I was just thinking. If we could build a small transmitter tuned to the same frequency as the Marizan control signal then we might be able to block commands from the Cerebri.'

'That is indeed a possibility, Mills. 'But such a device would have a low power output. We could only immobilise Marizans that were very close to the unit as such a device would have a limited range.'

'Yes that's true. But there's more. I was also thinking that the Marizans are controlled by the Cerebri's voice. If we connected a microphone to any device we created and amplified the mike's output then we could...take control of a Marizan. It's a long shot Captain, but I think it might work. But I'm going to need your help to build such a device. Davy knows about basic auto electrics but electronics is not his field. I know a bit about the subject but probably not as much as you sir.'

'By jove, I think you are onto something, Mills. I suggest you get on with it. I will join you and Davy as soon as I can. But first I have a patient to treat.'

'That's fine sir. We've set up a temporary workshop in one of the rooms in the fort. The one next to the sick bay, sir.'

'Good. I'll join you there as soon as I can.'

Landser Peiper lay on an old wooden table inside the makeshift sick bay. The room was filled with a mixture of British and German medical supplies retrieved from both sides' trucks. Peiper's head rested on a sandbag. Private McTavish, who had once worked as a porter at Greenock Royal Infirmary before the war, was Lee's assistant.

'I 'm going to give you an injection of a barbiturate drug into one of the veins of your good right arm. It may make you fall asleep, or just feel a bit woozy. Either way it will make the following procedure more bearable.'

Lee applied a tourniquet to Peiper's upper right arm and slapped the veins on the back of his right hand a few times to make them dilate. Then he rubbed the skin over the veins with a piece of cotton wool soaked in methylated spirit and gently inserted the needle of a glass syringe filled with sodium amytal into one of them. Slowly he depressed the plunger of the syringe and watched as Peiper's eyelids fluttered and then closed.

Now he had to get to work. Peiper had two large lacerations in his left forearm plus a broken wrist. He thought the best technique to induce anaesthesia would be the so – called Bier block in which a blood pressure – measuring cuff is applied to the upper arm and then inflated to stop all blood flow. Then local anaesthetic would be injected into the veins of the forearm to make it free of sensation, allowing the otherwise painful resetting of the bones to be carried out.

'I am going to carry out a Bier block,' he told McTavish. Ever see it being used to help set fractures at the casualty department at Greenock Royal Infirmary?

'Beer block! Oh aye, sir. I remember a guy who drank ten pints of Tennent's at the Oban Bar after he had finished his shift at Scott's Shipyard. He got beaten up outside the pub and was brought to the Royal Infirmary by ambulance. His face was swollen up like a football. Absolutely pissed he was. He was so drunk the doctor stitched up his scalp lacerations without any anaesthetic and he didn't feel a thing.'

'Well I suppose you could call that a Beer block, McTavish. Actually I was meaning a Bier block, spelled B-I-E-R. Named after its inventor, August Bier, who created the technique in 1908. It is also known as intravenous regional anaesthesia. A blood pressure cuff is applied to an upper limb and inflated to thirty millimetres above arterial pressure. This stops all blood flow. Then you inject some local anaesthetic into a vein and you have a very effective temporary anaesthesia.'

'Oh, I see.'

McTavish helped Lee apply the blood pressure cuff to the upper left arm. Then Lee inflated it by pumping a black rubber bulb. After making sure the cuff was fully inflated and checking the pressure, Lee injected some procaine into the back of Peiper's left hand. He waited five minutes for the local anaesthetic to take effect and then began suturing the two lacerations after cleaning them with an iodine-based antiseptic. Peiper felt nothing and snored loudly.

The next job was to reset the broken wrist. This was not difficult, but was easier with an assistant. Lee applied traction in the correct directions and felt the bones click into place. Then, with the help of McTavish, he applied a wooden splint, bound tightly in place with bandages. It would never be as effective as a plaster cast but would do until Peiper could be seen at a field hospital.

'That's you all fixed up, Peiper,' said Lee. But the young German soldier had not woken up. Instead he was muttering in incomprehensible German. Lee guessed he was not truly asleep . Neither was he fully awake. Instead he was in that twilight state between sleeping and waking, what scientists called a hypnopompic state, akin to a hypnotic trance in which suggestions could be passed into the unconscious. It was widely known that barbiturate drugs could induce this state.

Lee had read a few books about hypnosis and was familiar with the work of the American psychiatrist Dr Milton H. Erickson, who practised in Michigan. He knew there was a technique called hypnotic regression in which it was possible to take people back in time to discover the cause of a psychological problem. And —as a result of his extensive reading —he knew exactly how to do it. He had a golden opportunity to find out why Hans hated heat and loved cold. And perhaps also the reason he loathed Jews so much.

Lee elected to speak to Hans in German as he thought this would be more readily accepted by his unconscious.

'I wish to speak to the back of Hans' mind, what is

commonly called the unconscious. Hans' unconscious, are you willing to work with me to discover the reason why Hans hates heat and loves cold?'

'Yes, I am,' said Hans.

'Excellent. Now I want you to think of a recent time when you had this feeling of hating heat. Now allow this feeling to intensify, it is growing stronger, you can think of nothing else. Now I want you to imagine you are on a railway train which is going back in time. You are getting younger and smaller, smaller and younger. You are now on a bridge which is taking you back to the very first time you ever had this feeling. I am going to count from one to ten. When I reach ten you will be back to a few minutes before the very first time you ever had this feeling.'

Lee counted slowly from one to ten.

'I have now reached ten. You are now back to just before the very first time you had this feeling. Where are you? Are you indoors or outside?

'I am outside.'

'Are you alone or is someone with you?'

'I am with my friend Manny.'

'How old are you? Look at your feet?'

'I am five years old.'

'Report what's happening!'

'It's a cold night in January. I am playing with my friend Manny. He is eight years old. He is Jewish. We have made a bonfire.'

'What happens next?'

'I fall into the fire. Manny must have pushed me. My back is burning. Pain. Awful!'

Lee was sceptical of this story. Why would his friend Manny push him into a fire?

'I want you to run through this event again, Hans. But this time I want you to view it from a different angle, as though you were seeing it through a camera set up on a tripod well to the side of the bonfire. So you can see yourself this time instead of seeing everything through your own eyes.'

'I am seeing what happened once more. And I can see I am wearing a red jumper. I am illuminated by the flames of the bonfire. I have slipped on some ice and I have fallen into the flames. Aargh! Pain! My jumper is burning. I smell burnt wool. But now Manny has pulled me out of the bonfire. He has put me on my stomach and pulled up my jumper. He is piling snow onto the burnt area.'

Lee smiled. He knew that the treatment of burns was changing. Up until now there had been a belief in Medicine that some kind of cream or lotion should always be put on burns. Some people even applied butter as a first –aid measure and topical tannic acid was still used in most hospitals. But some doctors had started to question these methods and believed that the best first aid measure was the application of local cooling in the form of cold water or even ice. It was known that burned RAF pilots who parachuted into freezing cold salt water did better. So Manny's instinctive treatment was actually excellent first aid. As well as relieving pain, it probably limited the extent of the burnt area.

'So Hans, can you now see it was all an accident? And Manny pulled you from the flames and carried out some first aid. He saved you.

'Yes I now realize this'

'So you now have no reason to hate the Jews. Manny saved your life and applied first aid.'

Lee realized that both of Peiper's problems —his contempt for Jews and his love of cold and hatred of heat—stemmed from this one incident, which had been forgotten by his conscious mind. Now he had to complete his healing work.

'Where is Manny now?'

'He's dead. He was sent to Auschwitz where he was gassed and cremated.'

'I want you to imagine that Manny is up there in heaven. What words would you say to him now?'

'Manny please forgive me. I had no idea what had really happened.'

'And what does Manny say back to you?'

'I forgive you, Hans.'

'Now put your arms round one another and feel the love flowing between you. From Hans to Manny. And from Manny back to Hans. Manny will always be with you, Hans, and you now have a chance to atone for your past sins and become a good person. Hitler is evil, Hans. Just imagine you can see Hitler with a pair of horns coming out his head. He is possessed by Satan. He will not save Germany, he is going to destroy it. He will even destroy the entire world if he gets the chance. But you can help prevent this happening, Hans. Work with the Allies to ensure Hitler is defeated. But first we must beat the Marizans and the Cerebri and get back to Alexandria.'

'Yes, I will help you. Hitler is evil and he must be defeated. And we must also beat the Marizans and the Cerebri.'

Peiper's eyes opened slowly. He was still groggy from the barbiturate that was circulating in his bloodstream. Suddenly, there was a loud buzzing noise, which made all the medical instruments in the room vibrate. Lee pushed the door open and climbed up the steps to the parapets. All the soldiers —British and German —pointed at a large, silver, disc – shaped craft which had appeared above the fort. It was another Marizan saucer, double the size of the three others that had previously touched down. The craft orbited the fort and then landed in a cloud of dust on flat ground about eight hundred yards to the north -west. A large ramp lowered from the underside of the craft, and several Marizans pushed out two silver, wheeled contraptions. Each had a barrel and two wheels. They were obviously artillery pieces of some kind. And they were both aimed at the fort.

# Chapter 30

## Electric Guns

Mayne, Lee and Seidel stood on the parapets and studied the newly-arrived Marizan transport ship through binoculars. Six creatures had emerged from the craft and were setting up what looked like two field guns. The warriors attached various odd-looking devices to the barrel, and one Marizan carried a crate of shells. Everything was made of a gleaming, silver metal which sparkled in the sunshine.

'These guns don't look that big,' said Mayne to Lee who was standing beside him. 'What sort of firepower do they have? Are they equivalent to our own 25 – pounder field guns, perhaps?'

'Oh, I think they are considerably more powerful than that,' said Lee. 'And I don't think they work using conventional explosives, either. Everything to do with the Marizans involves electricity, have you noticed that? And I can see the Marizans are attaching thick electric cables to the weapons, which lead all the way back to their craft. No, I think what we are looking at here is some form of electromagnetic cannon which fires projectiles at enormous speeds.'

' Really, I find that hard to believe.'

'Oh, but scientists here on Earth have been working on such a weapon since the mid-19th century. In 1845 Professor Kristian Birkeland of the University of Oslo suggested that it would be possible to build what he described as a coil gun. Then in 1918 Louis Octave Touchon Villeplee wrote a paper about a so -called electric cannon.'

'How do you know all this? Don't tell, me I know! You read about it in a book in the Mitchell Library didn't you? But how does such an electric cannon work?'

'The principle is really quite simple, Paddy. You will already be familiar with the conventional rotary electric motor, which uses an armature. Now just imagine one of these rolled out flat and you have the so-called linear induction motor which propels metal objects in the horizontal plane as well as levitating them. After the war it is likely that Britain, and other countries, will build monorails which work using such motors. I believe the Marizan guns work using the same method. They employ a powerful electromagnetic field to send metal projectiles at high speed towards their target – which happens to be us!'

'So what sort of explosive warheads do the projectiles carry?'

'They don't need one. They fly so fast —quicker than any artillery shell we have in our inventory — that they destroy their target through sheer kinetic energy. I would estimate that a hit from one of these Marizan rounds would have the same destructive power as an eight inch naval shell.'

'Really! So what we can do to stop them?'

'Nothing, absolutely nothing! If we still had *Honeychile* we could plaster them at long range with her 75mm, but she has been destroyed. Our fifty - calibre Brownings could just about reach them but at that range the rounds won't penetrate the Marizans' body armour and we are almost out of ammunition anyway. The smartest thing we can do is evacuate the front of the fort at both ground floor and parapet level and move all our troops and weapons to the rear. Once the Marizans open fire, the entire front of the fort will collapse. I suggest you do this immediately, Paddy, while I check on Davy and Private Mills.'

'OK ,will do!'

Mayne lifted up his bullhorn and screamed orders to his troops, which Seidel immediately repeated in German:

'Attention all soldiers! The fort is about to be hit by heavy artillery! We believe the front of the building is in danger of imminent collapse. All soldiers are to pick up their weapons and move to the back of the fort. And hurry!'

All the soldiers —British and German —began to dismantle their machine guns and the troops on the parapets made their way down the stone stairs to the ground floor level carrying their personal weapons. Lee entered the room at the side of the courtyard where Davy Atkins and Private Mills were working. Suddenly, there was a loud bang as a supersonic projectile hit the front of the fort. Two further rounds followed, just a few seconds apart. Lee estimated that each Marizan electric cannon had a rate of fire of six rounds per minute, and there were two of them. Within just one minute, the fort had been hit by twelve rounds, each causing a large hole and extensive cracking. The inevitable happened and a few seconds later the entire front of the building collapsed. The sound of shearing masonry was deafening. Where there had once been thick, stone walls fifty feet high there was now a pile of rubble. A large cloud of sand-coloured dust rose into the sky, temporarily blotting out the sun.

Most of the soldiers manning the fort were buried under the debris. Any who were not already dead would die soon from blood loss, dehydration and suffocation. In the meantime, the buried casualties screamed with the pain of their broken limbs. Mayne survived unscathed as he had been standing at the back of the courtyard, on the southern side, when the collapse occurred.

Lee, Mills and Davy Atkins were also unharmed as they had been in one of the small rooms at the side of the fort when the front disintegrated. A sleeping Peiper was in the same position in the adjacent chamber. Unfortunately, broken masonry was piled up against the doors of both rooms, preventing them from being opened outwards. The only other survivor was Oberst Seidel who was lying in the courtyard with a bleeding head wound. He had been hit by a flying stone and knocked out but was still alive.

Mayne knocked on the upper part of the door of the

makeshift radio workshop.

'Lee, Mills, Davy are you all right in there?'

'We're unharmed. But there's rubble piled up against the door. We can't get it open. Can you shift it for us?'

'I'll do my best. But I'll have to hide for a while. A force of Marizans is marching towards the fort. They will be looking for survivors for recycling. I suggest you also hide from view. I'll be back soon.'

Mayne looked over the pile of rubble that had once been the front of the fort. A large force of Marizans was heading towards him from the transport saucer, untroubled by defensive fire. Mayne opened the heavy wooden rear door of the fort and looked around for somewhere to conceal himself. He spotted one of the captured Bedford OY lorries that the Germans had brought over and got into the back of the vehicle, lying down on the wooden truck bed and pulling a tarpaulin over himself. It was not a perfect hiding place but it would have to do.

Back inside the fort, Lee looked through the small barred window in the door and saw several Marizans climbing over the pile of rubble that used to be the front of the fort.

'Marizans coming! Everyone hide!'

All three soldiers flattened themselves against the wall next to the door. If a Marizan happened to look in the window, he would see only the makeshift workbench.

Lee heard footsteps. It was a Marizan walking up to the door. The air was filled with choking dust and Lee prayed that no-one would cough and give the game away. The Marizan came very close to the small window, and checked out the inside of the room with its tiny inbuilt camera. All the creature could see was a pile of electronic junk on the table. There were no humans. Inside the room, on either side of the door, the three British soldiers remained motionless, holding their breath. Would the Marizan remove the rubble, open the door and search the room thoroughly?

After a moment the Marizan lost interest and

investigated the room next door, in which Peiper lay sleeping. The door to this room was also jammed with rubble. Furthermore the small window was covered on the inside by a makeshift privacy curtain made from a piece of sacking. Once again the Marizan paused and wondered whether this chamber should be investigated further.

The Marizan's thought process was interrupted by a series of electronic bleeping tones. The creature turned round and faced another of its kind which had two horizontal black stripes painted on its chest armour, suggesting some kind of rank. It had two blinking cylindrical red lights on its shoulders which looked like epaulettes. Lee risked a brief glance through the window. *So that is how the Marizans communicate with one another*, he thought. *They don't speak.*

The Marizan with the black stripes emitted a few more electronic tones from its red lights and pointed at the rubble in the courtyard. It was giving a command to the more junior Marizan to drag some of the more accessible casualties out of the debris. Lee guessed they would be taken back to the main ship for recycling.

Meanwhile, at the back of the fort, Mayne sweated under a heavy tarpaulin. How long could he stay hidden like this? The temperature in the shade must be at least 120 degrees Fahrenheit. His mouth felt parched. Right now he could drink a gallon of cold water. Or better still, a couple of pints of cool Guinness at his local back in Northern Ireland. And he also needed a pee. And a crap.

Then Mayne heard the sound of the rusting hinges of the rear door of the fort creaking. The Marizans had arrived to check the lorries. From the sound of their footsteps on the concrete strip behind the fort, Mayne estimated there were two of them.

Slowly and systematically, the Marizans checked every vehicle. They looked inside each cab, inspected under the chassis and then investigated the truck bed. After a further ten minutes, Mayne heard the sound of his truck's tailgate being unlatched and pulled down. He held his breath as even the slight movement of his chest might be spotted by the Marizans.

The two creatures studied the tarpaulin which was draped over the truck bed. Something was under it. Should they lift off the tarpaulin and see what was there? For a few seconds the Marizans' electronically enhanced brains considered the problem with computer logic and came up with a solution. They would scan the area with their infra – red sensors. If there was a human underneath the tarpaulin then its body heat would show up on their scan. That was standard procedure. Lifting the tarpaulin would waste energy.

The tiny camera mounted in each Marizan's metal headband glowed red for a moment and then the result flashed up in the Marizans' inner vision: *scan negative*. The Marizans turned round, their task complete, and re-entered the fort through the back door.

Mayne heard the creatures go back into the fort and waited five minutes before shedding the tarpaulin. He ran up to the back door and opened it slightly. The Marizans had all gone. And they had taken Seidel with them. As he had a quick pee against the wall of the fort, he reflected on his good fortune. He had no idea why the Marizans had failed to spot him. In fact, it was the high ambient temperature which had saved him. It was so hot that his body had failed to show up as a 'warm' area on an infra – red scan as the truck bed was the same temperature as his body.

Mayne downed a full canteen of water and then made his way to the door of the room in which his three comrades were trapped. He rapped on the door. 'Peter, Davy, Mills. Can you hear me? The Marizans have all gone so I'm going to remove all this rubble from outside the door so I can free you. It will probably take me twenty or thirty minutes. And I have to take a dump first.'

'OK, Paddy, that's fine,' said Lee before turning to his colleagues.

'It will be half-an-hour or so before we get out of this

room. I suggest we use this time to work on the Marizan control device. Mills, what have you done so far?'

'Well sir, I've taken the Number 11 radio set out of Truck Six. And I also have the rather crude transmitter that the Jerries planted to enable them to track us. Just as well you stopped the Major from wrecking it because it is has been an invaluable source of electronic parts.'

'So what are you proposing, Mills?' said Lee.

'Well sir, as I said earlier , we could build a device which emits a simple carrier wave at the same frequency as the Marizan control signal. That would stop the Cerebri from controlling the Marizans. I think the technical term is jamming, sir.'

' Well that would help us,' said Lee. 'But it would only work at close range because of the limited power output of such a device. So we wouldn't be able to immobilize every Marizan, just ones that were within say, 100 feet of the device.'

'That's true sir. But as I explained earlier, the Cerebri controls the Marizans with voice commands. This little unit on each Marizan's back converts these speech signals into electronic impulses the creature can understand. If we connected an audio circuit to the device and plugged in a microphone then we could control a single Marizan. I would need to rewire the Marizan receiver unit slightly to make sure it would make a radio – frequency connection with our device.'

'We may need to reverse the polarity. Do you have a microphone?' asked Lee. 'I thought the number 11 set was for Morse code transmissions only?'

'At great distances we only use Morse code,' answered Mills. 'But the Number 11 set can also be used for speech transmissions and we have a moving – coil microphone as part of our basic radio kit.'

'Well let's get started then,' said Lee. 'But what are we going to use for a soldering iron? We don't have electric power in the fort.'

'That's no problem. The Weller company in the USA

has manufactured a special soldering iron for the US military that works off six volts, and we have one. Look, Captain. '

Mills pointed at the dirt floor. One of the six-volt lead-acid batteries from the Chevys was sitting on the ground, next to the Enigma machine, which was wrapped in a blanket. Attached to the battery by two large, copper alligator clips and a long black cotton - covered lead was a chunky soldering iron with a Bakelite handle, which was lying on the table. A thin wisp of white smoke rose vertically from the hot tip of the instrument.

'Well it looks as though you have got everything we need, Mills. Let's get started! Davy, while we are working on the circuits see if you can knock together a portable power pack. We want this thing to be easily transportable so a vehicle battery will be too big and heavy.'

'OK ,Captain. How about a couple of zinc -carbon dry cell six- volt lantern batteries strapped together and wired in parallel? The box – shaped sort with connectors that look like springs. There are a few of them in a crate over there.'

'That would be ideal.'

While the three soldiers worked on creating the electronic control device, Mayne had arrived from the latrines and started the back – breaking work of lifting the masonry from the front of the door. After thirty minutes he had completed the task.The door swung open towards him on rusty hinges.

'Perfect timing, Paddy. We're just about ready to test the device,' said Lee.

The captured Marizan control receiver lay on the table. Lee connected it to the six-volt supply and two tiny light bulbs on the back of the unit glowed. One was red, the other green. Lee guessed that red signified power and green that a signal had been received. Or maybe it was the other way round? He wasn't sure.

'Right. So far so good. Let's switch on the blocking unit and see what happens.'

The device that Lee had created with the help of Mills and Davy was based on the chassis of the Number 11 set but with the casing removed to save weight and allow adjustments. A few components from the German radio bug had also been incorporated. Davy connected the power supply lead to the two six-volt batteries and pushed down the toggle switch. After a couple of minutes the heater filaments of the four thermionic valves glowed cherry red. If the device was working then it would now be emitting a radio signal on the Marizan frequency. But how could they tell if it worked?

As the four soldiers watched, the green light on the Marizan control unit flickered, went out and then came on again.

'It's working. I think. The unit is now receiving our blocking signal,' said Davy.

'We can't be sure of that,' said Mills.

'He's right,' said Lee. 'We will have to test it properly.'

' And how are we going to do that?' asked Mayne.

'There's only one way,' replied Lee. 'We're going to have to go back into the chasm and test out the device on a live Marizan.'

'Is that not going to be rather dangerous?' asked Mayne.

'I'm afraid it is going to be risky. Very risky indeed. And I have a horrible feeling that we may die in the attempt!'

# Chapter 31

# Weapons of Mass Destruction

'Stay calm, Peiper,' said Lee. 'We'll have you out of there in a jiffy.' The four British soldiers lifted the heavy pieces of broken masonry which prevented the door from opening outwards. It was back-breaking work but with four pairs of hands, the job was done in ten minutes

Lee and Mayne entered the room while Davy and Mills stood outside. Peiper lay on the table, only half – awake as he was still affected by the intravenous barbiturate that Lee had administered. The room smelled of blood and antiseptic.

'Captain Lee. I have had time to reflect on things and am now ashamed at the conduct of my nation during this war. I am a patriotic German but I now realise that we were misled by a madman who was obsessed with the idea that the Aryan race is superior to all others. We were wrong to blame the Jews for all Germany's economic woes. By wiping them out, Hitler has destroyed much of German culture. He's insane and may even be possessed by Satan.'

Lee was gobsmacked. His impromptu regression hypnotherapy had worked even better than he had expected.

'How very true,' said Lee. 'And his policies before the war lead to an exodus of Jewish scientists to the USA. Many of them are now working for the Allies, like Professor Albert Einstein for example.'

'I profoundly regret my past actions,' said Peiper. 'But now I wish to make amends. I want to help the Allies to defeat Hitler because he is evil and he lied to us. I will do anything you ask.'

'Well, well, well. A Damascene conversion indeed,' said Mayne. 'Yes, we will accept your help, won't we

Peter? But first we have to defeat the Marizans and the Cerebri. Then we have to get a certain item back to Alexandria, by hook or by crook. However, the odds are not on our side. We started this mission with eighteen men, including myself. Now only four of our force are left. All our heavy weapons have been destroyed. Most of our trucks have been wrecked. All we have left are our personal weapons, a small quantity of ammunition and some grenades. There is no prospect of a rescue force arriving as the Eighth Army is retreating to a new defence line at El Alamein. The only light at the end of the tunnel is that Captain Lee —with the assistance of Mills and Davy – has built a device which just might help us fight the Marizans. But it hasn't been tested yet. We don't really know if it will work. That is why we intend to go back into the chasm to try it out on a Marizan.'

'Then let me come with you. I will help you fight the Marizans and the Cerebri. You have a saying in your language, have you not : my enemy's enemy is my friend,' said Peiper, not realising he was repeating Seidel's exact words.

'But you are in no fit state to take part in combat,' said Lee. 'You are still drowsy from that barbiturate I gave you. And you have a splint on your left hand. You can't fire a rifle or a sub-machine gun with one hand ....and how are we going to get you into the chasm?'

'I can still fire my Luger pistol and use a fighting knife. Perhaps you can lend me one of your British Sykes-Fairbairn commando knives. I have heard it is the best weapon of its kind in the world. And you can lower me into the chasm on the end of a rope.'

'Very well. On your own head be it,' said Mayne. He handed Peiper his commando knife before turning to Lee.

'Peter, assuming we can get into the chasm without injury and succeed in overpowering a Marizan and then take control of it, what do we do after that?'

'You know Paddy, I have no idea. I don't have a plan. And that both scares me and excites me! But when the time comes, I am sure I'll think of something!'

Moments later, the four British soldiers stood on the edge of the chasm. There were no Marizans in sight. The distant electric cannons and the saucers appeared unmanned. *For some reason all the creatures have been recalled to the main ship*, thought Lee. *Perhaps they need to recharge their batteries?*

Peiper had a thick rope round his chest just under his armpits and was being lowered into the fissure by the four British soldiers. He held onto the rope with his good right hand. It was hard, slow work. The four British troops carried Thompson sub - machine guns on slings and Davy was wearing a backpack containing the electronic gizmo that he had built with Mills and Lee.

Eventually Peiper reached the flat corridor floor at the bottom of the chasm and shouted up to Mayne:

'I'm down!'

'OK, Peiper. Slip the loop of rope off your body and we'll pull it up. We're coming down one at a time.'

Mayne, Davy and Lee were all lowered into the chasm using the same method. Then Mills,who was the best climber of the four, abseiled down the rope. Two of the light fittings in the corridor were still broken so Mayne shone a torch to get a better view. There were no Marizans. Surely there would be at least one on sentry duty?

Suddenly, two pairs of glowing white eyes appeared in the darkness at the end of the corridor. 'There's two of them,' said Lee. 'We only need one so we'll have to destroy the other.'

'Leave this to me,' said Mayne as he pulled a grenade from his webbing pouch and pulled the pin.

'No, we can't use grenades,' said Lee. 'One of them must be left undamaged.'

'Kill the left one,' ordered Mayne. 'We'll capture the one on the right.'

Mayne and Mills raised their Thompsons and fired a few short bursts at the left-hand Marizan. The slow-moving forty-five calibre rounds bounced harmlessly off the chest armour. Both soldiers aimed at the vulnerable neck area just below the Marizan's transparent visor but the Thompson was notoriously inaccurate and sprayed bullets everywhere. The Marizan continued relentlessly towards Mills and touched his face with its outstretched right hand. There was a blue flash, a crackling sound and a smell of burning flesh as Mills fell dead.

Mills' sacrifice was not in vain because it distracted the Marizan for a vital moment. Mayne got behind the creature, put his left arm around the warrior's head, tilted it back and stabbed the creature in the centre of the front of the neck. Mayne's first knife thrust severed the windpipe but did not penetrate the tough cervical vertebrae. He repeated the move, aiming a bit higher. This time the blade penetrated the soft intervertebral disc and severed the spine. The creature slumped to the ground, paralysed from the neck down.

Now the three surviving British soldiers concentrated on immobilizing the second Marizan. Mayne rugby tackled the creature. It crashed to the ground with a clang of metal. Then Mayne sat on top of its chest to keep it down, pulled its dart gun from its holster and threw it away. Lee and Davy both gripped the creature's right forearm as they struggled to prevent the Marizan from touching any of them with its right hand.

'We've got to roll the Marizan onto its front so that we can get at the control unit on its back,' said Lee. 'On the count of three, I want you to roll the creature over. One, two ,three… roll.'

The three soldiers flipped the Marizan into a prone position. It was still struggling to break free, and it took the combined muscle power of three soldiers to keep it down.

'Davy get the signal blocker out your back pack and switch it on,' said Lee.

Davy slipped the backpack off his shoulders and carefully pulled out the makeshift device. He clicked the main power switch on. A red light glowed.

'It's not working,' said Mayne, who noticed the Marizan was still struggling.

'Give it time,' said Lee. 'Remember the valves take a couple of minutes to heat up.'

Two minutes later, the heater filaments of the four thermionic valves glowed cherry red. Almost immediately, the tiny green light on the Marizan control unit on the creature's back went out for a couple of seconds, then came on again.

'Paddy, Davy you can get off the Marizan now. It's quite safe….I think!' said Lee.

The two soldiers stood up, leaving the Marizan lying face down on the ground. It had stopped moving.

'Oh my giddy aunt, it's working,' said Lee. 'We've blocked the Cerebri's control signal. Now we need to test the voice control system. Davy, remove the Marizan control box from the back of the creature and replace it with our own modified unit.'

It took Davy only two minutes to remove the device from the creature's back and replace it with the captured unit which had been altered to accept signals from the control device. Lee took a moving- coil microphone from Davy's backpack, plugged it into a jack socket in the side of the British machine and spoke a few words into it:

'Marizan, stand up.'

With a clank of metal, the creature got up from the ground and stood erect, as still as a statue.

'Marizan, lift your right arm.'

The creature obeyed Lee's command.

'Marizan, lift your left hand.'

Once more the creature did as Lee requested.

'Amazing,' said Mayne. 'Does that mean we can get the creature to do anything we want? And could we take over more of them?'

'In theory, yes,' said Lee, who was rubbing his hands together with excitement. 'But we would need more of the Marizan receivers – the little black things on their backs

— to do that. However, we only need one Marizan to help us carry out my plan.'

'I thought you didn't have a plan?' asked Mayne.

'Oh, that was fifteen minutes ago. I've just had an idea which might work, although it is highly dangerous!'

As Davy held the makeshift radio device in front of him, Lee spoke once more into the microphone:

'Marizan, we need your help to prevent the end of civilization. From now on you will accept only voice commands from me. If you pick up any transmissions from the Cerebri they will be ignored. Indicate your understanding.'

The Marizan nodded.

'And we are going to give you a name, to distinguish you from the other Marizans. From now you will respond to the name Roger. Is that understood?'

Again the Marizan nodded.

Lee put the radio device back into the canvas backpack and allowed the top of the microphone to project slightly under the flap, which was secured by two brass press-studs. Then he slipped it over his own shoulders, removed the creature's dart gun from its holster and gave it to the Marizan. Lee turned his head to the right so his voice was picked up by the mike and spoke once more.

'Marizan...or should I say Roger.... we're going to leave all our weapons on the ground and walk slowly in front of you with our hands in the air. We're going to walk along the corridor and enter the ship where we'll go to the main chamber containing the Cerebri. It will look as though we have laid down our arms and surrendered. Is that command understood?'

'Roger' nodded once more.

*******

Just a few hundred feet away, deep inside the alien ship, Oberst Seidel lay slumped in a chair, his wrists secured to the arms of the seat with straps as two Marizans removed a metal skull cap from his head. Numerous curly coloured wires connected the skull cap to a nearby control console. The mind transfer had been completed and the Cerebri had absorbed all Seidel's memories and intellect.

The giant brain floating in the huge tank felt a sensation akin to pleasure. Suddenly, a pair of metal power-operated doors at the far end of the chamber opened with a faint electric whine. Four men in beige uniforms entered, their hands held high. Three were British, one was German. They were followed by a Marizan, who was pointing a dart gun at them.

The electronic voice of the Cerebri boomed out from the speaker grille.

'What is this? Four humans surrendering. You have always resisted. Why the change of mind?'

'Oh, once we saw the overwhelming power of the Cerebri and your foot soldiers, the Marizans, we realised there was no point in fighting,' said Lee. 'We have therefore decided to capitulate and I submit myself for mind processing. I want my intellect to help the Cerebri achieve its worthy goals. You are without a doubt the supreme organism in the Universe. Your power and wisdom are awesome.'

'That is logical. Come forward.'

Lee chuckled inwardly. A little flattery went a long way, even when you were dealing with a brain in a tank.

'Yes, we humans do have our weaknesses,' said Lee. And so do the Cerebri. Your own life-support system, for example, is controlled by that unit next to your fluid-filled tank.'

Lee pointed to a silver console bedecked with flashing lights and a display screen rather like an oscilloscope.

'If someone was to destroy that, you would become unconscious immediately and die from oxygen starvation within three minutes.'

'But you cannot destroy it. It is too strongly made to be damaged with your bare hands and you have no explosives.'

'Quite so. A human cannot destroy that unit. But a Marizan can!'

Lee turned his head to the right and shouted into the microphone.

'Roger, destroy that life-support unit.'

'Stop them!' said the Cerebri.

But the Marizan guards in the chamber were too far away to intervene in time. Roger moved forward to the console and placed his right hand on it. There was a blue flash and a burning smell as thick, black smoke issued from the vents on each side of the unit. All the flashing lights on the front went out.

'Aaargh..... help me!' said the Cerebri. 'I feel dizzy. Everything is going grey......aaaargh!'

Most of the Marizans, except Roger, collapsed on the ground, their control signals gone. Others froze like statues. Lee watched the huge brain in the tank and checked his watch. The Cerebri was no longer conscious as its supply of oxygenated blood had been cut off. The mechanical pump which served as its heart had stopped. Three minutes later, the colour of the giant brain changed. Originally an overall light grey, dark areas appeared, which spread, until the whole of the cerebral cortex was a gooey black. Then bits of the brain started to fall off. Some fell to the bottom of the tank and others floated. The fluid in the tank, once crystal clear, became murky.

Lee knew what had happened. The entire brain had suffered an infarction. All the tissues were undergoing irreversible ischaemic necrosis – a death of all the brain cells, in common parlance. Soon the brain would be mush and eventually all that would be left would be dirty water. Lee was fascinated. He was the first person in the history of medicine to actually see a cerebral infarct happening with his own eyes. If only he had recorded it with a movie camera he could show it at one of the Thursday evening meetings of the Glasgow University Medico – Chirurgical Society.

Mayne also found the spectacle fascinating but he knew

they still had a job to do – they had to get the Enigma machine back to Alexandria. He nudged Lee.

'Well done, Peter. The Cerebri is dead. And the Marizans have been neutralised. But now we have to get out of here and deliver the Enigma machine to our intelligence people in Alex.'

'Yes, of course you're right, Paddy. We must leave immediately.'

Davy looked a bit disconsolate. 'Excuse me Captain. I know I don't have your level of education. I'm really just a mechanic and all that. But is there not something you've forgotten?'

'What's that?' said Lee, rather irritated.

'Well, when we were up on the parapets of the fort, being spoken to by that silver ball thing, I remember the Cerebri said something about a homing beacon and a million alien ships heading towards Earth.'

'Damn, blast, the homing beacon. I'd forgotten about that,' said Lee. 'Maybe Roger can answer a few questions.' He turned to the tame Marizan.

'Roger, I'm going to ask you a few questions. I know you can't speak. Nod for Yes and shake your head from side to side for No. Indicate your understanding.'

Roger nodded.

'Roger, first question. The Cerebri is now dead. Is the homing beacon still active?'

Roger nodded.

'Do you know where the homing beacon is located?'

Roger shook his head .

'Well that figures. An ordinary foot soldier wouldn't know a thing like that. We could search the ship from top to bottom. But it could take forever as this craft is probably a mile across. And we have no idea what it looks like or how to turn it off. However, there may be another way. Roger, the Cerebri mentioned weapons of mass destruction. Are there any on this ship?'

Roger nodded.

'Do you know where they are?'

Again the creature bowed forward.

'Roger, I want you to lead us to the place where the devices are stored.'

The Marizan turned and walked down the corridor for about a hundred yards. The four soldiers followed the creature, taking care not to trip over the many deactivated Marizans that were lying on the ground. Roger stopped outside a metal door and pressed a red button. The door slid open with an electric whine to reveal a room about a hundred feet long and twenty feet wide. Stacked along one wall were about fifty cylindrical objects. The smallest were about the size of a Thermos flask, the next size up was about as big as a milk churn and the largest were six feet in height. Lee guessed that he was looking at different sizes of tactical nuclear weapons.

In one corner were two wooden crates packed with straw. One contained British hand grenades which looked like small metal pineapples. The other crate had their German equivalents, which resembled potato mashers. Lee guessed the Marizans were evaluating the relatively primitive weapons that were used on Earth.

'So these are nuclear weapons,' said Mayne. 'Tell me Peter, what sort of explosive power do they have?'

'Well I guess the smallest one is really a kind of nuclear hand grenade with a relatively low yield. I would go for the one about the size of a milk churn. The next size up may be too powerful for our purposes. We don't want to wipe out half of Egypt.'

Lee pointed to the middle - sized weapon. 'Roger, will this be big enough to totally obliterate this ship and destroy the homing beacon?'

The Marizan nodded.

'Now I need to know how to set it off. Does the device have a time fuse?'

Roger shook his head.

Lee looked at the milk-churn sized weapon again. It had a slot on one side, at the top of which was a lever which could slide down, plus a switch.

'I get it. The devices are set off manually by the Marizans. The Cerebri uses individual Marizans as suicide bombers. Remember, we saw one Marizan destroy the German armoured car with a backpack full of explosives.'

'Roger, can you detonate the device for us at an agreed time?'

Roger shook his head from side to side.

Lee was perplexed. How was this possible? Then he had an idea.

'Roger, are you fitted with an inhibitor which prevents you from carrying out actions which may harm yourself?'

Roger nodded.

'Does the Cerebri deactivate this inhibitor when a suicide bombing is required?'

Roger nodded once more.

Lee slapped his head. 'We're back to square one. I have no idea how to switch off Roger's inhibitor.'

'We still have some Nobel 808 plastic explosive in the trucks,' said Mayne. 'Supposing we fitted a charge to one of these bombs and attached a time pencil and detonator. We would have enough time to get away.'

'Unfortunately I don't think that would work,' said Lee. 'If we detonated a conventional explosive charge next to one of these bombs it would very likely damage it and maybe cause leakage of radioactive material, but I don't think it would cause a nuclear explosion.'

The three British soldiers looked despondent. Was there no solution to their dilemma? Then Peiper stepped forward and turned to face them all.

'I have a solution to your problem, my friends. I will set off the device for you. I will be your suicide bomber!'

# Chapter 32

# Resurrection

'You can't be serious, laddie!' said Mayne. 'You're planning to sacrifice yourself to detonate this bomb. We don't do things like that in the British Army……and I'm sure it's not an approved method in the Afrika Korps, either.'

'It's the only way!' said Peiper. 'We can't set a time fuse. The only option is for me to pull down this lever when the time comes! The Reich's Japanese allies do this sort of thing all the time. During the attack on the American Pearl Harbour base in 1941 one of their Zeroes was damaged by anti-aircraft fire and deliberately crashed into a hangar. The carnage was enormous.

'Besides, there are a couple of other things I must tell you about. My entire family was killed in an RAF bombing raid on Cologne a few weeks ago—the so called 1,000 bomber raid — so there is no-one in my life. And am I ashamed to say that I did a terrible thing in France in 1940. I was responsible for the deaths of a platoon of Scottish soldiers of the 51$^{st}$ Highland Division. They had surrendered and I had them executed.'

Lee shuddered. That was his regiment and he had heard of this incident.

'After the war is over the Allies will put me on trial. I will probably be hanged.'

'But if you help us, then this will be taken into account when you are put on trial. I will make a personal plea for a lenient sentence. I used to be a solicitor before the war, you know,' said Mayne.

'That's very generous of you, Major, but I'm certain that all that awaits me is the hangman's noose. I said I will help you, and best way I can assist the Allied war effort is by pulling that lever when the time comes. But I've said enough, it' s time for you to go.'

'I'm afraid he's correct in everything he says,' said Lee. 'It really is the only way.'

Mayne looked down at the floor for a moment. He had spent much of the last two years killing Germans, sometimes with his bare hands. And now he was trying to save the life of a former SS man who had been responsible for the deaths of British POWs. Such were the ironies of war.

'OK Peter, you and Peiper are right. We have to leave now. Tell me, what is the likely explosive power of this bomb, and how far will we have to travel to be out of harm's way?'

'I can't be certain but from what I have read, a nuclear bomb of this size is likely to have an explosive power equivalent to 60,000 tons of TNT. We'll have to get at least twenty-five miles away to be safe, preferably more. There will be an initial bright flash which could burn our retinas. The best protection from this would be welding goggles, but we don't have any. So the next best option would be to cover our eyes and lie face down on the ground. Everything within a few miles of the bomb will be incinerated and there will be a blast wave extending for twenty miles or more which could cause structural damage. The immediate area of the blast will also be left radioactive for years and this could cause long-term problems such as birth defects, leukaemia and other cancers. However, as the Qattara Depression and the Great Sand Sea to the north are largely uninhabited that is not going to be a major problem.'

Mayne was gobsmacked. He had thought that Nobel 808 was a powerful explosive but it paled into insignificance compared with a nuclear warhead. He processed the information for a moment and then came to a decision.

'OK ,this is what we are going to do. Peiper will stay in the ship and detonate the bomb when the time comes. Myself, Peter and Davy will climb back up to the surface

221

and find a truck that still works, and get the hell out of here. We'll be taking the Enigma machine with us. And I think it might be an idea to take one of these bombs, the smallest example about the size of a Thermos flask. Our boffins back home will want to examine it. It will probably take us fifteen minutes to get to the surface and another ten to get the truck ready. I would allow another two hours for us to get well clear of this area. The Chevy can do thirty miles per hour but over rough ground we might only average twenty. And we have to allow time for the odd puncture or getting stuck in the sand. Peiper, I suggest you detonate the bomb exactly three hours from now. I wouldn't wait any longer because that Marizan fleet could arrive at any moment . If it does, I want you to detonate the bomb immediately, even if we're not clear.'

Peiper looked at his watch. 'Very well, it is agreed.'

The three British soldiers shook hands with the former SS man and turned to leave the room. Peiper had a last few words for Mayne.

'Major Mayne, it has been an honour to serve under you. I have learned a lot about the British in the last twenty-four hours. You are a brave and honourable man and a clever and resourceful soldier. It seems that not everything we were taught about the British was correct.'

Lee was last to leave the room and, as he left, Peiper saluted him. 'Farewell Captain Lee, or should I say *Shalom Aleichem*. And I hope your people manage to establish a homeland in Palestine after the war and live in peace with your Arab neighbours.'

As the British soldiers made their way along the corridor to the bottom of the chasm where two ropes still dangled, Peiper sat on a wooden ammunition crate, lit a cigarette, drank some water and ate some chocolate. It would be a long wait, he thought, and he had nothing to occupy his attention. In the corner of the room Roger, the tame Marizan, stood motionless awaiting instructions. The makeshift control unit lay on the floor in a backpack.

Back in the main control room of the ship, the Cerebri lay dead in its fluid tank. The once-clear water was stained an inky black and pieces of necrotic brain lay at the bottom of the tank. The life support unit was burned and blackened. But about twenty yards away was a second identical unit hidden from view, which the British soldiers had failed to spot. This was the Cerebri's reserve life support system. At present it was not powered up, but exactly five minutes after the British soldiers left, a single red light flickered into life on the front control panel, followed by two more. Then the oscilloscope display came on as the back-up system booted up. The ship's main computer re-started and —as various systems came back on line—it analysed what had happened. The Cerebri had died because its life support system had been destroyed. The back-up system was now working but the Cerebri had undergone ischaemic necrosis. It was a condition which doctors on the planet Earth regarded as irreversible. But the Cerebri had technology which could reverse this pathological process. Within a minute, the large fluid tank was bathed in a pulsating violet light as individual brain cells travelled back in time to the moment before the supply of oxygen stopped. Slowly, the black staining in the water cleared, and the debris in the bottom of the tank started to float up towards the centre of the huge glass container where the dark mass of dead cells was slowly changing colour, first to dark grey and then to light grey. To an observer standing outside the tank, it would have looked as though a film of the Cerebri's demise was being run backwards. Five minutes later the giant brain was fully functioning and awake as it barked out its first commands to its army of foot soldiers.

'Marizans, awaken and serve the Cerebri! Search for intruders! Seek and kill!'

The Cerebri was back in business. And it wanted revenge!

# Chapter 33

# Escape!

Mayne, Lee and Davy climbed over the southern lip of the fissure and headed for what had once been the front wall of the fort. All that was left was a pile of rubble, in the middle of which was the burned-out, smoking hulk of a German four-wheeled armoured car. The air was thick with smoke and beige dust. The charred corpses of the three crewmen of the armoured vehicle were still at their fighting positions. Three of the five surviving British Chevys lay buried under the rubble. Of the other two, one had been badly crushed by falling masonry.

Davy tried the starter motor of the only intact truck. The six-cylinder engine fired up instantly. The vehicle had a flat tyre but that was easily sorted. And the all-important Enigma machine was safe as it had been moved to the makeshift radio room before the fighting started.

'Let's get this truck loaded with as much water and fuel as she can carry.' said Mayne. Plus any rations we have left. Peter, you can help me with this while Davy sorts the wheel. I want to be out of here in fifteen minutes.'

Fourteen minutes later, Davy opened the rear doors of the fort and steered the truck through the narrow doorway, edging past the parked German lorries. It was a tight squeeze. Davy drove due east for the first half mile to avoid the fissure and the remaining landmines, and then turned north towards the rough track which lead to Alexandria. The road went past two Marizan saucers and the wrecked German vehicles, which both lay north-west of the fort. There were a few nervous moments as the truck crept by, but the saucers appeared unoccupied as all the warriors had been summoned to the main ship. Two Marizan field guns lay abandoned at the side of the road.

*******

As the British vehicle began its long, arduous journey towards Alexandria, back in the alien ship Peiper sat on a wooden ammunition crate and ate his last bar of Manner's chocolate. He had less than three hours to live. Who would have thought that his life would end like this, all alone in a metal-walled bomb room inside a giant spaceship deep below the Qattara Depression, with only an electrically-operated zombie for company?

In the USA, prisoners facing execution were offered a last meal. What would he choose? He had enjoyed one of the best meals of his life when he had visited Salzburg, Austria in April 1936. A hot, steaming *bratwurst* from a street vendor, served on a white china plate with a fresh bread roll, salty butter and tangy mustard. All washed down with a bottle of *Schartner Bombe*, that delicious lemon-flavoured soft drink that Austrians loved. Afterwards for 'pudding' he had a slice of Bavarian cream cake and a large cup of freshly -ground coffee at a nearby *Konditorei*. Or maybe he could have some *Wiener Schnitzel* and *Sauerkraut* followed by a large helping of *Apfelstrudel* with whipped cream. Another thing he craved was fresh Hungarian *Gulasch* or a bowl of his mother's home-made *Gulaschsuppe*,a broth so thick it was often eaten as a main course with bread. To wash it down he would have a large one - litre *Stein* of Beck's beer. Peiper salivated at the thought.

His gastronomic fantasies were interrupted by the sound of metal grinding against metal. Peiper finished his chocolate and walked along the corridor to investigate as the last square of Manner's melted in his mouth. What he saw stopped him dead in his tracks. The Cerebri was still in its tank but apparently now in a healthy condition as it was intact and light grey in colour, not black. The nutrition fluid was clear and bubbles rose from the giant brain to the surface of the liquid. *How had that happened?* And several Marizans —who had collapsed earlier—were rising from the floor. Others who had simply 'frozen' while in a standing position were moving their limbs slowly, as though they were awakening from hibernation.

Peiper had no idea what had happened but he knew he had to get out of the room …and fast! He turned round and fled a hundred yards back down the corridor towards the bomb room. As he did so, he noticed vertical slots at regular intervals along the left-hand wall.

Peiper charged into the bomb room, almost colliding with Roger who was standing as motionless as a statue. He picked up the microphone of the control unit and spoke to the creature:

'Roger, the slots in the wall. Do they contain power-operated fire doors?'

Roger nodded.

'I know you can't speak but can you show me how to trigger them?'

Roger walked into the corridor and pointed at a circular object in the ceiling.

'I get it! It's a smoke detector. When it is stimulated the fire doors close automatically!'

Peiper rummaged in one of the crates of grenades and found some straw and old newspapers. He rolled some straw in a couple of sheets of newspaper, lit the end with his cigarette lighter and held it aloft just below the smoke detector. Would his makeshift blazing torch produce enough smoke to set off the fire alarm?

'Come on! Come on!' he screamed. Several Marizans had appeared at the end of the corridor, having returned to normal wakefulness. They were marching towards him.

BLEEP! …BLEEP!…BLEEP!...BLEEP!

The noise of the fire alarm resounded through the ship. With a faint electric whirr, several metal fire doors closed. One Marizan was caught between a closing door and the opposite wall. Other creatures arrived and pulled the door open with brute strength, freeing their fellow warrior. But four other stout metal doors slid shut between Peiper and the approaching creatures. For the moment he was safe.

But, thought Peiper, it wouldn't take the Cerebri long to work out what had happened and take counter-measures.

Peiper spoke into the microphone once more.

'Roger, can the Cerebri deactivate the fire alarm?'

The Marizan nodded.

'Do you know a way that we can stop the doors from opening?'

Roger nodded and walked into the corridor. He approached a metal panel on the wall held in place with four rivets and ripped it off to reveal a mass of thick red and black electrical cables and junction boxes. Then the creature put the palm of its right hand on the wires. There was a blue flash, a few small orange flames and black smoke. The cables melted, leaving a gooey mess of burnt plastic and melted copper. Roger had cut the power supply to the doors.

'Well done, Roger,' said Peiper.

A moment later, the beeping noise stopped, but the doors remained closed. Peiper knew the Cerebri would surely find a way for the Marizans to get through them. They might have to force them open or burn a hole in them. But at the very least, he had bought some time for his British friends to get away. He studied his watch. Forty-five minutes had now elapsed since the three British soldiers had said their farewells. They would be fifteen minutes or more into their journey to Alexandria. He would need to hold off the Marizans for another hour or two. Would he manage that?

*******

Several miles away, Lee perched on the hard, canvas - covered front passenger seat of the Chevy truck as Davy drove as fast as he dared towards Alexandria. The road was nothing more than a rough dirt track littered with potholes and large stones. In 1942 there were very few tarmac roads in Egypt. Lee's back ached with the discomfort of the crude seat and the ancient cart- spring, live rear axle suspension, which gave passengers a hard ride. Every bump and rut in the road seemed to jar his spine. He hoped that after the war was over, vehicle designers would specify seats which offered decent lumbar support and sophisticated suspension systems which cushioned bumps. The jolting, uncomfortable ride didn't seem to faze Mayne, who was taking a much-needed nap on the wooden bench seat in the rear of the truck.

Lee consulted his watch. They had been driving for just twenty minutes and covered only a few miles. Not nearly far enough to escape a nuclear blast. He hoped Peiper would keep his word. And what would happen if the entire Marizan space fleet arrived in the next couple of hours?

*******

Seven miles away, Peiper and Roger dragged some wooden ammunition crates into the corridor and piled them on top of one another to form a makeshift barricade just twenty yards from the nearest fire door. Most of the boxes were empty, but some contained British and German grenades and 0.303 inch ammunition. The rifle-calibre bullets were useless against Marizans but Peiper did find three German *Stielhandgranate* stick grenades and five British Mills bombs. This would help him hold off the creatures for a while, but the problem would be the sheer number of them. He had seen only a handful but there could be hundreds, even thousands, being brought out of hibernation

Everything was quiet for ten minutes. Then Peiper heard a loud crackling sound accompanied by an electronic buzz. He edged around the crates and put his ear to the nearest fire door. The noise sounded like an electric arc-welding unit. But how long would it take to cut a Marizan-sized hole in the door? He checked his watch and waited. Eleven minutes later there was a loud clang which he assumed was a large rectangle of metal hitting the ground. The Marizans had three more doors to burn through. That would take them another thirty-three minutes. How on earth was he going to defend himself against a massed attack? Could Roger help?

*******

Thirteen miles away, the Chevy truck continued its slow, uncomfortable journey towards the north-east. Mayne had woken up and was now fully wide awake. Like most Special Forces soldiers he had developed the ability to sleep almost anywhere, regardless of the ambient noise and discomfort, and then awaken feeling refreshed.

Lee decided that it was time to have a chat with his two colleagues and found he had to shout to be heard over the noise of the six-cylinder engine and the slipstream.

'We all need to be clear about what we have to do when the bomb goes off. The first thing you will be aware of is a brilliant flash of white light which will reflect off the sand, even in broad daylight. When that happens do not …and I repeat ….do not…look back at the blast. It is so bright it will burn your retinas and cause permanent blindness. When the flash occurs, Davy I want you to stop the vehicle immediately. Then we must all get out, get well clear of the truck and lie face down in the sand. If we can find some kind of hollow in the ground or even a cave, so much the better.

The flash will come first, followed by the sound of the explosion. Just like in a thunderstorm as light travels much faster than sound. We will need to remain stationary for thirty minutes, during which time a hot blast wave will pass over us. It will be the like the worst sandstorm you ever encountered. After that we can move on.'

'Will the truck still work after the blast?' asked Davy.

'That's a good question.' said Lee. 'From what I have read, a nuclear explosion is likely to cause an electromagnetic pulse which will fry any kind of electronic circuit. However, I don't think it would affect the very simple electrics of the Chevy's ignition system, which relies on nothing more than a contact breaker and an ignition coil. On the other hand, the blast wave might wreck the truck. If that was to happen we could be stranded in the desert, far from help!'

*******

Fifteen miles away, Peiper crouched behind the ammunition crates as the Marizans slowly cut their way through the last metal fire door. The creatures were creating an oblong hole just large enough for one of their warriors to climb through. Peiper checked the time again. In three minutes the first Marizan would be through the hole, followed no doubt by many more.

Peiper had an idea and spoke to Roger using the microphone, 'Roger, can you kill another Marizan using your dart gun?'

Roger pointed at his chest armour and shook his head. Then he put a finger on his neck, touched the area of his windpipe and nodded.

'I get it,' said Peiper. 'The dart is likely to bounce off chest armour. But if you aim for that weak spot in the neck it will kill. Roger, I want you to use your dart gun against the first Marizan that climbs through the hole. Aim for the neck. Wait for my command.'

There was a loud clang as a large rectangle of shining metal fell on the corridor floor. A Marizan clambered through the rectangular hole, which had scorched and melted edges It was just large enough to allow a single creature to get through.

'Roger, shoot!' said Peiper.

A small dart shot through the air from Roger's gun and struck the Marizan in the front of the neck. Electricity crackled. Small blue lightning bolts fizzled down the creature's limbs and torso. Then it froze. Motionless.

The attacking force now had a big problem as their way was blocked by a dead Marizan, which was wedged in the hole. Three other warriors tried to pull their moribund colleague out the hole but a kind of electronic *rigor mortis* seemed to have set in and it was a difficult task.

Now Peiper exploited the Marizans' momentary confusion by delivering his own attack. With only one useful hand he couldn't pull out the pin of a Mills bomb in the usual way. But he could use his teeth to do the job and — after priming a British grenade this way — pushed it into the small gap between the dead Marizan's head and the remaining section of the door. He heard it hit the ground and then delivered two more of the British bombs the same way. Four seconds after priming, each grenade exploded, sending splinters of metal everywhere. Two Marizans behind the door were killed and three damaged. But more were coming. Lots more.

Black smoke poured out of the space around the dead Marizan, making Peiper cough. Everything went quiet for five minutes. Then, four pairs of white hands wrenched the dead creature backwards out of the hole and a Marizan burst forwards through the aperture followed by two more.

'Roger, shoot them all,' said Peiper.

Roger's dart hit the neck of the left-hand creature, which died immediately. But he missed the second which was moving too fast. That creature fired back with its own gun. Peiper and Roger ducked and the dart hit the front of an ammunition crate. The German soldier pulled out the pin of a Mills bomb with his teeth and chucked it at the creatures, followed by another. There were two loud bangs as shrapnel flew everywhere. Peiper and Roger were well protected behind the crate, but one Marizan was killed by the metal fragments while a second was damaged. Now five more creatures climbed through the hole in the door and headed towards Peiper. He had used up all the Mills bombs but had a few German stick grenades. But the creatures were now too close to use them.

'Roger, fall back to the bomb room! Now!'

Peiper grabbed the backpack containing the control unit and microphone and raced into the bomb room, narrowly avoiding the outstretched right hand of a Marizan. Roger followed and pressed a large red button to the left of the door. It slid shut, just closing in the faces of five approaching Marizans. Then Roger ripped off the metal panel to the right of the door and used his electrified right hand to fry the wires. The door was now stuck in the shut position.

Peiper approached the cylindrical, silver, milk churn – sized atom bomb which was standing upright a few feet from the door, and flicked the arming switch on the side. A pilot light next to it glowed red. All he had to do now was push down the black detonation lever on the side of the weapon and it would explode.

He turned round and saw that a tiny hole had appeared near the top of the door. The borders of the hole glowed red hot and a shower of sparks fell on the floor. In eleven minutes the Marizans would be through the door and it would all be over. He could detonate the bomb now but if he could wait another eleven minutes – or even longer – then it would give his British friends more time to get clear of the blast.

'Roger, get your dart gun ready. Shoot any Marizans that come through the door.'

\*\*\*\*\*\*\*

Twenty- three miles away, Davy struggled with the heavy steering of the Chevy truck as it negotiated the badly rutted, potholed road.

'Cor blimey this is some road, Captain! Could do with some tarmacadam! And I think one of our leaf springs is gone. We really should stop to replace it.'

'No,' said Lee. 'We must get as far away from the blast as possible. We can look at the suspension later. Keep going! As fast as possible. That's an order, by the way.'

\*\*\*\*\*\*\*

Back at the bomb room, the Marizans' electric cutting

torch had completed its work. A warrior pushed on the burned - out panel and a rectangle of scorched metal fell on the floor with a loud clang. Roger shot the first creature which came through the hole, but this time the Marizan staggered forward as it died, allowing two further creatures to enter. Roger fired again, killing one more Marizan but the second fired back and hit Roger in the neck. The 'tame' Marizan convulsed with the electric shock and fell on the floor, dead.

Peiper had left the remaining grenades in the ammunition boxes in the corridor but he had his 9mm Luger pistol in a holster on his belt. He pulled it out and fired seven rounds in quick succession at the Marizan that had killed Roger. Five bullets bounced off the chest armour but two hit the front of the creature's neck. It collapsed on the floor.

Peiper had no more bullets left so he chucked his gun at the creatures and pulled out his British Sykes-Fairbairn fighting knife. He lunged forward, putting all his body weight behind his thrust and plunged the razor-sharp blade into the front of a Marizan's neck, severing the creature's spine. The warrior slumped onto the floor. But three more warriors had entered the room and one touched him on the face with its right hand. The powerful electric shock burned his face and caused his heart to go into ventricular fibrillation. In his last two seconds of consciousness, Peiper fell on the bomb's lever, pushing it down. The last thing he saw before he died was Manny's face.

*******

Twenty-seven miles away, Lee, Davy and Mayne saw the entire desert plus the bonnet and front wings of the Chevy illuminated by a brilliant white light. It was like a lightning flash but much brighter and lasted far longer. Three years later, an American scientist would describe a nuclear explosion as being 'brighter than a thousand suns.' Two minutes later there was a loud roar which nearly deafened them and left their ears ringing.

As previously instructed, Davy brought the Chevy to a complete stop.

'Everyone out,' said Lee. Keep looking to the north-east. Don't look back. Get at least twenty-five yards from the vehicle and lie face down. Don't move until I give the command.'

The three soldiers scrambled clear of the vehicle, lay face down in the desert and waited, hands covering their eyes. Fourteen minutes later, the blast wave hit them. It was scorching hot and consisted mainly of sand. Fortunately there were no trees which might have been uprooted by the blast. After a few minutes the wind subsided.

'OK,' said Lee. We can get up now. And it's quite safe to look back now.'

Lee, Mayne and Davy turned towards the south-west and saw a sight they would never forget. A huge glowing cloud shaped like a mushroom was rising high into the sky. Lee thought it must be two miles high. Inside the pillar of rising black, brown and white smoke were glowing orange flames and multiple lightning bolts. A rapidly – expanding doughnut of white cloud surrounded the mushroom.

*******

Fifty miles away to the north-west, the observer in the dorsal Perspex bubble of a twin-engine RAF Bristol Beaufighter heavy fighter flying at 15,000 feet spotted the explosion.

'Crikey, what is that?' he said to his pilot over the intercom. 'Has a Jerry ammunition dump exploded or what?'

*******

Twenty-three miles to the south-west of the British

aircraft, the three British soldiers stood in awe at the spectacle that was unfolding in front of them. The power of the atom had caused the biggest technologically-generated explosion that had ever occurred in the history of the planet Earth. Nothing they would ever see for the rest of their lives would compare with this.

'Well, I think we've done enough sightseeing. Let's get back to the Chevy and finish our mission.' said Mayne. The three soldiers turned round and looked at where the Chevy had been standing. Lee felt a lump in his throat as he saw what had happened. The vehicle had been flipped over by the blast wave and was partially buried. Only the four wheels and the chassis were projecting above the sand. There was only one thing they could do now. Walk back to Alexandria. But would that be possible or would they die in the attempt?

# Chapter 34

# Ordeal

'Could we not dig it out?' asked Davy. 'Then we could flip it over, get it back on its wheels and drive back to Alex. A lot easier than hoofing it!'

'That wouldn't work,' said Lee.' These trucks weigh thirty hundredweight. Three thousand three hundred and sixty pounds. 'We would need an Army recovery vehicle with a crane to right it. A Scammell or an AEC Matador, perhaps. And right now, I bet there isn't one within a hundred miles of this spot.

'No, what I think we should do is recover as much as possible from the truck. We will need to dig with our hands as we don't even have a spade. Then we will have to walk towards Alexandria carrying as much as we can,' said Lee.

'I agree,' said Mayne.

For the next hour, the three men excavated the sand under the truck. They found a single spade which made things easier. Eventually they recovered the Enigma machine and Lee's pack containing the small tactical nuclear weapon. They also found two partially - filled jerrycans of water, some bars of chocolate and a few cans of bully beef.

'We don't have a compass,' said Mayne. 'But if we stick to this track it will eventually lead to Alexandria. With recent Axis advances on the battlefield, I have no idea where our front lines are. They could be twenty miles from here or a hundred. But there's always the chance we might come across one of our own long-range patrols.'

'Or a German or Italian patrol,' said Lee. 'Have you thought about that?'

'Yes I have,' answered Mayne. 'But we'll have to risk it.'

The three men set off in single file. Mayne was leading, carrying a jerrycan . Lee followed behind, holding the precious Enigma machine in front of him. In his backpack was the alien nuclear weapon. Davy brought up the rear, gripping the handle of the second jerrycan. All three men carried chocolate and canned bully beef in the pouches of their webbing sets. They left their guns behind to save weight.

In his youth, Lee had gone on many country walks. On a few occasions, he had gone hillwalking in the Campsies, and in 1938 had even climbed Ben Lomond. But these were relatively short walks in cool conditions. Even in midsummer, the temperature in Glasgow rarely exceeded 68 degrees Fahrenhcit and was often much cooler, with considerable rain.

The Egyptian desert in late June was one of the hottest places on Earth with temperatures of up to 120 degrees Fahrenheit. With a high blazing sun, no cloud and low humidity, the human body soon lost water at an alarming rate through perspiration and breathing. Lee knew from his medical training that even in cool conditions, without any exertion, the human body needed at least a litre and a half of water a day to remain hydrated. The two partially- filled jerrycans of water they carried would sustain three men for a couple of days at most. Maybe even less than that with all the walking they were doing. After a couple of days of marching in the hot sun, their water would run out and they would rapidly become dehydrated. Eventually they would die.

On the first day of their march towards Alexandria, the three men walked for seven hours and then collapsed exhausted in the sand. They took shelter under an abandoned British Army Bedford QL truck which was lying by the roadside. The three men searched the vehicle for rations or water but there were none. Mayne suggested they all drink the water from the vehicle's radiator but they found it was dry as it had a bullet hole in it.

On the second day, the three soldiers had a quick

breakfast of bully beef and some water and then took a dump in the sand before heading along the track to Alexandria. Davy's jerrycan was now empty so he discarded it and took Lee's backpack on his shoulders.

Five hours later, Lee was thirstier than he had ever felt in his life. His mouth felt dry and his tongue had swollen up to the point that it was difficult to speak. His lips were covered with painful sores and his face was red and blistered from the constant sun exposure. His legs felt like jelly and it was an effort to put one in front of the other.

Ten minutes later, Mayne collapsed. Davy and Lee went up to him at once and gave him some water. Mayne's lips and tongue were badly swollen and he could barely speak.

'I can't go any further. Too hot. Too thirsty. Too weak. You must get the Enigma to Alex.' Then Mayne closed his eyes. Lee felt his pulse. It was fast and weak. And he was still breathing. He was still alive but would die if he wasn't rehydrated soon.

Lee and Davy drank the small amount of remaining water from the jerrycan and headed north-east along the track. They had to find help for Mayne ….and soon. But there were no troops or vehicles to be seen. There weren't even any aircraft in the sky.

Thirty minutes later, Davy collapsed. There was nothing Lee could do for him. He didn't even have any water to give to him. Hoisting Davy's pack onto his shoulders, Lee headed along the track to Alexandria. But how long could he keep going in this energy -sapping heat with no water, while carrying a backpack and an Enigma machine?

Lee felt dizzy and light - headed. Then he saw images appearing in front of him. He knew he was becoming delirious because of dehydration. Soon he would be suffering from heatstroke which could be fatal if untreated.

*I am seated in the University Café in Byres Road enjoying a tall glass of Barr's Iron-Brew with ice. Lots of ice. The glass is so cold that condensation is forming on it.*

*Now Dino speaks. 'Would you like another glass of Iron-Brew, Mr Lee? Or maybe some ginger beer? Or some Barr's American cream soda? And perhaps a large helping of my home – made ice cream?'*

Lee felt his legs turning to jelly. He wanted to fall to the ground but let himself down gently so as not to damage the precious Enigma machine. Then he rested his head on the warm sand. He was going to die alone of thirst more than two thousand miles from home. Just before he closed his eyes he saw an aircraft flying overhead. It turned round and circled his position at low level. The pilot waved from the cockpit. It had a heavily-framed glasshouse canopy and two round engines. Lee recognised it as a Junkers Ju 88. He was either going to die or be captured by the Germans. To be honest he didn't care. All he wanted to do now was sleep. Sleep forever. Lee closed his eyes.

*I am playing in the sand on the beach at Brodick on the Isle of Arran with my brother Leslie. The date is 19th July 1927. I hear the sound of seagulls and the waves crashing on the shore. The beach smells of salt water, hot sand and Nivea cream. The sun is shining and there are a few fleecy white clouds high in the blue sky. They look like clumps of cotton wool. The large mountain, Goat Fell, looks magnificent in the bright summer sunshine, all green and brown. A black Model T Ford makes its way along the tarred road next to the seafront at fifteen miles an hour, emitting clouds of white exhaust smoke. I am licking an ice cream cone. It tastes sweet and creamy. Leslie is building a sandcastle. A paddle steamer with twin black and yellow funnels, a black hull and white superstructure is tied up at Brodick Pier. It is the 'Jeanie Deans'. My mother sits in a black and yellow striped wooden deck chair reading 'The Scottish Daily Express' while my father is smoking his pipe. Someone is playing an Al Jolson record on a portable clockwork gramophone.*

*I am excited because at five o' clock we are all going for high tea in a local café. Haddock and chips and Heinz tomato ketchup served with buttered Mother's Pride bread. And American Coca Cola to drink. And then then we are all going to Brodick's tiny cinema to see the latest Charlie Chaplin comedy.*

Lee opened his eyes. 'Easy, Captain,' said a voice which had a foreign accent. Lee thought it was probably German. An officer gave Lee cool water from a canteen. He felt the cold liquid wet his parched lips. Some ran down his chin and wet his battledress top.

'Once you've finished this one, you can drink two more.'

Lee looked around. Three soldiers stood ten yards from him in front of a vehicle which looked like a German four-wheeled armoured car. Lee was sure they were talking in German.

'Captain Peter Lee. Royal Army Medical Corps. 76896527.'

His benefactor laughed. 'Relax Captain, we're not Germans. We're South Africans. I 'm Captain Van Der Graaf of the South African First Infantry Division. Some of us speak in Afrikaans. It is based on Dutch, but sounds a bit like German. And you think our armoured car is German, don't you? No, it's a Marmon Herrington. Built in South Africa.'

'How did you find me?' asked Lee.

'Simple detective work,' answered Captain Van Der Graaf. 'An RAF Beaufighter crew spotted a huge explosion in the Qattara Depression from a considerable distance. We thought it might be a secret Jerry ammunition dump going up so we sent out aircraft to investigate. A squadron of Bristol Blenheim IV light bombers, to be precise.'

'Just before I passed out I saw a Junkers Ju 88,' said Lee.

'No, that Junkers was actually a Blenheim. The two aircraft are often confused because they do look a bit alike with their glasshouse canopies and twin round engines.'

'There are two others in my party, back down the road. They need urgent medical attention.'

'Don't worry, we've already found them and given

them some water. We are going to take all three of you to a field hospital and after that to Alexandria for further treatment.'

Lee felt himself being lifted onto a stretcher and then into the back of an Austin K2 Ambulance. His lids felt heavy and he fell asleep …. and resumed his dream about Brodick.

# Chapter 35

# Recovery

Lee leaned forward in his blue and white striped pyjamas to allow the Army doctor to examine his chest. After lifting up Lee's pyjama jacket, the physician went through all the stages of clinical examination as he had been taught at medical school. Inspection, percussion, palpation and finally, auscultation. The doctor listened to all the zones of Lee's thorax with his stethoscope and smiled in satisfaction.

'Well there are no signs of any chest infection or a pleural effusion. Clinically, you now have no signs of dehydration either. We took the saline drip down yesterday and I understand from Sister that you are now eating and drinking normally. Your urine output is fine. How about your bowels?'

'No problem. I moved them this morning. And I'm pleased to see you have lovely Izal Medicated toilet paper in your W.C.s. '

'Good,' said the doctor. 'If there are no further problems then we can discharge you tomorrow. You and your two friends have been given a week's leave to complete your recovery before you return to your units.'

In the bed to Lee's right, Mayne was sitting up reading a copy of *Picture Post*. In the bed on the other side, Davy was sipping a glass of orange squash while he read a 1938 copy of *Autocar* magazine. It had a road test on the latest version of the Austin Seven.

'I'll put the radio on for you before I leave,' said the doctor. 'I think it is about time for the BBC news.' The physician turned a Bakelite rotary switch on the large, varnished wooden Bush radio which stood on a table nearby. The circular tuning dial was already set to receive the BBC Overseas Service. After a couple of minutes, the valves warmed up, the 'magic eye' tuning aid glowed bright green and a deep male voice emanated from the brass grille on the front of the radio.

'This is the BBC Overseas Service broadcasting on Short Wave from London. Here is the latest news read by Alvar Lidell. The War Office has just announced that the RAF carried out a spectacular raid on German positions just north of the Qattara Depression in Egypt last week. Two squadrons of four - engine Handley Page Halifax bombers of the RAF's Desert Air Force attacked a large ammunition dump using a new type of bomb developed by British scientists. This extremely large weapon weighing 4,000 pounds contains a considerable quantity of magnesium, resulting in a very bright flash and a large smoke cloud resembling a mushroom. The mission was completely successful and the target was totally destroyed. The attack was pressed home with great determination despite ferocious anti-aircraft fire. Three of our Halifaxes are missing.

'In Washington, President Roosevelt has confirmed that American industrial position is at an all - time high. Factory output in May 1942 was … '

Mayne turned the radio off so he could talk to the others.

'So the cover - up has started already,' said Mayne. 'Lots of people would have seen the nuclear blast from a considerable distance. The War Office had to say something or people would get suspicious. However, I am not interested in fake news. What is important is the future of the SAS and the LRDG. The three of us make a good team. We should work together again some time. How about it, Peter? We could do with a doctor on our missions. Especially someone like you who is bit of a know - all. When you are in the SAS, you never know when you're going to come across electro-zombies from outer space controlled by an alien brain in a tank in a giant spaceship. How about it, Peter?'

'I'm going to have to pass on that, Paddy. It has been the most exciting adventure of my life. But I don't think I'm cut out to be an action hero. I see my future as being an ordinary doctor, whether in the Army or civilian life.'

Mayne sighed and turned to Davy.

'How about you, Davy? Do you fancy being seconded to the SAS on a permanent basis? We are always looking for mechanics. David Stirling has told me that we are adopting a new tactic for our airfield raids. We are going to drive onto the airstrips at night using large numbers of the new American Willys MB jeeps and shoot up the enemy planes with machine guns. You've probably heard of the new American jeep. It's a mechanical marvel. Four-wheel drive. Light, manoeuvrable and with a powerful four – cylinder Go Devil engine. It can travel where no other vehicle can go.'

'Sounds good. Count me in,' said Davy.

'Just one more thing,' said Mayne. 'The SAS is a young organisation. We've only been in existence for less than a year. But we have a tradition that we have a piss – up at the end of each mission. To celebrate the success of the operation and toast those who didn't come back. In short, the three of us are going to get hammered tomorrow night. When I was in Tobruk, I met an RAMC Captain. What was his name? …Captain Hudson I think it was. He looked a bit like the late Private Mills. Anyway, he said there was a bar in Alexandria that served beer that was so ruddy cold it had a kind of dew on the glass. I suggest we all go there tomorrow night and get rat-arsed. I believe the beer they serve is Carlsberg.'

'That's impossible,' said Lee. 'Carlsberg is only brewed in Denmark, which was occupied by the Germans in 1940. It is more likely to be Stella which is actually brewed here in Egypt.'

'Carlsberg…Stella…whatever the beer is! Are the two of you coming?'

'I'm up for it,' said Davy.

'Not me,' said Peter. 'I don't really drink. It doesn't agree with me …and I get a sore stomach into the bargain.'

'OK, how about you have just one bottle of beer to be sociable and then stick to tonic water for the rest of the night? One bottle is hardly going to kill you! After all, even teetotallers absorb alcohol from their gut every day. It is produced by fermentation in the intestines and is said to be equivalent to a half pint of beer a day,'

'How do you know that?' said Lee.

'I read it an hour ago in a copy of the *Reader's Digest*. I told you I was going to read more,' answered Mayne.

The Major grinned mischievously. Tomorrow night, Lee would be accompanying him and Davy on a visit to that bar in Alexandria. And he would make sure the short, teetotal Captain with the little moustache drank considerably more than one bottle of beer. And woke up the following morning with the mother of all hangovers. Plus a sore stomach.

# Chapter 36

# Retribution

The huge, gleaming, silver Boeing B29A Superfortress bomber cruised at 31,000 feet as it approached its target, the Japanese city of Hiroshima. Built just three months earlier at the Glenn L. Martin plant in Bellevue, Nebraska, the aircraft represented the pinnacle of American aviation design. First conceived in 1940, the giant Boeing incorporated the very latest technology including cabin pressurisation, air conditioning and four remote – controlled gun turrets aimed using gyro gunsights linked to analogue computers.

This particular B-29, *Enola Gay* was one of a small number that had been converted to *Silverplate* specification for the carriage of a single atomic bomb. The four remote - controlled gun turrets had been removed and the aircraft's sole defence was the tail turret containing two Browning fifty-calibre guns. However, no fighter opposition was expected. At this stage in the war the Japanese Air Arm was a spent force. Short of fuel, planes and pilots, the Japanese never bothered to intercept single aircraft which, in their experience, were always reconnaissance planes.

As the giant bomber approached the target, the aircraft's commander, Major Paul Tibbets (who had named the plane *Enola Gay* after his mother), pulled a lever to open the bomb bay doors, revealing the payload, an 11,000 lb atomic fission weapon named *Little Boy*. At the front of the glasshouse nose, the Boeing's bombardier, Major Thomas Ferebee, looked through his Norden bombsight— another American technological marvel —

246

and flipped the switch which allowed the Norden to control the aircraft through the automatic pilot.

At exactly 08.15 hrs the *Enola Gay* dropped the bomb from a height of 31,060 feet. As the projectile plunged towards the ground, Tibbets pushed the aircraft's nose down to gain speed and executed a perfect 180 degree turn. As the bomb doors closed, flight engineer, Staff Sergeant Wyatt E. Duzenbury, who was sitting at his control panel behind Tibbets, opened the throttles to give maximum combat power from the four 2,500 horsepower Curtiss-Wright R-3350 engines,which would allow the B-29 to exit the target area at 360 miles per hour.

When the falling bomb reached a height of 1,968 feet it detonated as planned. By this time the *Enola Gay* was more than eleven miles from the target and, although severely buffeted by the blast, it sustained no damage. 80,000 people were killed in the raid and 70,000 injured but—combined with a similar attack on Nagasaki three days later—it resulted in a Japanese surrender and the end of an ultimately pointless conflict which had cost tens of millions of lives.

On the long journey back to base on the Pacific island of Tinian, Major Tibbetts started to feel tired and went for a sleep in one of the four bunks in the gunners' compartment towards the rear of the plane, which was accessed by crawling along a pressurised tunnel above the bomb bay. His co-pilot Captain Robert A. Lewis and the two flight engineers could fly the plane for the next few hours.

As Major Tibbets started to drop off, he reflected on how the Allies' fortunes had changed over the last three years. In July 1942, Britain appeared to be on the verge of losing the war. After eighteen months of disasters and defeats, the British Eighth Army had been pushed back to a defence line at El Alamein. Then something seemed to change as the summer progressed. The appointment of a new, more confident commander, General Bernard Law Montgomery, had helped. But there was more to it than that. Up to the summer of 1942, Rommel seemed to know all of the Eighth Army's moves even before they made them. It was as if he was being tipped off. Now it was the other way round. In October 1942, superior Allied forces had crushed the Afrika Korps at the Battle of El Alamein, helped no doubt by the fact that they were now winning the Intelligence War.

Yes, some kind of intelligence breakthrough had been made in the summer of 1942. Tibbets was not to know that this had been made possible by the recovery of a crucial Enigma coding machine from the North African theatre in late June 1942. The apparatus had been flown back to Britain in an RAF Consolidated B-24 Liberator bomber and had been taken to the top-secret decoding centre at Bletchley Park where it was of great assistance in breaking German codes and producing 'Ultra' intelligence. The existence of the Enigma machine and the decoding effort at Bletchley Park was not made public until 1975. The Enigma capture at Dieppe on 19 August 1942 was not revealed until the 21st century.

Furthermore, Tibbets did not know exactly how the Allies had managed to produce a working atomic bomb by the summer of 1945. In April 1942, J. Robert Oppenheimer, the head of the Manhattan Project, had informed Roosevelt that that such a device would not be possible before 1948 as there were so many technical problems to overcome. Roosevelt had to prepare himself for an invasion of Japan in 1946 and a million Allied casualties. Then in July 1942, a strange cylindrical device about the size of a Thermos flask had been flown to the USA in a US Army Air Force Douglas C-54 Skymaster. Rumour had it that it had been recovered by British Forces in the North African desert and that it was extraterrestial in origin.

After dismantling the device, American scientists managed to reverse- engineer certain key components, resulting in the production of several atomic bombs by the summer of 1945. All of these bombs had a much smaller explosive power than the nuclear weapon that had exploded in the Qattara Depression in 1942, but they were still potent enough to bring about the surrender of Japan and avoid the massive casualties which would have resulted from a land invasion.

Tibbets knew none of these things as he closed his eyes and fell asleep on a bunk in the gunner's compartment of the *Enola Gay*. He would have no difficulty sleeping for the next sixty-two years.

# Chapter 37

# Bondage

Ian Fleming turned the wheel of his 1935 four-and-a-half litre Blower Bentley and drove through the open gates of Chartwell House, the private residence of former Prime Minister, Winston Spencer Churchill MP. It was a beautiful late autumn day. The low, weak sun illuminated the red brickwork of the house and its extensive gardens. Situated 650 feet above sea level, Chartwell had a grandstand view of the surrounding Kent countryside. The lawns and paths were strewn with dead, golden, leaves and the gardener, Clements was doing his best to rake them up. A bonfire of garden rubbish burned on a slabbed area to the rear of the property, issuing a plume of white smoke, which rose vertically in the still autumn air.

Fleming wore civilian clothes. A navy - blue wool suit, white silk shirt, knitted black woollen tie and a thick grey overcoat to keep out the autumn chill. Plus a hat. In 1945 everyone wore hats.

Fleming pressed the brass push button to the left of the heavy, varnished oak door. Churchill's wife Clementine answered.

'Ian, how nice to see you again. And how punctual you are.'

'Well , that's what comes from my years in Naval Intelligence. Admiral Godfrey was always a stickler for punctuality.'

'Winston's in the study. I'll take you through.'

Former Prime Minister, Winston Spencer Churchill stood at the window of his study, puffing a cigar. He wore a dark grey, three -piece suit, a white shirt with separate starched collar and a dark blue bow tie with white polka dots. He turned to Fleming and looked at him over the top of his half-moon specs.

'Hello Ian, good to see you again. Long time since I've seen you in civilian clothes.'

'I've been demobbed,' said Fleming. 'I've even got one of these demob suits the Government gave to every discharged serviceman. Rather cheap and nasty though. Like something out of Woolworth's. I never wear it.'

'That's a nice car you've got.'

'I'm glad you like it. A 1935 four-and-a-half litre Blower Bentley with an Amherst Villiers supercharger. Don't like the colour though. British Racing Green. I plan to have it resprayed in Battleship Grey.'

'How many miles per gallon do you get?'

'Not many!'

Their conversation was interrupted by Churchill's housekeeper, Maisie, who knocked on the door and entered, pushing a large wooden two-tier trolley laden with a very appetising breakfast. There were white china cups, matching saucers and plates and a large bowl of freshly-prepared scrambled eggs made to Fleming's own recipe:

*Twelve eggs whisked in a bowl for exactly two minutes. Heat in a pan with six ounces of butter until the eggs started to cook. Then take the pan off the heat and continue to agitate the eggs with a wooden spoon until they were fluffy. Salt and pepper added to taste and served immediately with lashings of hot, buttered toast. One can never get enough toast. Don't add milk. Milk ruined scrambled eggs though a little cream was permissible.*

Churchill served them both and the two men ate greedily, using the huge antique desk as a dining table. In 1945 eggs were strictly rationed to just one per person every five days and so were regarded as a great delicacy. Fleming had no idea where Churchill's housekeeper had got so many but ex - Prime Ministers who had won the war for Britain would have their sources.

'You must excuse me,' said Fleming as he consumed

his breakfast with relish. 'But I take great pleasure in what I eat and drink. It comes partly from being a bachelor, but mostly from a habit of being meticulous about detail.'

After just ten minutes of eating, Fleming chased the last bit of scrambled egg round the plate with his fork and put it in his mouth. There was still plenty of toast left and Fleming devoured it with some Frank Cooper's vintage Oxford marmalade. To drink, Churchill had Earl Grey tea while Fleming had three cups of strong black coffee purchased from De Bry in Oxford Street and brewed in an American Chemex. He hated tea, which he regarded as 'mud' and one of the causes of the decline of the British Empire.

But there more to come. As Fleming was drinking his last cup of coffee, Maisie entered the room once more with a tray on which were two blue china bowls of yoghurt and a large plate of fresh figs.

'You are probably wondering where I got those?' asked Churchill. 'You won't find them in any greengrocers in Britain. An Avro York transport aircraft arrived at RAF Northolt from Libya last night. The same one I used as a personal transport during the war. Serial number LV633, also known as *Ascalon*. It was carrying important diplomatic papers. Plus a few trays of fresh figs and dates. Being a former Prime Minister has its perks you know.'

The two men devoured the figs and the yoghurt which was a deep yellow colour with the consistency of thick cream, and then retired to large brown leather armchairs on either side of the fire. Three large logs were crackling in the grate as they burned. The room smelled of burning wood and wax furniture polish.

'I am glad you enjoyed your breakfast,' said Churchill. 'I know you regard it as your favourite meal of the day.'

'You know me so well,' replied Fleming. 'And I have a great love of eggs.'

'Quite so. However, I 've not asked you here today to discuss food. As you know, I 'm no longer Prime Minister. Last summer the British electorate voted for a Labour

Government. I guess they concluded that I was the best person to lead them while we were at war but socialists would be better at rebuilding Britain. Within a few years we're going to have a Welfare State and a National Health Service. Actually, I don't disagree with that. If we had stayed in power we would probably have done the same thing.'

Fleming nodded and listened attentively.

'We both have an interest in writing, Ian. I know that you are now working as Foreign Manager at the Kemsley Group which owns the Sunday Times.'

'That's correct. I oversee the paper's worldwide network of correspondents. My contract also allows me three months' holiday a year, which I take in Jamaica. In a few years I hope to move there and write novels for a living. I plan to create spy adventures based on my wartime experiences.'

'How very interesting!' Churchill puffed at his cigar and continued. 'You saw a lot of secret documents during your time with the Intelligence Branch of the Royal Navy. The German Enigma machine, for example. The various Enigma captures during the war. The decoding work at Bletchley Park and Ultra Intelligence. It has already been agreed that all this will be kept secret for another thirty years. However, I bet you haven't seen these documents.'

Churchill handed Fleming two thick Manila folders. One had *Alien Incursion 1942* written on it. The other was labelled *Operation Archer*. Fleming was a fast reader and quickly scanned both documents.

As a journalist and writer, he was amazed at what the reports revealed. In 1942 an Enigma machine had been recovered from a German radio truck in the North African desert. He already knew about that and the capture of another decoding machine at Dieppe on 19 August 1942. Both had proved vital to the decoding effort at Bletchley Park. Everything else in the reports was new to him.

In June 1942, the small force of LRDG and SAS troops that had got the Enigma out of Tobruk had taken refuge at a fort just north of the Qattara Depression. They had then come under attack from strange warrior creatures called Marizans, zombie - like beings which had been created by a giant brain in a tank, deep inside a huge alien spaceship underneath the Qattara Depression. The British and Germans had joined forces to defeat the aliens and the threat of an invasion had only been thwarted by the detonation of a nuclear device. A small atomic weapon of extraterrestial origin had been brought back to Britain and flown to the USA where it had helped accelerate the Allies' own nuclear programme.

The *Operation Archer* file was equally incredible. The Germans had developed flying saucer craft which could travel through time. They were possibly based on alien technology. The threat posed by these *Haunebu* (as they were called) had been ended by a commando raid on the factory producing them. An RAF Lancaster pilot called Simon Culver had played a crucial part in the operation. And there was a suggestion he might be a time traveller from the year 2019.

After just forty minutes of reading, Fleming put the two files on his lap. It was all so unbelievable. He had to remind himself that the date was really the 4th of November, not the 1st of April. Electrically-operated zombies, flying saucers, an alien brain in a tank, nuclear weapons. He intended to be the writer of serious spy thrillers, not a science fiction author.

'You're probably wondering if all this really happened,' said Churchill. 'But I can assure you that every word in these reports is true. The War Cabinet took the view that all this information would be too much for the general public to handle. It won't be made public until 2045. It might cause mass panic if everyone knew that there are alien races out there that want to attack us. And during the war years, we didn't want people to know that the Allies and Germans had cooperated to defeat the aliens. It would have been bad for morale. We wanted our troops and the public to hate our enemy. And we didn't want everyone to know that a former SS man who had committed atrocities had detonated the nuclear device which saved the world. There are some things the British public must never know, at least for another hundred years.

'Before I left 10 Downing Street, I had a copy of these two files made and that is what you are holding now. I cannot let you take them away but you are welcome to make a few notes for your own personal use.'

'I quite understand,' said Fleming. 'Some of this stuff is incredible. But I won't breach national security, you have my word. All the same there are some interesting names and ideas I can use.'

Fleming frantically scribbled a few pencil notes in the notebook he carried everywhere. *Honeychile ... man called Gumbold...nuclear weapons...a German tank with the number 007 on its turret ...that's an interesting number ...a golden gun...a golden eye (good name for a house!) .... and an Arab spy used a radio bug to allow the Germans to locate the vehicle.*

Churchill puffed on his cigar again and began to cough. The coughing continued for ten minutes.

'That's a nasty cough you have there, Winston, Have you seen your doctor about it?'

'Doctor…no,' replied the former Prime Minister.

'Doctor….no. That's an interesting juxtaposition of words,' said Fleming, scribbling in his note book. That could be book title.'

'But now I must leave,' said Fleming, as he rose from his armchair, putting his notebook back in his jacket pocket. 'I have a lunchtime meeting in London.'

Churchill showed him out. As Fleming stood on the front steps buttoning his coat, he turned towards the former Prime Minister.

'Just one more thing,' he said. 'That fort in the desert. Did it have a name?

'It was named after the General who ordered its construction in 1855. General Harold Knox.'

' Fort Knox,' said Fleming. 'That's the same name as the town in Kentucky where the US Army has its armoured forces HQ.'

'That's correct,' said Churchill. 'It's also where the USA stores its gold reserves.'

'How very interesting,' said Fleming as he turned to leave.

Fleming started his Bentley and drove out of the open gates of Chartwell House. Churchill waved goodbye from his study window and then dumped the two reports on the log fire. As they were slowly consumed by flames, he reflected on Fleming's plans to write spy novels in Jamaica. He admired the former Naval Commander's enthusiasm but privately, he doubted the books would ever be a success. They would probably sell about a hundred copies each. And as for his hope that they might eventually be filmed, that was also pie in the sky. Who would ever go to see a film about a British secret agent? It would be the biggest flop in film history.

# Chapter 38

# First Date

**7 October, 1946**
**The Malmaison Restaurant, Hope Street, Glasgow**

Dr Peter Lee's brow furrowed with anxiety as he looked at the Timex self-winding watch on his left wrist. It was 8.07 p.m. She was seven minutes late. Where was she?

Several months earlier, he had started a job as a senior house officer in General Medicine at Glasgow's Southern General Hospital in Govan and had become instantly attracted to his registrar, Dr Agnes Montgomerie Knight Culver. She was one grade above him but was actually two years younger, having graduated in 1943. Nancy had made rapid progress up the career ladder, having worked in Psychiatry and General Medicine, and had recently passed her M.R.C.P exam.

However, it wasn't just her intelligence and professional qualifications that had impressed him. She had nice legs and Lee was a 'leg man.' She also looked a bit like Hollywood actress Ingrid Bergman, especially when she wasn't wearing her glasses. Lee had asked her out a few times and she had always refused. But last Tuesday she had finally relented.

A moment later, Nancy Culver burst through the revolving front doors of the Malmaison, part of the huge Glasgow Central Station Hotel. She was wearing a simple red dress, flat heeled black shoes and a matching black raincoat. Nancy shook the rain from her umbrella, put it in the stand next to the doors, waved at Peter, and hurried to the table.

'Sorry I'm late,' she said. 'The tram from Dennistoun was delayed by flooding caused by the heavy rain. But here I am now….at the heart of the big city.'

Nancy smiled. With no glasses and bright red lipstick she did indeed look a bit like Ingrid Bergman in *Casablanca*. Peter held up his glass of water.

'Here's looking at you kid!,' he said, in his best attempt at a Humphrey Bogart accent. Then he remembered that Bogey had made a film called *Sahara* in 1943, about an American tank crew that had helped some Allied soldiers defend a fort in the desert. The British contingent included an RAMC Captain. *I wonder where that idea had come from?* The tank in the film – an M3 Lee —had been called *Lulu Belle* and had the same type of 75mm gun as *Honeychile*. He wondered how Sergeant Gunn (as Bogey's character was called) would have fared against the Marizans.

Nancy picked up the menu and studied it carefully. 'I hear this is the best restaurant in Glasgow,' she said. 'Quite an impressive choice of dishes, despite rationing.'

Lee also looked at the menu and realised he had a problem. It was all in French and he didn't know even one word of that language. He would just have to make an educated guess at what everything meant.

The waiter arrived with his notepad. He was smartly dressed in a full dinner suit, his dark hair slicked back with Brylcreem.

'I'll have *soupe aux oignons* to start , followed by the *coq au vin*,' said Nancy. 'No *legumes*, I'll just have a bowl of *salade maison* on the side.'

'Excellent choice, madame. And you Monsieur?'

'I'll have *Escargots* to start and *Les Pommes De Terres* as my main course,' said Peter. Nancy raised her eyebrows in astonishment but said nothing.

'Oui, oui, monsieur,' said the waiter.

'I don't need a wee - wee,' said Peter. 'I went to the station toilets thirty minutes ago.'

Nancy laughed. Peter was a bit of an unconscious comedian. The couple chatted about the poor weather in Glasgow as they shared a jug of water. Then the waiter brought the starters. Peter's eyes nearly popped out of his head.

'Oh no, it's a slug. I can't eat this!'

'It's not a slug, it's a snail. Look it's got a shell,' said Nancy, viewing the glistening creature. 'At least it's dead and cooked. Don't you know the French will eat just about anything as long as it's cooked with garlic?'

Lee left his starter untouched. After Nancy had finished her soup, his main course arrived – nothing more than a plate of boiled potatoes.

'I can' t eat this either,' he said. 'It's just plain boiled potatoes. No meat, not even corned beef. This is even worse than the food I had in the Army. Even a tin of McConnachie's M&V would be better than this.'

Nancy chuckled. 'Didn't you know that *Pommes De Terres* is the French term for potatoes? It literally means *Earth Apples*. It was in the section marked *Legumes*, which is French for vegetables. Look, I think I should order in future. Let's have some *Crème Brûlée* for dessert. It's a kind of rich custard, which has some slightly burnt brown sugar on top. If you're still hungry after that we can get some chips across the road and eat them on the way home.'

Soon Nancy and Peter were tucking into two generous portions of delicious sweet, *Crème Brûlée* followed by freshly ground French coffee. Peter liked coffee and it was a real treat as very few British people drank it in 1946.

Nancy spent the next hour talking about her family. Her father was a civil engineer and had been involved in the construction of the defences at Scapa Flow naval base. Her mother was a teacher. Her older brother, Jimmy was a final year medical student while her younger brother, George was still at school.

Peter had never met anyone who could talk so much. And non-stop. As comedian Arthur Askey had once said about his mother-in-law, 'She had a slight speech impediment...she paused to breathe occasionally.' Or as Groucho Marx had once remarked, 'I have had long conversations with her but I've never actually said anything myself.'

At 10.00 p.m., Peter finally asked a question. ' So what do you see yourself doing for the rest of your life?'

'Oh, I could become a Consultant Physician I suppose, but it's hard for women to rise to the top in a profession that's dominated by men. I see myself going into a speciality, Ophthalmology, perhaps. And I'd like to have three children eventually. Maybe two sons and a daughter. I've even got names for them. Sally, Alastair and Ninian.'

'Ninian!' said Peter. 'What kind of name is that for a boy? Would that not lead to a lot of bullying at school? People would call him a ninny.'

'The name comes from St Ninian's Bay on the Isle of Bute. We used to go there a lot for holidays before the war. I suppose you have a point, though. But I have talked enough about myself. I know you served in the Army during the war. And you were in North Africa. What kind of a person was General Montgomery? And did anything exciting happen while you were there?'

Peter thought for a moment. There was so much he wanted to tell Nancy about what had happened. His dangerous sea journey to Tobruk and how he had shot down a Stuka. His secondment to the LRDG and SAS. All the battles with German Forces. Honeychile. The fort. The Marizans. The Cerebri. Flying saucers. His use of hypnosis to turn an SS man into a good person who supported the Allies. Yes , Peiper…towards the end he had actually liked him. The fact he had personally witnessed the first nuclear explosion on the planet Earth. And played a crucial role in defeating an alien invasion. And all the sacrifices…and the good men who had died.

But he couldn't say anything. The security services had told him that he could never talk about what happened. If he did he would be thrown in jail. Peter thought for a moment and then spoke.

'No, absolutely nothing of importance happened to me while I was in North Africa. The most boring time in my life. On the other hand, I had many exciting experiences in

North West Europe in 1944. Did you know I liberated a Belgian village single-handed when I made a wrong turn in my jeep?'

*******

In 1949 Peter and Nancy married and bought a house in Greenock, 25 miles from Glasgow, where Peter became a General Practitioner. They had three children - Sally, Alastair and Colin (who was mightily glad that he was never called 'Ninian'). Peter spent the next twenty – nine years treating thousands of patients in the Greenock and Port Glasgow area. He retired in 1978. Nancy temporarily retired from medicine in 1950 but then resumed her medical career in 1960, this time as an ophthalmologist at Greenock Eye Infirmary and then Inverclyde Royal Hospital. She retired in 1980.

Peter never spoke a word about what had happened in Egypt in June 1942. At least not until late 1995 when he was admitted to a nursing home in Callander, suffering from vascular dementia. On a few occasions,while in a confused state, he was heard to mutter something about the 'Marizans in the Qattara Depression.' The nursing home staff mis-heard this as 'Marathons in the Qattara Depression' and wondered how anyone could go running in that part of the world as it was so hot!

Sometimes he would wake up after having a brief daytime nap, screaming , 'The brain in the tank! The brain in the tank!' A GP who personally witnessed one of these episodes thought he was remembering a time in the late 1930s when he had visited the Anatomy Museum at Glasgow University.

Peter died in February 1996, eighteen years before Nancy. His obituary —written by his son ,Colin — was published in *The Greenock Telegraph*, the *Glasgow Herald* and the *British Medical Journal*. Mention was made of his distinguished medical career, but not of the key role he had played in one of the most important missions of the Second World War, an operation that had reversed Allied fortunes and also led to an acceleration of the atomic bomb programme, resulting in the defeat of Japan in 1945. Peter had also been largely responsible for the defeat of an alien invasion.

None of this was made public. At least not until 2017 when an investigative journalist discovered some previously unseen files in the National Archives at Kew which had accidentally been sent there due to a clerical error. The two files—one about time - travelling Nazi flying saucers and the other about events at the Qattara Depression in 1942—were made public on the internet. The British Government claimed they were fakes, works of pure fiction. Most people who read the two files thought they were too unbelievable to be true. But sometimes the truth can be stranger than fiction.

# Codename Enigma - Fact and Fiction

For my second WW2 novel ( which like my first, features a large dollop of science fiction) I have chosen a plot which centres around the recovery of a German Enigma coding machine and adds on various disparate elements. But how accurate is the story and how likely (or unlikely) are the various plot points?

The German Enigma machine was used by the Wehrmacht in all theatres of war, including North Africa. So it is entirely plausible that one might have been captured during the desert campaign, although this did not happen. Commander Ian Fleming's plan to seize an Enigma machine from a German Air- Sea Rescue launch (*Operation Ruthless*) was proposed but never carried out for the reasons explained in my book. However, evidence has emerged in recent years that the true purpose of the Dieppe raid on 19 August 1942 (*Operation Jubilee*) was indeed the capture of an Enigma machine from a building in the town.

**The LRDG and SAS**

The LRDG was formed in the summer of 1940 and the SAS was established the following year. The LRDG used two main types of vehicle – stripped down Chevrolet 30cwt light trucks and Ford lorries with V8 petrol engines and four-wheel drive. The first SAS mission in November 1941 involved insertion of troops by parachute. This was a disaster and most of the attacking force was killed or captured. Lieutenant Colonel David Stirling, the founder of the SAS , then realised that a better plan was to have his troops taken to the target area and back in LRDG trucks. Later, the SAS acquired its own vehicles, which by the summer of 1942 included the new American Willys MB jeeps. However, the LRDG and SAS continued to work together on joint missions, with the LRDG often providing drivers for SAS raids. Later, the LRDG acquired its own jeeps, the first of which were SAS vehicles which had broken down and were recovered and repaired by LRDG mechanics.

The SAS also pioneered the use of Vickers K fast-firing machine guns in their jeeps. These weapons were originally produced for use in RAF bombers but were replaced by the belt-fed Browning 0.303 machine gun. Consequently, large numbers became available to the SAS who found them very effective at close range against parked Axis aircraft. The LRDG copied this idea and also the use of the heavy American M2 Browning fifty-calibre machine gun. By late 1942, SAS jeeps would often mount a pair of twin Vickers K guns plus a single M2 Browning fifty – calibre weapon, giving them awesome firepower.

One of the main 'characters' in the book is actually the fictitious 'Super Valentine' tank called *Honeychile*. There never was a 'Super Valentine' but it is entirely plausible that such a machine might have been built. Constructed by Vickers – Armstrong, the Valentine Infantry Tank played a key part in the battles in the North African campaign between 1941 and 1943. Originally equipped with a 40mm two – pounder gun, the tank was later fitted with a more powerful 57mm six – pounder cannon which could knock out most German tanks. Towards the end of its production run, a version fitted with a 75mm gun in a larger turret was developed (the Mark XI), so the up- gunned 'Super Valentine' is entirely feasible. No armour upgrades were fitted to these later versions but they would also have been possible.

The heaviest American tank of WW2 was the T26/M26 Pershing which was fitted with a 90mm gun. Just twenty were shipped to Europe in early 1945 and saw combat in the last few months before the German surrender in May 1945. A single improved version known as the *Super Pershing* mounting a more powerful, longer-barrelled variant of the 90mm gun and thicker armour saw some action and was credited with the destruction of one German tank. Some accounts state that the Super Pershing knocked out a Tiger II (King Tiger) but recent research has suggested it was only a Panzer IV. US industry also produced a variant of the M4 tank known as the Sherman 'Jumbo' with extra – thick frontal armour, while the Israelis produced a post – war version of the M4 called the M51 *Super Sherman*. These reconstructed tanks, which were fitted with Cummins diesel engines and long-barrelled, high – velocity French 105mm guns, had devastating firepower and some accounted for the latest Soviet super-tanks during the 1973 Yom Kippur war.

My book also mentions the superior M61 armour – piercing round for the 75mm M3 gun. Again this existed in reality but few were shipped to Europe, and Allied Sherman crews often had to use the inferior M72 round. Large quantities of the M61 round were sent to the Soviet Army, who used them in their Lend – Lease Shermans and even found them capable of knocking out German Tiger tanks.

All the Valentine engine upgrades depicted in the book existed in reality, even the fuel catalyst pellets, which were indeed used to boost the performance of Hurricane fighters on the Russian front. I have several such devices in the petrol tank of my Jaguar X-type.

Part of the plot of the book involves a German spy building a radio bug to enable the LRDG vehicles to be tracked. This is entirely plausible. The 1949 James Cagney movie *White Heat* has a scene in which an FBI technician creates a simple transmitter from a domestic radio receiver. The bug is then hidden in the chassis of a suspect vehicle and tracked with direction-finding equipment.

Ian Fleming's 1959 novel *Goldfinger* features a simple radio tracking device which Bond creates just by wiring a dry battery to a radio valve. This would not work as the valve would have to be part of a tuned oscillator circuit, so several other components would be required. The 1964 film adaptation is actually more accurate in this respect as Bond uses two compact tracking devices similar to what are used today by the Security Services of many countries.

In my book, Rashid reads how it is possible to turn a radio receiver into a transmitter by using the speaker as a microphone, amplifying the signal using the audio amplifier and then feeding the output into the local oscillator. This is entirely correct and is described as such by Jon Pertwee's Doctor in Episode Two of the *Doctor Who* serial *The Sea Devils*, first broadcast on BBC -1 on 4 March 1972. However, in this episode the Doctor builds such a device using modern (1970s) transistor radios. This would be impossible since radios made in this era had all their components soldered to a printed circuit board, making rewiring unfeasible.

In this same serial, Pertwee's Doctor utters the immortal line 'reverse the polarity of the neutron flow' in Episode Six. This is widely regarded as his catchphrase though in fact he only ever uttered it once. He did say 'reverse the polarity' a few times during his tenure and, accordingly, I have had my character, Captain Peter Lee say the phrase as he is building the Marizan control unit.

The second half of the book contains the notion that an alien creature could evolve to the point where it was pure brain, living in a nutrition tank. I believe this would be scientifically possible, though it would be quite a miserable existence!

What about the warrior Marizan creatures themselves? Could they exist? My original plan for these creatures was that they should be 'scientifically plausible zombies.' Lee's explanation about dead muscles being stimulated by electricity is entirely correct. The scientific problem with any type of zombie though, is that dead tissue soon undergoes necrosis and cannot function. Brain tissue dies after as little as three minutes without oxygen. That is why I introduced the plot point about how the Cerebri had used time - travel technology to reverse necrosis. The Marizans' field guns - which work by electromagnetism - are also entirely plausible. Known as coil guns or rail guns these have been suggested as future naval weapons.

The book has been influenced by many well-known

films and TV series. For example the first half contains more than a nod to *Ice Cold In Alex (1958)* , *Tobruk(1966)* and *Sea of Sand(1957)*. The fort sequences were inspired by the 1943 Humphrey Bogart movie *Sahara* in which an M3 Lee tank named *Lulu Belle* and commanded by Sergeant Gunn helps several Allied soldiers defend a building in the desert against German attack. The film was remade in 1995 with James Belushi in the starring role. The British film industry made its own version in 1943 which was called *Nine Men*.

The second half of the book is also inspired by several classic *Doctor Who* stories including *The Moonbase (1967)*, *Tomb of the Cybermen (1967)*,*The Web of Fear (1968)*, *The Invasion (1968)*, *Spearhead From Space (1970)*, *The Ambassadors of Death (1970)* and *The Brain of Morbius (1976)*. Others influences include a number of stories from *The Avengers* TV series including *The Cybernauts (1965)*, *Return of the Cybernauts (1967)* and *The Positive Negative Man (1967)*. By the way 'Roger', the tame Marizan, is named after the principal robot in *The Cybernauts* who Dr Armstrong referred to as 'Roger.'

The book also features an interesting character called Hans Peiper, a former Waffen SS man turned *Afrika Korps* soldier who undergoes a *volte face* and changes from a die-hard, anti-Semitic Nazi to a supporter of the Allied cause who also champions the right of Israel to exist.

Is that really likely? The name 'Hans Peiper' was inspired by the real Waffen SS tank commander Oberst Joachim Peiper who lead a column of King Tigers during the Battle of the Bulge in December 1944. After the war Peiper was convicted of war crimes because of his alleged involvement in the Malmedy massacre on 17 December 1944 when a large number of American prisoners were killed. Peiper was subsequently sentenced to death. This was later commuted to life imprisonment. However, Peiper was released from prison after twelve years and later went to live in France where he was eventually murdered by former members of the French Resistance .

Robert Shaw's character in the 1965 film *Battle of the Bulge* was originally to be Joachim Peiper but — after the former SS officer made legal threats—the character's name was changed to the fictitious Major Martin Hessler. Peiper always denied any involvement in the Malmedy massacre, as he was not in the area at the time and there is some evidence that he actually treated American prisoners according to the provisions of the Geneva Convention.

In my novel, Hans Peiper is involved in the massacre of soldiers of the 51$^{st}$ Highland Division in France in 1940. This is inspired by the real-life incident in which soldiers from the 2$^{nd}$ Battalion of the Royal Norfolk Regiment were killed at Le Paradis in Northern France on 27 May 1940.

There is also the real – life case of Otto Skorzeny, the SS Officer who rescued Mussolini from captivity in 1943 and lead a column of German soldiers disguised as Americans during the opening stages of the Battle of the Bulge in 1944. Skorzeny survived the war and (rather unbelievably) ended up working for the Israelis by 1963. He even helped the Mossad to assassinate a number of German rocket scientists who were working for the Egyptians.

In my novel, Peiper undergoes his 'Damascene conversion' as a result of hypnotic regression facilitated by the administration of a barbiturate drug. Not many people (including most doctors and hypnotherapists) know that the hypnotic state can be induced by various drugs, notably barbiturates. When I read my father's hypnotherapy textbooks in the sixties, mention was made of drugs being used to facilitate the hypnotic state. This is not mentioned in current textbooks, probably because no-one wants to encourage hypnotists to use potentially dangerous drugs in their practice. In any case the use of barbiturate drugs is now heavily restricted, even to the medical profession. If you want to learn more about hypnotic regression then I suggest you read another of my books *Practical Hypnotherapy* (New Generation Publishing 2018).

The penultimate chapter of my novel features a fictitious encounter between Churchill and Ian Fleming in late 1945. This never happened but the two men did know each other and Churchill was a personal friend of Ian Fleming's father. What is entirely true is that Fleming drew on his wartime experiences as an inspiration for his Bond stories. The novel and film *Thunderball* draws heavily on the wartime exploits of the Royal Navy frogman 'Buster' Crabbe, particularly his underwater adventures between 1941 and 1943 (see my book *Victories at Sea* - Extremis Publishing 2018 for further details).

Many of Bond's traits come from Fleming himself, particularly his love of certain foods especially eggs, which feature heavily in the books. James Bond's recipe for scrambled eggs which is mentioned in the short story *007 in New York*, is actually Fleming's own recipe.

The penultimate chapter of my novel suggests, rather mischievously, that the events in the Egyptian desert in 1942 were the inspiration for some of the names in the Bond books. This is just a bit of whimsy on my part, but is not entirely impossible. For example there was a very famous German tank with the turret number '007', namely the Tiger I in which German ace Michael Wittmann lost his life on 8 August 1944 after a battle with British Sherman tanks.

**Dr Peter Barron – the real life Captain Peter Lee**

As some of you may have guessed, the character of Captain Peter Lee was based on my father Dr Peter Barron. My father was born in Glasgow in 1918 and studied Medicine at Glasgow University. As his family was poor, he suffered from childhood rickets and also could not afford to buy all the required textbooks. Much of his studying was carried out in the Glasgow University Reading Room and the Mitchell Library.

My father was due to graduate in 1940 but elected to join the Home Guard. Being Jewish, he was fearful of a

German invasion and wanted access to weapons. He subsequently graduated in 1941 and – after a spell in General Practice in Wales – was inducted into the British Army in early 1942. By late spring 1942, he was a Captain in the Royal Army Medical Corps and served in North Africa, Sicily, Italy and north-west Europe. He was demobbed in 1946 but remained an Army reservist until 1959.

My novel features a scene in which Captain Lee takes over a 20mm Oerlikon gun and shoots down an attacking Stuka. This may seem far-fetched but is based on a real-life incident involving my father. In 1942, my father was travelling in an Army convoy which was overflown by an Italian Breda reconnaissance aircraft. One of the officers shouted 'someone shoot down that bloody aircraft' and my father responded by firing at the plane with a pintle-mounted Bren gun. Fortunately for the Italian pilot, he missed.

It is also true that Jewish people who joined the British Armed forces often changed their names to conceal their religion. The example of Klaus Adam (who became 'Ken Adam' when he joined the RAF) is true. Adam flew rocket – firing Hawker Typhoons with the 2nd Tactical Air Force and later became a production designer on several James Bond films in the Sean Connery and Roger Moore eras. Two of his most famous creations were the volcano rocket base in *You Only Live Twice* (1967) and the tanker submarine pen in *The Spy Who Loved Me* (1977).

After the war, my father worked at Glasgow's Southern General Hospital where he met my mother Dr Agnes Montgomerie Knight Culver. My parents married in 1949 and moved to Greenock where my father was a GP in Greenock and Port Glasgow until 1978. My mother became a Clinical Assistant in Ophthalmology at Greenock Eye Infirmary in 1960. In 1973 she was promoted to consultant and remained in this post until her retirement in 1980. My father died in 1996, and my mother passed away in 2014. In the novel Captain Lee is a non –

270

smoker. In reality my father smoked cigarettes until he was forty.

My father was very interested in electronics and built various devices though, as far as I know, he never built a control unit for an alien zombie! I took up the same hobby in late 1969 and seriously considered a career in electronics, though in the end I chose to study Medicine. Both my parents were a great influence on my life and I like to think that wherever they are now, they approve of this book...and may even have helped me to write it!

# References

*Wikipedia was used as a basic reference source during the writing of this book. In addition the following publications provided invaluable information :*

**The Long Range Desert Group 1940 -1945 : Providence Their Guide**
David Lloyd Owen
Pen & Sword Books Ltd. 2000.
ASIN B00JYHOEUW

**The Men Who Made the SAS : The History of the LRDG**
Gavin Mortimer
Constable Publishing 2016
ISBN-10 1472122097
ISBN -13 978-1472122094

**For Your Eyes Only Ian Fleming + James Bond**
Ben MacIntyre
Bloomsbury Publishing 2008
ISBN 978 0 74759866 4

**James Bond : The Man and His World**
Henry Chancellor
Ian Fleming Publication 2005
ISBN 0 7195 6815 3

**Britain at War (Magazine)**
Issue 140  December 2018
Article on pages 74- 85 about the Valentine Tank

*My late father Captain Peter Barron RAMC , pictured here in Spring 1942 just before he was posted to North Africa.*

*My mother Dr Agnes Montgomerie Knight Barron, pictured in the 1970s.*

*Near the author's home in Dunblane is this monument to Lieutenant Colonel David Stirling, founder of the SAS*

*Near the David Stirling statue is this memorial to the LRDG.*

**ABOUT THE AUTHOR**

Colin Barron was born in Greenock, Scotland in 1956 and was educated at Greenock Academy (1961 -74) and Glasgow University (1974-79) where he graduated in Medicine (M.B. Ch.B.) in July 1979. He worked for the next five years in hospital medicine, eventually becoming a Registrar in Ophthalmology at Gartnavel General Hospital and Glasgow Eye Infirmary.

In December 1984 he left the National Health Service to set up Ashlea Nursing Home in Callander, which he established with his first wife and ran until 1999.He was the chairman of the Scottish branch of the British Federation of Care Home Proprietors (BFCHP) from 1985 to 1991 and then a founding member and chairman of the Scottish Association of Care Home Owners (SACHO) from 1991 to 1999.

Colin has a special interest in writing – his first non - fiction book *Running Your Own Private Residential and Nursing Home* was published by Jessica Kingsley Publishers in 1990. When he was at Glasgow University he was editor of *SURGO* (Glasgow University Medical Journal) between 1977 and 1979. *SURGO* subsequently won an award from the *The Glasgow Herald* for best student magazine in 1979. In late 1978 Colin was asked to write an article *How to Improve a Student Medical Journal* which appeared in the *British Medical Journal* in March 1979 and has been reprinted and revised in three separate editions of the BMA's *How To Do It* book.

He was also the Art Editor and Motoring Correspondent of *Glasgow Medicine* between 1984 and 1986. He is a former cartoonist, having contributed to *Glasgow University Guardian, Ygorra, Glasgow Medicine, Scottish Medicine* and *BMA News Review*. In February 1977 the Greenock Arts Guild held an exhibition of his work along with that of two other local cartoonists.

He has also written about 150 articles for various publications including *This Caring Business,The Glasgow Herald, Caring Times,Care Weekly , The British Medical Journal ,The Hypnotherapist, The Thought Field* and many others. He was a regular columnist for *This Caring Business* between 1991 and 1999 and the editor of *SACHO Newsline* between 1991 and 1999.

Colin has always had a special interest in hypnosis and alternative medicine. In 1999 he completed a one –year Diploma course in hypnotherapy and neuro-linguistic programming with the British Society of Clinical and Medical Ericksonian Hypnosis (BSCMEH) an organisation created by Stephen Brooks who was the first person in the UK to teach Ericksonian Hypnosis . He has also trained with the British Society of Medical and Dental Hypnosis (BSMDH) and with Valerie Austin, who is a top Harley

Street hypnotherapist. Colin has also been a licensed NLP practitioner. In 1992 he was made a Fellow of the Royal Society of Health (FRSH)). He is a former member of various societies including the British Society of Medical and Dental Hypnosis - Scotland (BSMDH),the British Thought Field Therapy Association (BTFTA),the Association for Thought Field Therapy (ATFT) ,the British Complementary Medicine Association (BCMA) and the Hypnotherapy Association .

Colin has been using TFT since early in 2000 and in November 2001 he became the first British person to qualify as a Voice TechnologyTFT practitioner. He used to work from home in Dunblane and at the Glasgow Nuffield Hospital.

Colin has also had 40 years of experience in public speaking and did some training with the John May School of Public Speaking in London in January 1990.

In May 2011 his wife Vivien, then 55, collapsed at home due to a massive stroke. Colin then became his wife's carer but continued to see a few hypnotherapy and TFT clients. In late July 2015 Colin suffered a very severe heart attack and was rushed to hospital. Investigation showed that he had suffered a rare and very serious complication of myocardial infarction known as a ventricular septal defect (VSD) effectively a large hole between the two main pumping chambers of the heart.

Colin had open heart surgery to repair the defect in August 2015 but this first operation was unsuccessful and a second procedure had to be carried out three months later. On November 30 he was finally discharged home after spending four months in hospital. Unfortunately he also developed epilepsy while in hospital which meant he had to give up driving for a year.

As a result of his wife's care needs, and his own health problems, Colin closed down his hypnotherapy and TFT business in April 2016 to concentrate on writing books and looking after his wife. His second book *The Craft of Public Speaking* was published on 30 June 2016 and was followed by *Planes on Film* (2016), *Die Harder : Action Movies of the 80s* (2017), *A Life By Misadventure* (2017), *Battles on Screen : WW2 Action Movies* (2017), *Practical Hypnotherapy*(2018),*Operation Archer* (2018), *Victories at Sea : On Films and TV* (2018) and *Travels in Time : The History of Time Travel Cinema* (2019).

His interests include walking, cycling, military history, aviation , plastic modelling and reading. He can be contacted via his website **www.colinbarron.co.uk**

OPERATION ARCHER

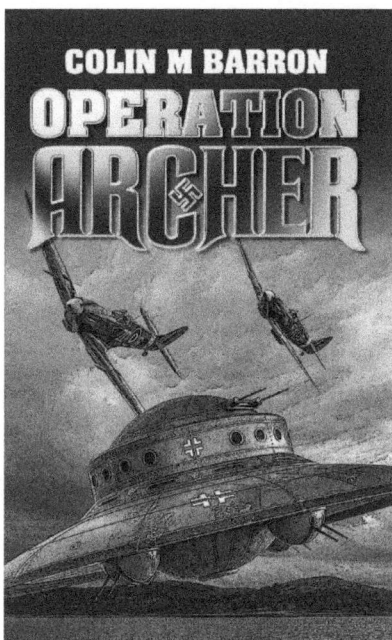

Destroy the Saucers – or die!

They called them *Haunebu*. Flying saucers which can travel at 5000 miles an hour and win the war for Nazi Germany. In a desperate bid to destroy them, Churchill sends a crack commando team to Germany. Their mission – destroy the *Haunebu* in their underground hangar whatever the cost in human lives! The team are joined by an RAF pilot who has a tragic past. And there is a traitor in their ranks!

Operation Archer is an exciting war thriller in the style of Where Eagles Dare and The Guns of Navarone. Packed with action, it takes the reader on a rollercoaster ride of excitement and danger which never lets up.

281

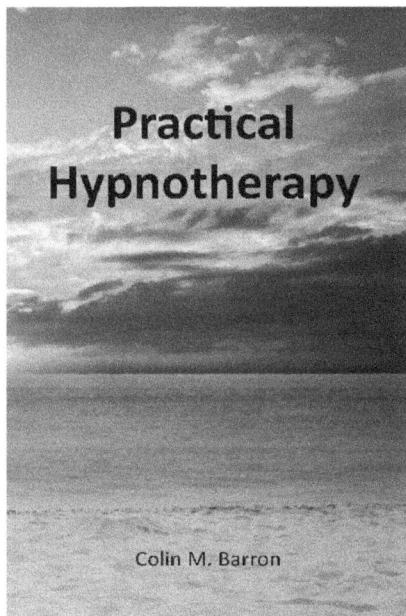

Dr Colin M. Barron has had a lifelong interest in hypnosis. After graduating in Medicine from Glasgow University in 1979, he worked in the NHS for a few years and was then the business manager of a private nursing home from 1985 to 1999. From 1999 until 2016 he was a hypnotherapist and, in this comprehensive book, he explains what hypnosis can be used for and how it can be integrated with other techniques such as TFT and NLP. The book will be of interest to practising hypnotherapists , doctors, dentists, psychologists, anyone contemplating a career in hypnotherapy and even members of the general public wishing to know more about the technique.

Lightning Source UK Ltd.
Milton Keynes UK
UKHW040646271119
354332UK00002B/480/P